MAFIA TO THE MAX

Mafia to the Max is the second in a series of Max Snow adventures. In the first—***Murder to the Max***, the suspicious death of Maxie's best friend is judged *accidental* by the local powers that be. Love and loyalty leave him no choice but to launch a by-the-seat-of-his-pants investigation to prove his theory of foul play. The third installment—***Morbid to the Max***, has our hero doing his reluctant best for Homeland Security as stylist and makeup artist for a funeral home where the undertakers are terrorists, and the stiffs are stuffed with government secrets. Visit Maxie's website at www.maxsnowmysteries.com.

Mafia to the Max

A Max Snow Adventure

Paul Chmielewski

iUniverse, Inc.
New York Lincoln Shanghai

Mafia to the Max
A Max Snow Adventure

All Rights Reserved © 2004 by Paul Chmielewski

No part of this book may be reproduced or transmitted in any form or by any means, graphic, electronic, or mechanical, including photocopying, recording, taping, or by any information storage retrieval system, without the written permission of the publisher.

iUniverse, Inc.

For information address:
iUniverse, Inc.
2021 Pine Lake Road, Suite 100
Lincoln, NE 68512
www.iuniverse.com

ISBN: 0-595-32997-7

Printed in the United States of America

Everything I do is for Patty

The author wishes to thank the following people for their much needed assistance—Robin O'Grady, Linda White, Sue Galli, Carol Sigler, Dianna Lipp, Debbe Krause, Bev Piskorski, Alice Sipes, Chuck Tice, and especially my wife and best friend, Patty, without whom none of this could have happened. Thanks, Babe! You're the best!

PS
In the beginning of my twenty-five plus years as a hairstylist, I never appreciated what a goldmine of hopes, dreams, and schemes I was about to share with my clients. Many of them became good friends. All of them are invaluable windows into the infinite perspectives on the human condition. I am a lucky man for having this opportunity. Thank you all from the bottom of my heart.

Prologue

"I was just thinking about it, Lieutenant. No need to get your thong in a knot."

"Well, un-think about it, friend. People like you don't become private investigators."

I flashed a tight smile. "People like me?"

"Look, Maxie, you know I love you. And I'd never try and tell you what to do…"

"Ha!"

Riff ignored my curt comment. "…but this P.I. idea is the worst."

"You are the one who suggested it."

"Hel-lo. That was sarcasm. For a while there, you were starting to think you were James freakin' Bond."

"You still haven't answered my question. Why can't people like me become private investigators?"

She topped off her coffee from the carafe on the kitchen table and looked at me over the rim of the cup. "You don't need another job. You're rich. Stick to cutting hair and squandering the millions you copped in the lotto."

"I'm not leaving the hair biz. I just want to try something different."

"So take up the violin. Or better yet, how about becoming the first hairstylist to fly on the space-shuttle?"

"I helped your department break Andra's murder case."

"Luck, Maxie."

"I'll say the same, next time you solve a mystery."

She swallowed some coffee and sighed. "Are you just jerking my chain about this P.I. thing, or what?"

"Could be. It's so much fun."

We locked eyes as she ran slim fingers through her spiky-short blonde hair. "What about you being in love with the mysterious Zed?"

"She's still in Belize."

"But she'll be back, right?"

The tender question hung between us.

"What has that got to do with me trying for a P.I. license?"

"Investigations can turn nasty," she insisted.

"And?"

"And you could find yourself dead, or worse."

"Worse than dead?"

"There are worse things."

"Oh yeah? Like what?"

CHAPTER 1

▼

The petite hooker leaned against the doorway of my private hairstyling studio; hands on hips, her leather jacket bound breasts projecting out over her lithe body like an awning. A snug black miniskirt was barely there and she balanced skillfully atop five-inch stilettos that looked sharp enough to carve up a cheap steak. I had met the woman, picture Betty Boop's twin sister, a month ago when I decided to crawl out on a very shaky limb to search for my best friend's killer. Bette popped into that scene uninvited but her wacky input, plus the fact that she's either fearless or crazy, helped me uncover evidence needed to solve the case. At the time I promised my help if she ever needed it. From the look on her face, she was about to claim the marker.

"Good to see you, Maxie," she said, in her high pitched, cartoon like voice. "Looking fine, honey."

"Right back at ya, Bette," I said. "Plying your trade in the mall now?"

"No," she said, stepping inside the room and closing the door behind her. "I'm happy in my own neighborhood. I came to see you."

Swallowing the lump that formed in my throat whenever the unpredictable Bette came around, I invited her to sit in my styling chair.

"What's up?"

"A friend of mine is being held prisoner where she works. I thought you'd like to help me rescue her."

I kept my expression neutral but Bette took that as an invitation to continue.

"Like, there's this house in Grosse Pointe where Petey works," Bette said. "That's my friend. Petey. It's short for Petrova."

"Cool name."

Bette nodded as she checked out the blood-red finish on her fingernails. "Petey went to work three days ago and I haven't seen her since."

"Have you tried calling there?"

The woman looked at me like I was simple.

"Well what did they say?"

"That Petey never showed up for her shift."

"And you don't believe them."

"Nope. I dropped her off there the day she disappeared and watched her walk in the door. They're definitely holding her."

"Who are they? And why would they do that?"

Before answering, Bette lifted a pair of scissors from my station, snipped off one of the corkscrew curls that framed her heart-shaped face, and stretched it taut above her upper lip like a mustache.

"Because she owes the house a ton of money," Bette said, miming faces in the mirror.

"For what?"

"Coke. Petey was snorting truckloads for a while there, and dealers connected to the house were supplying her."

"Have you talked to the police?"

"Hell no," Bette answered. "Too many big-shot cops hang there."

I raised an eyebrow. "What kind of work does your friend do?"

"She's a dominatrix," Bette said, mimicking my surprised expression.

"In Grosse Pointe?"

"You got it, slick."

"We're talking money, mansions and conservative Republicans up the wazoo, girl."

Bette stretched the lock of hair across her forehead like a single eyebrow. "So? You think rich people don't do kinky?"

"Sure, but how do they get away with it in a city like that?"

"There's no sign out front," Bette answered before flinging the strand of hair at me. "This is a class act."

"And you'd like me to do, what?"

Bette's big blue eyes dilated with excitement. "Go there with me tomorrow and pretend to be a customer."

I raised a hand in an attempt to stop her but she barreled past it.

"Once we're inside I can look for a way to get her out."

I shook my head and Bette started clucking like a chicken.

"I'm not afraid," I snapped.

"Yeah, right."

"I'm not."

"Then why won't you do it?"

I sighed heavily because I didn't have an answer.

"Nobody's gonna rape you," Bette insisted. "All we have to do is get Victoria to show us around."

"Victoria?"

"The madam of the house. She books appointments and keeps everybody in line."

"I'm picturing an old Marlon Brando in drag here."

"Wrong," Bette said. "Petey describes Victoria as visual Viagra."

Because I don't need Viagra, at least not yet, I was instantly intrigued. Bette, being skilled in the art of male manipulation, picked up on my interest and jigged the bait.

"You got a thing for tall, intellectual babes, right?" she asked.

"Yeah. So?"

"So Victoria is 6'1", has her Masters in Business Management, and is working on a Doctorate at Wayne State."

I chewed on the madam fantasy, setting Bette's hook firmly in place. "Okay. I'll go with you. But if I do this, we're even, right? It'll settle our score?"

"Sure," the little hooker said. "Whatever you say."

I awoke the next morning at six, remembered it was my day off and ducked back beneath the covers. The cell phone woke me again at nine. It was Bette and she sounded way too perky for a woman whose profession is practiced mostly at night.

"Hey, lover," she teased. "Come to my apartment around noon and I'll let you take me to lunch." Then switching to a breathy sexiness added, "Stop by an hour earlier and I'll let you take me to bed."

"Thanks, but I'll pass. I'm already going through some performance anxiety about helping you rescue your friend."

"You're not going to back out?" Bette challenged.

"No, but..."

"Good," she said, ending any further discussion. "Pick me up about twelve."

Three hours later, dressed in a rust colored Armani suit, Italian loafers, and a banded collar shirt of pearl silk, I pulled into a parking spot directly across the street from Bette's apartment building in Detroit. The squat three-story brownstone stood alone on the corner of the block. A light rain was falling. As I exited the car, a shrill voice yelled at me to get back in and start the engine. Looking up I saw that Bette, dressed totally in black leather, had burst through the building's entryway and was running barefoot in my direction; purse in one hand, heels in the other.

"Start the car!" she screamed, as her giant boobs bounced around on her chest like basketballs. "Start the damn car!"

Any uncertainty I may have had evaporated when a very large, totally naked and obviously pissed off black man exploded through the door of the brownstone and pounded across the sidewalk after Bette. If the size of the man didn't intimidate me, I assure you the gun he was carrying did. Without pausing, I hit the automatic door locks and threw myself back behind the wheel. Two seconds later Bette jumped in beside me and we took off, tires squealing.

Bette's pursuer stopped in the middle of the street, aimed the .45 long-barrel at my retreating car, and unloaded several rounds in quick succession. The first smacked into the rear window, causing it to implode and Bette to hit the floor. Number two took out the Jag's right taillight. And a third whizzed so close to my ear, I swear I felt its heat before it punched a silver dollar-sized hole in the windshield. Freaked, I jerked the wheel hard to the left. The car hydroplaned across the wet pavement, slamming into the opposite curb with a body-jarring thump. On impact, Bette peeked over the dash, caught sight of the shooter running full tilt in our direction and ducked down again.

"Unless you want a lead sandwich for lunch," Bette said, tucking herself beneath the dash. "I'd get us the freakin' hell out of here."

Ten feet away, the naked man stopped and flashed a spider-to-the-fly smile, but before the gun could come up, I punched the gas, clipped his thigh with my fender, and sent him sprawling. Slowing to a stop twenty yards away, I felt a strange sense of relief wash over me as the shooter pushed up off the pavement. He started after us again but sans the gun—which had been lost in the fall—he was a lot less threatening.

At a McDonalds a quarter mile down the road, I pulled Bette up by the jacket lapels and sat her in the passenger seat. "What the hell was *that* all about?!"

"Heeey," she said, straightening the front of her leather, "easy on the merchandise. Do you have any idea how many tricks I had to do for this jacket?"

In a desperate attempt not to strangle the woman, I clutched the steering wheel in a death grip. "Mind telling me why that guy was trying to kill us?"

"He came busting into my apartment with his Johnson in his hand," she said. "Told me I owed him a freebee for some repair work he did on my sound system. When he stripped down, I booked."

"So you know the guy?"

"Well, duh," she said, fishing a pack of Camels out of her jacket pocket. "I just told you he worked on my sound."

"Don't even play with me, Bette," I growled. "My car is trashed and I was almost made into Swiss cheese a minute ago."

Bette lit a cigarette, took a long drag deep into her lungs, then grinned at me through the escaping smoke. "Why do you always make a big deal out of everything?"

"What?!"

"It's not like you don't have any other transportation."

I just stared at her, afraid if I opened my mouth, I wouldn't stop bitching.

"And you're not like, hurt or anything. Right?"

I continued to stare at her.

"Cool," she said, buckling her seatbelt. "Then let's go to your place, change vehicles and get this gig off the ground."

An hour and a half later we were cruising down Grosse Point's famous Lakeshore Drive in my Lexus SUV. I looked over at Bette who had been primping in the vanity mirror for the last five minutes and tapped her arm. "Let's have the plan again."

"Piece of cake," she said, folding up the sun visor. "We go in; you flash Petey's business card, and ask for a tour."

"What do I say?"

"As little as possible," Bette said. "Let Victoria think you've done this before."

"But..."

She cut me off with a narrow eyed stare. "Just chill and pull into the next driveway. The one next to that old church."

That "old church" was St. Juliani's, a famous cloistered retreat for retired nuns. I remember visiting it as a Catholic schoolboy with my fourth grade class. After all these years, I could still recall the castle-like feel of the place.

"You plan to try to get Petey out today?"

"No," Bette said. "Today we find out where she practices her magic and get an idea of the layout."

I must have looked doubtful because she issued more instructions.

"Don't freak over the stuff you might see," Bette warned. "And look like you're ready to spend big bucks."

"Riiight," I said, tugging at my shirt collar. "Big bucks."

My heartbeat doubled as I proceeded up the long cobblestone drive and took in the opulent grounds surrounding the Tudor-style mansion. The front lawn was the size of a football field with giant oaks and pines dotting the rolling landscape. The house itself sat at the rear of the property. It was all stucco, stone, and rough-hewn wood. I estimated it to be an easy ten thousand square feet.

We parked under an arched portico near the front entrance and a valet in formal livery appeared out of nowhere to open the SUV's doors. Bette and I stepped down to the shining cobblestones. The man pointed out the mansion's carved front door with a sweep of his hand, then sliding behind the wheel, he drove around the side of the house.

As we neared the half-circle flagstone porch, a tall woman wearing a suit of shimmering black silk stood waiting for us.

"This has got to be Victoria," whispered Bette out of the corner of her mouth. "Hold on to your hormones."

The madam indicated for us to enter. Once inside, I found myself gaping like a horny teenager at what had to be one of the Top Ten sexiest women on the planet. Victoria was Marilyn Monroe, Pam Anderson, and Jessica Rabbit all rolled into one, with shoulder length hair the color of midnight, and a pair of wide-set aquamarine eyes that peered deeply into mine.

"Welcome," the woman said. "I am Victoria."

"Max Snow," I said, accepting the hand she offered.

"A pleasure," she said, eyes shifting to Bette. "And this charming creature?"

I looked at Bette but drew a complete blank. The madam's erotic persona had me so mesmerized; I could *not* remember her name.

"I'm Bette," she said, then shot me a venomous look. "Nice to meet you."

Victoria eyed Bette from top to bottom like she was perusing a restaurant menu, and then turned on pencil thin heels, gesturing for us to follow. Before I could take a step, Bette elbowed me in the gut for forgetting her name. A soft *ompff* escaped my throat, causing Victoria to pause and turn back in our direction.

Without missing a beat, Bette smiled and slipped an arm through mine. "You'll have to excuse Max," she said, while patting my stomach. "He has a problem with gas as well as his memory."

"How unfortunate," Victoria said, playing along with Bette's little joke. "If it becomes more of a problem, I'm sure we can locate some Mylanta."

Victoria's office was spartan but sumptuous. After slipping behind the single slab of white marble that served as a desk, she invited us to sit in the two high-back chairs facing her.

"Now," Victoria said; steepling ten perfectly manicured fingertips. "How may I be of service?"

I looked at Bette but she nodded the question back at me. "Well," I said, then cleared my throat. "I met one of your employees recently. She suggested I visit your house."

"I see," Victoria said. "The employee's name?"

In answer, I pulled Petey's card out, sliding it across the desk.

"Ah, Petey," Victoria said, barely glancing at the card. "Do you wish an appointment with her specifically?"

I cut my eyes to Bette.

"What we'd really like," Bette said, "is a tour, so we can get an idea of what's available."

"Certainly," Victoria replied.

"If I did want Petey, would she be able to work me into her schedule today?" I inquired, thinking we should determine if Bette's friend was actually on the premises.

"I'm afraid not," Victoria said, shifting her attention back to me.

"I'd be willing to double her fee."

"Sorry. Perhaps tomorrow?"

"I'm not sure I can make it tomorrow. What time?"

Victoria walked to the computer in the corner of the room, and her fingers danced lightly across the keyboard. "Would seven o'clock be convenient?"

I looked at Bette. "What do you think, babe?"

Totally into her part, Bette lifted a palm pilot from her purse and touched the screen. "I think," she said before nodding in agreement, "that you'll just be able to make it."

"Excellent," Victoria said, adding me to Petey's schedule. "Now, if you are ready, we'll begin the tour."

With Victoria in the lead, me close behind, and Bette bringing up the rear, we started down the wide stone hallway. She stopped abruptly at the foot of a curved stairway and for a moment I thought she was going to start up. Instead she grasped the carved handle of a heavy wood door on the opposite wall, slowly pulling it open. "It's this way," she said, eyes narrowed as if to challenge our resolve. "Please watch your step."

The basement of the house was quite large with a higher than usual ceiling. And the decorator—perhaps Vlad the Impaler—had succeeded in reproducing the eerie feel of the medieval torture chamber to the 'nth degree. Walls had been erected to divide the room into spacious cubicles, open in the front. Several were occupied, and as we walked along the corridor that split the basement in two, a variety of kinky scenes were being played out before us. For those who would like more detail, I'm sorry. Let's just say I saw enough latex, vinyl, and leather restraints to last me a lifetime. Maybe even two.

At the far end of the hall, we entered an empty cubicle that at first glance looked like a hair cutting station. It contained a chrome-and-porcelain barber chair, floor to ceiling mirrors on three surrounding walls, and an assortment of evil looking straight-razors laid out neatly on a side table.

"This is Petey's room," Victoria said, running a forefinger down the side of one razor. "And these…are the tools of her trade. They are very sharp. I do hope she's careful with them."

I wanted to ask, careful doing what, but decided to reserve the question for when Bette and I were alone. A quick glance at my little friend told me she was checking out the ground-level window outside Petey's cubical. It didn't take a rocket scientist to deduce what was going on in her mind. Bette's stepfather, a master locksmith, had taught his adopted daughter to excel at the skill. I had no doubt she was eyeing the lock in order to figure out what it would take to open it.

Minutes later, the three of us were headed back up the stairs. We had gone halfway when Bette suddenly remembered she'd left her purse in Petey's room.

"I know exactly where it is," she said when Victoria offered to retrieve it. "I'll only be a minute."

The madam and I continued up the stairs and into to her office. She had finished loading my credit card information into the computer when Bette rejoined us.

"Does anyone actually live in the house?" Bette asked casually as she slipped into her coat and sidled up to take my hand.

Before replying, Victoria lifted the phone and gave orders for my truck to be brought around.

"A few of the staff use the upstairs bedrooms for business purposes," the madam said, her gaze dropping momentarily to Bette's cleavage. "I live in an apartment at the rear of the house. Perhaps you would like to visit me there sometime."

Driving back to Bette's apartment, I asked if she had successfully opened the lock on the window near Petey's cubical.

"The inside was no problem, Sherlock," she said. "But I have no idea how the bars on the outside are secured. I'll tackle that little chore tomorrow."

"And if you can't?"

"Don't worry about it," she said dismissively. "Just tell Petey what's up and be ready to move when you see me."

Chapter 2

The hair salon I own is in the Rolling Pines Mall in the city of South Lyon, a true yuppie suburb, where houses are big; yards are small, and the kids smoke pot instead of crack. Rolling Pines is a three-story palace of temptin' temptation, no less skilled at separating you from your money than any Vegas casino. The entertainment is different—with the mall getting Santa Claus and the Easter Bunny—and Vegas getting Cher farewell concerts and Elvis impersonators. Except for legal prostitution, the two are pretty much on a par. My salon is on the second level, comfortably sandwiched between Victoria's Secret and Fantasy Footwear; a shoe store whose claim to fame is that they sell no heels under four inches, including summer sandals.

I called the salon that afternoon to see if I had any appointments past five the next day. The phone was answered by my usually calm and friendly receptionist, Gwen Wright, who sounded anything but.

"Something very weird is going on here, Max." Her voice was an octave above normal. "Fifty boxes of product were delivered today and we didn't order any of them."

"What kind of products?" I asked. I didn't exactly have my finger on all the inner workings of the salon, being a hands-off kind of business owner, but I knew we never got more than ten to twenty boxes at a time.

"Hair products," Gwen shouted into the phone. "Paul Mitchell, Sebastian, American Crew, Abba. Everything we sell."

"Where are they from?" I asked.

"I don't know. I was at lunch when they were delivered and none of the cartons have shipping labels."

"Come on, Gwen. How could they be delivered without shipping labels?"

"Damn if I know."

"How about a packing slip?"

"I can't find one," Gwen snapped.

"Well, who signed for the delivery?"

"Would you believe no one?"

I sucked my teeth in frustration. "Well I can't take care of it from here. I'll figure something out when I come in."

"How?"

My eyes rolled as far up into my head as they would go and I cursed inwardly. I hated making business decisions. I owned the salon only because a friend had asked me to go partners. I put up the money; Andra put up the brains, drive and know-how. After she was murdered several months ago, I was forced to take control.

"Don't sweat it, Gwen," I said, trying to sound confident. "I'll be in early tomorrow to sort it out."

I could tell by her silence that Gwen wasn't satisfied, but I had been through too much that day and wasn't up for another challenge.

"Are you still there, Gwen?"

"I'm here."

"Where are the boxes now?" I asked, watching Blue stalk a spider across the floor, bat at it several times, and then give it a sniff to see if it was still kicking.

"Outside in the delivery hallway. There's no place to put them in the stockroom."

"Why not?"

"Because your mother's storing her motorcycle in there for the winter."

"What?!"

"You heard me. She brought it in yesterday before we opened. Said you knew all about it."

I slapped an open palm across my forehead. "Shit. How the hell did she get it up there?"

"I don't know, but now there's no room for anything else."

"Well call her, dammit! And tell her to get it out."

"*You* call her," Gwen said. "I'm scared to death of the woman. You never know what she might have under that leather jacket of hers."

"Right, Gwen. Like my mother would be packing a gun."

There was total silence on the line. We both knew Marie Snow was capable of anything.

"Okay," I said, wishing I was as carefree as my cat. "I'll call Marie. In the meantime, stack the boxes in my office before the mall starts bitching that they're blocking the hallway."

"They're already bitching," Gwen said. "But there's no way I'm lifting fifty boxes."

"Fine," I said, trying hard not to sound pissed off. "Go next door to Fantasy and ask Chickie-Baby if we can borrow Stoney. Tell her I'll pay his wages for the day if she'll let us use him."

"I hate going in that store," Gwen whined. "It's…immoral. And I think that Stoney guy is high all the time."

"I'm not suggesting you date him, Gwen. Just ask if he'll move the cartons into my office."

Work the next day was busy. The few breaks I managed to snag were spent trying to track the source of the mysterious product delivery. Like a good P.I. wannabe, I eliminated the obvious first by checking with our regular wholesale distributors. Two denied any knowledge of the shipment. I was in the middle of dialing the third when it hit me. There was no way it could be any of these companies. Each one sold a different selection of product lines, so none could have possibly sent the variety represented in the delivery. For lack of anything better, I started opening boxes, looking for a clue. After the fifth, I gave up the search.

A little creative rearrangement relieved the congestion in my office. Stoney had indeed transferred the fifty boxes from the hallway but his placement left a lot to be desired. Twenty were stacked on top of my desk in four neat rows. The remaining thirty stood like the Great Wall of China, blocking off access to the computer and the Mr. Coffee machine.

Carly Fox, the young woman who manages my salon, was seeing caffeine deprivation as the major issue here. When I cleared a path to her liquid jones, she practically lunged at the coffeemaker.

By six that evening, I was on my way back to Bette's apartment. Parking directly in front of the ancient brownstone, I looked for signs of trouble. Can you blame me? Little Bette could be upstairs beating the devil at Yatzee for all I knew. If he came down mad, and ready to waste someone, I wanted to be able to blast out of there in a hurry. The street scene looked reasonably safe, so I exited the SUV and walked to the locked entrance of the building. Six doorbells with nametags matched residents with respective apartments. Before I had a chance to pick my poison, a high-pitched voice shouted at me from above. I looked up to see Bette leaning out a second floor window. She was naked as a jaybird, at least the parts I could see, and her nipples stared down at me like a second set of eyeballs.

"Here's the key," she yelled, tossing a tiny bundle out into space. The thing floated down with the aid of a white, plastic parachute and landed at my feet. It was a tiny Betty Boop figurine, dressed in a flowered halter-top and sarong. An attached silver ring held two keys marked "ent" and "apt".

Inside I made the climb to the second floor, pausing to catch my breath before knocking on Bette's door.

"Use the key," she yelled. "I'm on the phone."

I hesitated, not knowing what state of undress I might find her in. When I finally did unlock the door, I kept my eyes on the floor.

"Are you ready?" I asked; trying hard not to think about how fine Bette had looked framed in that window. My resolve was tested when she stepped from the bedroom dressed in fishnet pantyhose, four-inch matte black pumps and absolutely nothing else.

"Ooh la la," she said, swivel-hipping her way toward me and taking in my black Levis, boots, and leather bomber. "You look good enough to eat."

"Thanks," I said, trying hard not to stare at her perfectly sculpted boobs. The doctor who created them ought to get a "Best Imagination of the Year" award. "You look pretty tasty yourself, but if we don't get moving, we're going to be late."

Bette eyed me, a prick teaser smile curving up the corners of her kewpie doll lips. "If that's what you want," she said, walking toward the bedroom slow enough to give me time to appreciate her flip side. "Don't complain later about lost chances."

Bette reappeared five minutes later dressed in camouflage capris with matching headband, a black spandex top that wrapped the twins like snakeskin, and a pair of freshly polished Dr. Martens.

"Well?" she asked, modeling the outfit, "what do you think?"

"That *Soldier Of Fortune* magazine should use you for their next cover shot," I answered, before taking in a last eyeful. "Now let's get the hell out of here."

Down in the truck, Bette ran a hand up the inside of my thigh. "Next time," she said, her eyes lusty with desire, "I might not let you get away so easily."

"Next time," I echoed, leaning over to kiss her on the cheek, "I might not want to."

It was 7:05 when we arrived at the house on Lakeshore Drive. We were met beneath the portico by the same valet who had parked the truck the day before.

Bette walked to the driver's side, gave me a quick hug and whispered, "Be ready," before she climbed in and sped off toward the road.

Inside Victoria's office, there was no mistaking the lady's anger at my tardiness. It could have been an act, but she was damn good at it.

"You're late," the madam snapped and pointed a finger at one of the chairs facing her. "Petey gets annoyed when people come late for their appointments."

"Sorry," I said and started to give some lame excuse about traffic.

Victoria cut me off with a glare; snatching up the cell phone on her desk.

"Mr. Snow is here for his appointment. Send Ivan and Dax to get him ready."

A minute later two burly men, who looked like bouncers for the WWF, filled the doorway. They were naked from the waist up, wore tight leather loincloths around their middles, and both sported a menacing black facemask that hid every feature but their eyes.

"These two gentlemen will prepare you for Petey," Victoria said, a cruel grin stretching her beautiful mouth. "Do yourself a favor—don't resist them."

A nod of her head signaled the man closest to me and a hand the size of a twelve-pound ham gripped my shoulder. "This way," the man growled from behind the zippered mouth-hole. As I was hustled from the room to the basement playhouse, serious doubts about Bette's plan started popping in my head. The S&M action here was certainly no game, and the two heavily muscled, barely-dressed monsters that herded me into a cubical like a cow to slaughter, weren't kidding around either.

I was ordered to strip and stand with arms at my side. A leather harness was fit roughly around me. And as they cinched the complicated straps a little snugger than comfortable, I realized it was too late to reconsider. My arms were pinned tight to my sides, leaving my genitals just sort of hanging out there in the breeze. When the gruesome twosome forced a ball-gag between my teeth, the niggling doubts of a moment before morphed to full-blown panic. After being escorted to Petey's room, and secured to the barber chair with more leather straps, the men abandoned me to my fate.

At the sharp click of stiletto heels outside the room, my gonads headed north. A moment later a seductive, dark-eyed woman appeared in the doorway. She was short, heavily muscled, and wore her flame red hair slicked high in a topknot. Two golden hoops pierced the corners of each finely penciled eyebrow. Her lips were stained a bloody vermilion. And the latex bustier, thigh-highs, and miniscule thong looked as though they were painted on.

"I am Petey," the woman announced sharply, a slight east-European accent blunting each word. "And *you*, Mr. Snow, are late!"

I shook my head, trying unsuccessfully to talk around the ball in my mouth.

"What's the matter?" Petey asked as she kicked a lever at the base of the chair, sending it into a reclining position. "Pussycat got your tongue?"

I stared upwards, desperate for her to read the message in my eyes.

"You'd like to speak to me, yes?" she teased and traced a shiny black fingernail around the ball.

I nodded; staring wide eyed as she lifted one of the razors and checked its gleaming edge in the spotlight. What she intended to do with it, immediately became evident when she tugged up several of my pubic hairs and sliced them cleanly off at the root.

"You are sorry for making me wait?"

"Mm hm," was all I could manage.

"And if I remove the gag, you will tell me how beautiful I am and how much you want me?"

Again I nodded.

"Better make it good," she growled, ripping the ball from my mouth. "I am not a happy woman today."

"I'm here with Bette," I gushed as soon as my mouth was clear. "We've come to rescue you."

Petey stared into my eyes, and then glanced to a back corner of the room. I followed her gaze and saw a tiny security camera mounted near the ceiling; its lens aimed directly at the chair.

"They can not hear us," Petey said. "But the camera can be activated at anytime. Just play along."

Nodding, I moved my jaw muscles back and forth to work out the kinks.

"Who are you?" Petey asked, lifting an ornate blue bottle from the side table and pouring a bit of the contents into her palm. It was spearmint scented oil. I caught a whiff as she warmed the slick liquid between her hands.

"My name is Max," I said. "Bette knew you were being held here so we came to get you out."

Petey glanced from the camera, to my face. "How?"

"The window," I said as she began working the oil between my legs. "Bette took care of the inside lock yesterday. Hopefully she worked her magic on the outside bars as well."

Petey's eyes darted to the arched window outside the room and grinned when she saw the lock was cracked open. "I love that tiny hooker," she said. "If we actually do get out of here, I'm going to hug the shit out of her."

A double thump against our escape window made us both look up. As the wood casement swung in, we saw Bette, dressed in a nun's habit and veil, kneeling just outside.

"Follow me to salvation," she said, then lifted away the iron security bars. "This is no place for children of the Lord."

Petey sliced cleanly through the straps of the harness with a straight razor and together we pushed the heavy barber chair against the wall. When it was directly under the window, I glanced back at the security camera and saw a tiny red light blink on beside the lens. We were made, and although I would have liked to reclaim my clothing, I thought better of it and followed Petey though the window.

"They are probably already hunting for us," Petey warned, glancing around for signs of pursuit. "I suggest we move."

A shout in the distance forced my already soaring adrenalin levels up a notch. Peeking around the front of the house, my worst fears were justified. Ivan and Dax were moving fast in our direction. I recognized the two muscle-bound bodies as they jogged through shafts of window light. Both wore sand colored running suits. One was talking nonstop into a cell phone.

Bette grabbed my arm and we all made a run for the hedge that separated Catholic cloister from S&M playhouse. When we reached it, Bette ducked down and slipped between a split in the tangled branches. Petey and I stared at each other before following her lead. Once on the other side, Bette called to us from a door of the church.

"We're going to cut through this joint," she whispered when we joined her. "Stay on my ass or be left behind."

We took two rights and a left, ran down a dimly lit hall toward what I assumed must be the main part of the church, stopping outside two closed doors to catch our breath. After a moment, Bette started for the door on our left, but paused like she was unsure.

"Well?" I said, impatient to get out of there. "Which one's it going to be, Sister?"

Bette grinned. "I'm not sure. *You* want to choose?"

I pushed against the door on the left and the three of us filed through, only to be met by a chorus of shocked murmurs and screams. At least two dozen nuns knelt on the floor of the chapel we had just entered. All stared wide-eyed at the unexpected burlesque show.

"Please excuse us, Sisters," I mumbled, snatching up the skirt of Bette's habit to cover myself. "We were ah…just passing through."

Scrambling back the way we came, each of us bounced off the other, Larry, Moe and Curly style, in our rush to escape. Once on the other side, Bette led the way through door number two and we scooted across a wide hall toward an exit. Two piles of clothing lay heaped near the door. When Bette picked one up, I recognized it instantly.

"I am *not* wearing that," I protested.

"Suit yourself," Bette said, unable to suppress a giggle, "but your truck's parked at the end of the driveway and those goons are probably still out there looking for us."

A few moments later, dressed as Brides of Christ, the three of us made our way carefully down the long, dark driveway. It was freezing, the wind was whipping up my skirt, and little pieces of gravel kept poking into my bare feet. We had gone maybe twenty yards and I had just made a promise to never get involved in one of Bette's hair-brained schemes again, when Ivan and Dax stepped out of the shadows.

My first inclination was to bolt, but dressed in the nun garb, I didn't think I'd get very far, so I stood still, bent my head low, and out of the corner of my eye saw Petey follow my lead.

"Excuse me, Sisters," one of the men said as they stopped in front of us. "Have you seen any strangers on the grounds?"

"Strangers?" Bette repeated; her voice a thin whisper like every good cloistered nun should have. "We are a closed order. No one may visit except by invitation."

"What about you two?" The same man addressed Petey and I directly. "You seen anybody around?"

"These good sisters," Bette said demurely, "have taken a vow of silence. They cannot answer your question directly. Perhaps if you state your request in writing to Mother Superior, they may be allowed to respond in kind."

I wanted to look up so bad I could taste it. It was frustrating to be unable to read the men's facial expressions. The only thing I could see was their shoes. When one pair moved in my direction, I almost wet myself.

"Young man," said Bette, a bit more forcefully as she stepped between us. "I'm afraid I must ask you to leave this sacred ground immediately."

The shoes stopped their progress and there was a strained silence for several beats before the two finally backed off.

"Sorry to have bothered you," the man said before drifting away. "Have a good evening, Sisters."

When we reached my truck, all three of us piled inside. I cranked the engine and took off down Lakeshore Drive, watching my mirrors for any sign of pursuit. Petey and Bette were in the back seat squealing like teenagers, hugging each other, and slapping the back of my head. None of us could believe we had actually pulled it off. At Cadieux Road, I turned right and moved steadily through traffic. Twenty minutes later, we parked in front of Bette's apartment building.

Upstairs Petey and I sat talking on the living room couch while Bette mixed a pitcher of martinis. Rejoining us, she filled three cocktail glasses to the brim, and passed them around.

The women had removed their nun habits but since the only thing Bette had in the apartment that might fit me was a hot-pink bathrobe trimmed in marabou, I left mine on. It was a little weird, I know, but with Petey still dressed in S&M latex and Bette sporting her urban guerilla sex kitten outfit, my body began to respond in an all too predictable way and I was glad for the cover. After my second drink, I got up to pee. When I returned, the living room was empty. Through a hazy buzz, I heard my name being called from a bedroom down the hall. Like a good P.I. in training, I went to investigate. Once inside, the two women stripped me of my habit.

"Bless us, Sister Max," Bette said as she and Petey each took a hand and pulled me toward the bed. "For we are about to sin."

Chapter 3

The next morning, over a breakfast of Pop Tarts and Mountain Dew, I talked to Petey about the debt she owed the S&M house. It wasn't all that much, so I told her I'd send a check to Victoria for the full amount. Why the hell I didn't think to pay the madam off in the first place was beyond me.

Preparing to leave, I re-donned the nun habit. Bette and Petey cracked up when I added the veil but I didn't care. It was just the right outfit to get me out of the building unmolested.

When I arrived home, I was met at the door by a howling pussycat. It wasn't my practice to miss Blue's mealtime and although there was still dry food in his bowl, no amount of apologies would soothe the furry little beast.

I had a full book of clients that day I would have gladly rescheduled. When I called the salon, Gwen answered, sounding miffed, so I decided it wouldn't be a good idea.

"Hey, Gwenster," I said, trying for light. "How are things there?"

"Crowded," she replied, obviously referring to the mystery products that filled my office. "Should we start selling that stuff or what?"

I thought about it. "No. Not yet. Let's see if anyone bills us first."

Gwen's silence spoke volumes. She liked every thing in her world neat and orderly. When it wasn't, she got a little bitchy. To ignite her efficiency streak, I asked who was on my book that day.

"You've got Sean and Ryan Sullivan at three," Gwen recited. "Kerry Walsh for highlights at four. A new client at five-thirty named Olympio Grillo and your mom's coming in at six for a trim."

"Olympio Grillo?" I said, repeating the name. "Is he a referral or what?"

"He didn't say."

I ran the odd handle through my memory banks. "I feel like I've heard the name before. Ring any bells for you?"

"Not really," Gwen answered, then jumped in with a question of her own. "Did you talk to your mom about getting her bike out of the stockroom?"

"No," I said, still trying to sort out where I had heard of Grillo. "But I will."

"When?"

"When, what?" I said distractedly. After a moment, I heard her sigh.

"Never mind," she said. "We'll talk when you get here."

After a shower, I spent the rest of the morning checking out my first mail order lesson on becoming a private investigator. The opening chapter gave a brief overview of the profession, including background checks, surveillance, and how to do a tail. A list titled "Don't Make These Mistakes" at the end of each section made me wonder if I really did want to take on what the book described as a new and exciting career.

I arrived at the mall that afternoon about 2:15. As I entered the salon, Gwen was just finishing a call. "Hey kiddo," I said, stepping behind her to check out the appointment book. "Anybody cancel?"

Gwen's smirk told me the answer was no. "Disappointed?" she asked.

I stroked my chin. "A little. I was hoping to get out of here early."

"The man starts work in the middle of the afternoon," she said, shaking her head, "and he hopes he can get out early."

My first three clients went smoothly and I was straightening up the studio when a tall, distinguished looking man in his late fifties walked in. He had a face like Valentino. Beneath the finely tailored gray on gray business suit, his body looked hard and distinct.

"Mr. Snow," he said, offering a deeply tanned hand. "Olympio Grillo."

"Mr. Grillo. A pleasure. Have a seat please, and we can discuss what you'd like done with your hair today."

The man sat in my styling chair, crossed his legs casually, and gazed at me with a pair of piercing steel-gray eyes. "As you can see," he said, running a hand through his finely trimmed hair, "I am not in need of your expert services. My purpose here is to invite you to join me in a no risk business opportunity."

I stepped around the chair and faced him, back to the mirror, arms crossed, suspicions in high gear.

Grillo caught the body language. "Please excuse me for approaching you this way. I understand from my research that Ms. Fox usually handles the salon's business matters, but I wanted to speak to you personally."

I nodded despite my reservations. The guy exuded a ton of charm. And although I normally would have shown any other salesman the door, I was curious about what he had to say.

"I own a beauty supply distributorship presently based in Chicago."

I snapped my fingers, remembering where I had heard the name. "Grillo Beauty Supply. I've seen your catalogs."

The handsome gray head nodded. "Having recently opened a branch here in Michigan, I would like you to consider buying your retail from us."

"A pretty unorthodox way of doing business, Mr. Grillo," I said, sure I had found our mysterious product benefactor. "Does the head man always send unordered stock and make cold calls?"

"Not always," he said; his smile a perfect white keyboard. "And please call me Olympio."

"A pretty unorthodox way of doing business, Olympio."

"If the account is important," he said, "I like to handle the first contact personally. And I wanted to meet you."

"Why?"

Before he answered, a voice in my head warned me against trusting him.

"Because you are a respected stylist and salon owner," he continued. "And well known in the industry."

I shooed the voice away and gave Grillo my full attention. "There are a lot of respected stylists around here. Why choose me?"

"Because you run a successful salon and turn over a great deal of product."

"How could you possibly know that?"

"I make it my business to know all about my customers," he said.

"But I'm not a customer."

"Not yet," he said, smiling warmly. "But I hope to make you one."

"And my incentive to buy from your company would be?"

Grillo's perfectly manicured fingertips came together and he touched them lightly to his lips. "What if I slice my competitors' prices in half?"

"In half!?" I said, my voice rising with surprise. "How can you do that?"

"We have," Grillo said, and here the fingers interlinked tightly, "an intimate relationship with our suppliers."

The greedy part of me said jump on it, but the voice in my head pushed for caution. "Your offer is generous, Olympio. I'll definitely consider it."

"Excellent," he said, lifting a slim gold business card case from an inside pocket. "Call this number if you decide to come onboard."

He handed me a powder-blue card with the initials GBS embossed in gold, and a phone number.

"If I'm not available, my secretary is authorized to make the deal." He stood up, pulled out a fat wad of hundreds, and looked at me. "You charge forty dollars for a man's haircut, correct?"

I nodded but waved away his offer.

Grillo smiled graciously, and as he pocketed the cash, I heard raised voices at the reception desk. A second later, my own pet Tasmanian devil, otherwise known as my mother, Marie Snow, pushed her way into the studio with Gwen hot on her heels. Marie was sixty-four on her last birthday but looks fifty. She's had almost everything north of her waist nipped, tucked, or reshaped, sits a motorcycle like a Hell's Angel, and has the tattoos to prove it.

"Tell this chick to back off!" Marie said, jabbing a thumb over her shoulder. "Or I'm going to have to deck her."

Gwen's face was flushed with anger. "I tried to explain you were with a client…"

"It's okay, Gwen," I said. "I'll take care of it."

The pissed off receptionist glared at Marie's back and I swear there was smoke coming out of her ears as she pivoted on her sensible heels and stormed from the room.

"Dammit, Mom," I said, turning on the petite silver-haired woman dressed in jeans, scuffed boots, and motorcycle leather. "If Gwen quits because of you, your butt's going to be down here answering the phone." I stopped when I realized what I was saying. But there was no need. Marie, ever on the prowl for her next boyfriend, tuned me out the second she caught sight of Grillo.

"Hello," she said; crossing over to him. "I'm Marie Snow."

I did the introductions.

"I had no idea my son had such good looking clients," Marie said as Grillo took the hand she offered and kissed the back of it. "You've been holding out on me, Max."

"The pleasure," said Grillo, taking her hand with both of his own, "is all mine. But surely you cannot be this gentleman's mother. If this is so, you must have given birth when you were a child."

Marie laughed gaily and I winced when I saw her eyes drop to Grillo's crotch.

"Max?" Grillo asked. "Would you and your lovely mother care to join me for dinner this evening? I have reservations at The Lark for seven, but my party had to cancel."

"Sorry, Olympio. I can't make it tonight. And Marie is here to get a haircut."

"But her hair looks perfect," the man said, playing a palm across the top of Marie's half-inch silver spikes. She'd been wearing it cropped close since her last trip to Hawaii and it looked great on her.

"Guess I could skip the trim," Marie said, slipping her right arm through Grillo's left. "Do they have a good wine list at The Lark?"

"If they do not have what you like," he said, leading Marie toward the door, "we will make them go out and buy it."

The couple paused just outside my studio and Grillo leaned back inside. "You are sure you won't join us, Max?"

"I'm sure," I said but before I could wish them goodnight, Marie tugged him away.

"My son is a workaholic," I heard her remark as they rounded the curved wall into the reception area. "Getting him to take a break is like pulling teeth."

I sat in my chair and thought about Olympio Grillo's offer. If he actually could provide retail for half the price I currently paid, the salon would make a hefty profit. The staff could get a raise with the extra income and I would be the hero. On the other hand, I had the feeling that if I *did* decide to do business with the suave Italian, somewhere down the line I'd get the real bill and it might be more than I was willing to pay.

On a whim, I called Lieutenant Linda Riff of the Southfield P.D., client, friend, and occasional—when I'm lucky—lover.

"What?" she said. "Zed's not back from Belize yet, so you're getting horny?"

Zed is the mysterious woman I fell big time for several months ago. She had returned to her home country of Belize and I hadn't heard from her in a while.

"What if I am horny, Lieutenant? You prepared to do anything about it?"

"Not unless you have written permission from the Amazon princess," Riff answered.

"You're off the hook, lady. It's not your body I want today. It's information."

"What kind of information?"

"The police kind. Do you have access to files in other cities?"

"Most," she said.

"How about Chicago?"

There was a pause. "What is this? Homework for P.I.101?"

"Nah, I just had a customer in here by the name of Olympio Grillo. Wondered if the handle means anything to you."

"You're shitin' me, right?" Riff asked with real surprise. "Olympio Grillo was in your salon? When?"

"A few minutes ago. Why? Do you know him?"

"Not personally, no," she said. "And I'm not complaining. The guy is like my rank in the Chicago *Family*."

"You mean the Mafia?"

"The one and only."

I shook my head and thought about Marie.

"Did he come in as a client?" she asked.

"He booked for a haircut but he was really trying to sign me up as a customer."

"In what?"

"A new wholesale hair product operation he just opened in the area."

"How's the deal?"

"Sweet. Want the details?"

"No," she said. "And if you're smart, you'll forget them."

"You saying I should be afraid of this guy?"

"I would be and I'm the one carrying a gun 24/7."

"Terrific," I said. "He just took my mom to dinner."

Riff laughed. "Could be he's met his match then."

I didn't comment. I was too busy thinking about the trouble Marie could get herself into.

"Soft pedal everything with this guy, Snowman. And don't let on that you know who he is. Just politely refuse his offer and maybe he'll go away."

"Maybe?"

There was a long pause. In the empty space, I could hear my heartbeat.

"Word is," Riff said. "When Grillo wants something, he's like a pit-bull with a soup bone."

"Wonderful."

"He's also been a suspect in several murders," Riff continued. "I've got a cop friend in Chicago who swears Grillo drilled his partner."

"He *saw* him do it?"

"No, but our boy was the only one around when his buddy bought it. Grillo was arrested but the murder weapon was never found, and a test of his hands for powder residue came out clean."

"How could he pull that off?"

"Gloves?"

"Did the cops find any?"

"Nope, but seconds after the shooting; a gang of teens charged into the alley, messing up the crime scene."

"You're thinking the kids copped the gloves and Grillo's piece?"

"What I'm thinking," she said, as a telephone rang in the background, and a voice called her name, "is that you should stay as far away from this bad dude as you possibly can."

Riff rang off and I thought about going to the restaurant to get Marie away from Grillo. Not that she would leave if she didn't feel like it. The woman was born stubborn.

At work the next day, I had just finished putting a foil-highlight under the dryer when Fawn Bessler, the salon's top booker, walked into my studio carrying a bottle of red wine. Fawn is short and plump, wears her white-blond hair in a spiky shag, and at the age of thirty-seven, has three ex-husbands.

"Thanks, Maxie," she said, displaying the label on the bottle. It was Toscana Solaia 1997 and although no wine expert, even I recognized the expensive vintage.

"Where did you get that?" I asked. "One of your exes trying to worm his way back into your pants?"

Fawn snorted. "Those chumps wouldn't know Toscana from Ripple."

"Then where?"

"A whole case was delivered to the front desk a few minutes ago. The card said it was a gift for the staff." Fawn looked at me expectantly.

"It wasn't me."

"It wasn't?"

I shook my head.

"Well, whoever it was has good taste in wine."

Olympio Grillo's face popped into my mind but I dismissed the thought, although the vision of the Mafia lieutenant made me wonder why Marie hadn't called yet that morning.

"Max?" Fawn said as she waved a hand before my unfocused eyes. "Earth to Max. Hello."

"Sorry," I said, shaking out of the trance. "I'm kind of worried about my mom. Who'd you say the wine was from?"

Fawn stared at me. "Boy, you are spacey today. I thought it was from you. Remember?"

"Oh yeah."

"So what's up with Marie?"

"Nothing really. She went to dinner with some guy last night and I haven't heard from her."

"Knowing how your mom likes to party, she was probably out till the wee hours. Why the concern?"

"Because according to Riff, the man's a big shot in the Chicago Mafia and probably a murderer."

Fawn's eyes narrowed with concern for a brief moment. "Marie's tough, Maxie. I've seen her handle guys twice her size."

"Me too. But none of them were backed by an army before."

I tried all that day to get hold of my mom but had zero luck. About three, I decided to call the number on Grillo's business card. After a pair of rings, the phone was answered by a soft, breathy voice, ala Marilyn Monroe.

"Grillo Beauty Supply. This is Candy. How may I help you?"

"Hello, Candy. My name is Max Snow. I'd like to speak to Olympio if he's available."

"I'm sorry, Mr. Snow. Olympio isn't here. He's out of town with your mom."

"Out of town?"

"Yes. They went to lunch at Everest."

"Everest?" I repeated, as my imagination took a flying leap to the top of the Himalayas.

"It's a wonderful French restaurant in Chicago's financial district."

I was temporarily relieved. Chicago was a hell of a lot closer than Tibet, but when I remembered the toddlin' town was Grillo's home base, my concern for Marie's safety inched up. "When will they be back?"

"Late this afternoon is my understanding."

"How?"

"On the company jet," Candy answered. "Olympio is a pilot."

"Of course he is," I grumbled, knowing that would impress the hell out of Marie.

"Excuse me?"

"It was nothing. Forget it."

"If you're concerned about your mom, Mr. Snow, there's really no need. I've flown with Olympio many times. He's a stickler for safety."

"Do you have a number where I could reach them?" I suddenly felt the urgent need to break up what I suspected might be a budding romance.

"You could try the restaurant but chances are—they're already heading back."

I blew out a long breath as Candy proffered an invitation.

"Why don't you join Olympio and me for dinner tonight?"

"Dinner?"

"Well, if you want to talk to him, it would be the ideal time."

I considered her offer and decided to accept. Dinner might provide the perfect opportunity to refuse Grillo's business proposition, and if things went well, maybe I'd get a shot at splitting up their romance before things got too cozy. "Where were you thinking of going?"

"How about the third floor of Grillo Beauty Supply?"

"Is that a good restaurant?"

"It's Olympio's residence when he's in Michigan. I'm sure he'd love to show it off to you."

"Are you cooking?"

"As a matter of fact I am."

"Then that's all the more reason to accept your invitation."

Candy laughed. "How do you know I'm any good?"

"I have a sixth sense about food," I bantered back. "That's why I weigh three hundred pounds."

"You don't sound like a fat man," Candy said. "And Olympio already told me how handsome you are. I hope you don't mind my saying that."

Candy emailed me one of those you-are-here and want-to-go-there Internet maps that plot the route to any location. The estimated travel time to the GBS building was 49.3 minutes.

I finished my last client of the day about five. And after assuring Fawn once again that I had not sent the Toscana, left for my dinner with the Mafia lieutenant. Traffic was rush hour heavy, something the magic Internet could not predict. By the time I arrived at the address on Franklin Road, it was 6:15.

Triangular in shape, with its narrow end pointing at the street, the amber mirror-sided, three story GBS building looked like a giant wedge of cheese. It was newly built, judging by the lack of landscaping. When I drove around back, my hunch was confirmed by several piles of post-construction rubble covering what was destined to become a lawn.

The moment I parked my truck, a ripe-bodied woman in a short black sweater dress stepped out of the building's rear entrance. She was tough-girl pretty—think Geena Davis in *Thelma and Louise*. Her shoulder length blonde hair was arranged in attractive tangles, and the three-inch pumps she wore complimented her superbly shaped legs.

"Mr. Snow?" she asked as I approached. This time she really did sound breathless, like she had just run down a flight of stairs. "I'm Candy Sprinkles."

My brows lifted and she rolled her eyes prettily.

"I know. It's a dumb name. But I assure you, I didn't make it up. My mom's name is Chocolate. Guess she wanted to keep the family joke going for another generation."

"Sounds sweet to me," I said, receiving a smile for my corny quip. "And please call me Max."

Swinging the thick glass door out on silent hinges, Candy nodded for me to enter. I stepped inside, glanced around at the building's first level office space and let out a low whistle. A buffed chrome customer counter split the triangular room at the wide end. Glass-enclosed cubicles ran the length of each flanking wall. And the twenty-some desktops filling the center each held a trio of flat-screened monitors.

"The tech industry must love your company," I said. "I've never seen so many PCs in one place."

"Olympio is an information freak," Candy said as she nodded at the sea of monitors facing us. "Some days I feel like I'm working at NASA." We walked to a door at the end of the customer counter and she led me into a dimly lit stairwell. "I'm sorry…but we'll have to use the stairs. They haven't completed work on the elevator yet."

Delicious cooking smells filled the air as we neared the third floor. Inside Grillo's apartment, Candy invited me to look around while she checked on dinner, and look around I did. I couldn't help myself. I was totally drawn in by the soft edge modernism of the double height living area that some very talented decorator had done entirely in distressed wood and stone. A rail-less balcony wrapped around three of the walls, all lined with illuminated paintings hung gallery-style. I recognized Gauguin, Matisse, Picasso, and from where I stood, they looked like the real McCoy. The wall facing the parking lot was solid smoked glass. Backlit by security lights, tree limbs near the building looked like long fingered silhouettes.

A few minutes later, Candy bustled out of the kitchen and sat a tray of hors d'oeuvres down on a terra cotta side-table. "Sorry I abandoned you," she apologized. "I didn't want the appetizers to burn."

"I love everything about this room, Candy. Who did the decorating?"

"Olympio. He's got a degree in Interior Design. In fact he was the architect for the entire building."

I ground my teeth and cursed under my breath. Was there no end to Grillo's accomplishments?

My hostess used wooden tongs to transfer three of the hors d'oeuvres to a square plate of almost translucent white china. After slipping a black silk napkin beneath the dish, she handed it to me.

"Use your fingers," she said, nodding at the tiny golden appetizers steaming on the plate. "That's how they're supposed to be eaten."

"What are they?" I asked, sniffing the tempting aroma.

"Apricot Chicken Wontons. They're a specialty of mine."

I picked up one of the delicate bundles and took a bite. The taste was pure heaven and when Candy's eyes asked my opinion, I smiled. "They're awesome," I said, popping the remainder in my mouth.

Candy laughed lightly and the sound eased any tension between us. "I worry every time that they won't come out right."

I reached for another and Candy took the third. "What's inside?"

"Ground chicken breast, cabbage, green onion, *miso*, black pepper, ginger." She paused and thought for a moment. "Oh yeah, and apricot preserves."

"Delicious," I said wiping my lips with the napkin. "Too bad we have to save some for Olympio."

"Actually we don't," Candy said, placing two more of the wontons on my plate. "He called when I was in the kitchen. The jet is being refueled at Detroit Metro, and he and Marie are continuing up to Traverse City for the weekend."

I paused with the second wonton halfway to my mouth. "I really wanted to talk to Marie," I said, suddenly remembering why I was there.

"You can," Candy assured me, "as soon as they get to their hotel."

I returned the wonton to the plate and set it on the table.

"It's okay, Max," Candy said. "Olympio is a perfect gentleman."

I knew she was right. Marie was probably in no danger. I just didn't want her falling for Grillo.

"You *will* stay for dinner, won't you?" Candy asked, locking eyes with me. I noticed for the first time that hers were a true sea green. "All my friends live in Chicago, so it gets a little lonely here."

"Sure I will," I said, retrieving my plate. "If the main course is half as good as the appetizer, I'd be a fool to miss it."

Dinner was delectable and full of robust flavors. Picture a peppery tomato-based vegetable chowder, mustard encrusted pork loin infused with whole cloves of garlic, tart apple slaw with poppy-seed dressing, accompanied by several glasses of a hearty St. Hallett Blackwell Shiraz. The lovely Candy was equally delightful. We discussed books we loved, authors we didn't, gardening, her adventures sailing on the Great Lakes, and creative ways to avoid too much exercise. Her love of the culinary arts was evident. When I clued her to my own passion for cooking, she asked me to email her my favorite recipe.

I was pleasantly buzzed on food, wine, and fine female company when Candy suggested a tour of Grillo's apartment. "Sure," I said, curious to see what else the handsome, charming, pilot, decorator, architect, restaurant gastronome, and Mafia lieutenant had up his sleeve. "But you could talk me into something chocolate and a cup of coffee first."

Candy nodded in agreement. "I'm thinking mocha almond cappuccino."

"Sounds excellent."

"And I made some chocolate chip cannolis yesterday."

"You make your own cannolis?" I said, appreciating Candy's zaftig-lite figure and full, sensuous mouth in a whole new way…translation…through my third glass of wine. "They're like my favorite food on the planet."

In the kitchen we sat knee to knee at a marble topped bistro enjoying the cappuccino and each other's company.

"You, Ms. Sprinkles," I said while tucking a loose lock of hair behind her ear, "are an excellent cook, and a very attractive woman. I hope you don't mind my saying that."

Candy smiled when she recognized the line she had used on me that afternoon. "I don't mind at all," she answered as her pink tongue darted out to catch a drip on the rim of her cup. "But I'll bet you compliment every woman you meet."

"It's the job," I teased. "Don't you know hairdressers are notorious for their flagrant use of flattery?"

Candy crossed her legs, revealing another two-inches of nicely tanned thigh. "So you're saying I shouldn't trust you?"

"Always trust a hairstylist," I said and winked. "We are a group of highly trained professionals."

The moment was irresistible and when Candy leaned forward, I met her halfway, stopping only when our lips were a breath apart. It was Candy who closed the gap and I felt that kiss all the way down to my…toes.

"Wow," Candy whispered against my cheek. "A man who can kiss. Imagine that."

"I can do other things well too," I said, trailing my lips down to the inviting base of her neck and nipping lightly at the tender skin. "Demonstrations are free, and highly encouraged."

Candy leaned into me and bent her head back. "Later, perhaps," she said teasingly. "I believe I promised you a tour earlier."

With her hand in mine, Candy led me down a corridor that ran the length of the apartment, tying together Grillo's master suite, a smallish guest bedroom, and at the far end, Candy's own sizable rectangle. After a second pass through the kitchen and dining area, we returned to the living room, approaching a set of French doors in the glass wall that opened out onto a dark, inset balcony.

"Olympio had a hot tub installed out there last week," Candy said, twisting a dimmer switch that illuminated a row of soft white lights on the balcony's flanking walls. "Shall we?"

"Absolutely," I answered. "Nothing I like better than outdoor hot-tubbing in the winter."

"Nothing?" Candy asked as she hiked the hem of her sweater-dress and pulled it up and over her head. "I find that difficult to believe."

The sight of her dressed in a sheer pink bra and matching thong zinged my libido up the stairway to heaven. "Well," I said as my eyes zeroed in on the plump nipples straining valiantly to be free, "maybe there are one or two exceptions."

I awoke the next morning in the arms of yet another woman and wondered what the hell was going on with me. Had I morphed into some kind of whore or what? I could blame the alcohol but that would only be half true. I had been hurting since Zed's return to Belize. Was having sex with other women my way of getting back at her? I lay in the dark pondering the question for a long while, finally deciding I wasn't sure. One thing I did know was that bedding the Mafia lieutenant's secretary—was that really all she was to him?—could very well prove to be hazardous to my health.

Slipping quietly out of bed, I padded to the kitchen and made a pot of coffee. I needed fresh caffeine and chocolate to clear my head. The moment I located an unopened package of Double-Stuff Oreos in a cupboard, I felt half my cares slip away.

Candy was sitting up when I returned to the bedroom and the sight of her bare breasts, nipples erect in the cool morning air, kick-started my ever-ready friend down below. "Morning," I said as I poured us each a cup of coffee. "Want anything in it?"

Candy shook her head and ran a hand through bed tousled hair. "Black is fine."

Leaning forward, I handed her the cup and kissed her on both cheeks. "You look exceptionally hot this morning, babe."

Candy smiled at the compliment but seemed lost in thought as she sipped her coffee. I joined her in the bed, placed a finger under her chin, and turned her head to face me.

"Anything wrong?"

"Guess I'm a little bit embarrassed," she said, obviously referring to our sexual adventures the previous night. "I'm usually not that easy."

I suddenly felt like a heel for letting my dick do my thinking after she had stripped down last night. Getting naked for the hot tub doesn't necessarily constitute an invitation to have sex. I read that once in *Cosmopolitan*. Maybe I interpreted her signals wrong.

Noticing my discomfort, Candy took my cup, set it on a side table, and hugged me tight to her. "I loved every minute of it though," she whispered as her hand snaked down to encircle me. "Especially the part where you…"

Chapter 4

When I walked into my house about ten that morning, the phone was ringing. I picked it up to hear my mom on the line. Her conversation was light and breezy which meant she had either popped a Valium that morning or got laid the night before.

"Ah, Maxie. Life is great, isn't it?"

"Yeah, Mom, great. Now about Grillo..."

"Mmmm," she sighed into the phone. "I know what you mean. He's a dream, isn't he?"

"More like a nightmare, Marie," I said in an attempt to snap her out of the love struck mood. "Grillo is a big-shot in the Chicago Mafia."

"Yes," she said distractedly. "He told me all about it."

I gripped the phone and took a deep breath, knowing I'd need it. "Don't fall for this guy, Marie. He's a criminal."

"He's not a criminal. He's never been convicted of a crime."

"That doesn't mean he isn't guilty of any. The guy's Mafia."

"So what? Your father sold Irish Sweepstakes tickets when they were illegal."

"This is a little different. The Mafia hurts people."

"Not anymore," Marie said. "Oli explained that his branch of the *Family* is into legitimate business now. All that rough stuff is history."

"Yeah, right."

"It's true," she insisted.

"Well I spoke with Linda Riff about him yesterday and she doesn't agree."

"What does a cop in Southfield know about a guy from Chicago?"

I was unable to stop my voice from rising. "She knows plenty. Police departments share information."

"I don't want to talk about it anymore," Marie said with finality. "And besides, you had a few scrapes with the law yourself."

"Like what?"

"I seem to remember you getting busted for smoking pot."

"I was seventeen for crissake."

"So you're saying I shouldn't hold your past against you? That you might have changed your ways?"

I could see where she was leading me but refused to go there. "Could you just do me a favor and not date Grillo anymore?"

"No, I couldn't," she said decisively. "Olympio likes me. I like him. We had a great time together and I'm going to see him again."

"But…"

"But nothing. I don't stick my nose into your love life, although God knows I should."

"And what's that supposed to mean?"

"It means you wouldn't recognize your soulmate if she bit you on the ass."

I bristled at the insinuation. "You seem to forget I was married for almost ten years."

"To a whacko."

"Susan is not a whacko," I insisted, picturing my ex-wife who had left me to become a Buddhist nun in Japan. "She just wanted something I couldn't give her."

Marie made a disapproving sound but offered no further comment.

"What about Zed?" I asked. "You like her, don't you?"

"Zed is the shit, Maxie, but you let her go."

"She'll be back."

"You hope."

"She will."

"You don't know that," Marie snapped. "Why don't you get your butt down to Belize and find her?"

"Because she asked me not to, that's why."

"So what? Go anyway. Show the woman that you love her and don't want to live without her."

I was tempted, I really was. Zed had been absent from my life for more than two months and I missed the hell out of her. But I also respected her right to privacy, which meant I would have to wait.

"No," I finally said. "I'm going to give her more time."

"You are such a bonehead."

"And you're not?" I shot back. "Riff told me Grillo was arrested for killing a cop in Chicago. Did he confess *that* to you?"

There was a pause before Marie answered. "Yes he did and I don't believe he would do anything like that."

"You don't sound convinced."

"Well I am," she said flatly. "And I told you, I don't want to talk about it anymore."

An hour-and-a-half later, I was at the mall preparing for my first two clients, Michelle and Edwina LeMeux, better know around the salon as "Les Girls" or Mike and Ed. "Les Girls" are conjoined twins, connected at the shoulder. They had called me out of the blue one day last year to explain their situation. I'll admit to initial shock, but after we worked out the physical dynamics, doing their hair became a piece of cake. Make that two pieces.

The twins are sort of infamous, having posed for a spread in a well-known men's magazine at the age of twenty. I've been searching for the issue but so far no luck. After that, they did cameos in two John Waters flicks, and by the age of thirty had settled down enough to become CAD designers for their mother's company.

Dad had been an industrialist, known in the auto trade for his innovations in sunroofs and tinted windows. Mama LeMeux stepped into the CEO position after her husband died ten years ago, building the company into a respected world leader.

The twins themselves are identical, although they jokingly claim not to see any resemblance. They're on the short side, solidly built, with blue eyes, auburn hair, and lips that would make Angelina Jolie jealous. When we first met, I was confused as to why they couldn't be separated. The connection at the shoulder doesn't look all that serious. They explained that to do so might cause them each to lose the use of an arm, so intricately intertwined are the muscles and tissue, and because Ed's liver is abnormally small, she could possibly lose her life. Neither wanted to take that chance. And the two insisted they would stay linked forever.

At noon, the twins walked into my studio. Both wore the same outfit; black silk slacks, black v-neck cashmere sweaters, and two-inch matte black pumps. Their hairstyles offer the biggest difference. Edwina wears hers in a full banged, one-length bob. Michelle's is short, heavily layered, and darkened to a shade of ripe plum, with a demi-permanent color.

"Yow," I said, after each put out an arm to offer a group hug. "Looks to me like somebody's been soaking up sunshine."

"We were in St. Martin last week," Mike explained. "You should have seen the tourists freak when we went topless on the beach."

"You got that right, girlfriend," Ed chimed in. "Guess they never saw four such fine looking titties in a row."

Ten minutes later the twins had been shampooed, and as they sat on side-by-side stools in front of the mirror, talked to me in tandem.

"How are your P.I. lessons going, Max?" Ed asked as I combed her hair straight down and blunt cut an inverted v-line against her neck. "Making any progress?"

"Slow but sure," I answered, glancing up from my work. "But I don't think I'll be giving Maxwell Smart competition any time soon."

"Too bad," said Mike. "We were kind of hoping you could help us out with a little problem."

"How little?"

Ed and Mike looked at each other and seemed to reach an unspoken agreement. "It's not really a problem," Ed said, taking the lead. "Not yet anyway."

I stopped cutting and gave them my full attention.

"You know about Mom being heavy into Asian art, right?" Mike asked.

I nodded.

"Have you seen her collection?"

"Only pictures," I said. "Love to see it in person sometime."

"It is sweet," Ed agreed. "And it's taken Mikala years to put it together. Now she wants to trade most of it for a single piece."

I blinked, wondering what might be worth trading an entire collection for. "What's she going after?"

"A fourteen-inch wooden statue called the *Sitting Tiso*," Mike said. "Carved in Japan's Kamakura period."

"Which would be when?"

"The Kamakura took up a big chunk of the thirteenth-century," Ed explained. "Tiso was a *Bodhisattva* that could grant wishes to tormented souls."

"What makes him worth so much?" I asked.

"All the known pieces crafted at that time portray Tiso standing. He's seated in this one, holding a sphere in his left hand and a staff, for driving off demons, in his right."

"And the sit-versus-stand thing makes him more expensive?"

"You bet your ass it does," Ed answered. "That's why we're concerned."

"About what?"

"That Mom's being taken," Mike insisted.

"The thing is, Maxie," Ed cut in, "we don't trust the joker setting up the deal. He's a weasely little guy by the name of Benny Shatts and he gives both of us the creeps."

"Benny Shatts?" I said, looking up and tapping my lips with a finger. "Didn't he shoot craps with Sinatra in *Guys and Dolls*?"

"This is serious, Max," Mike said. "What if this guy isn't legit?"

"Well is he? I'm sure you two Internet junkies have checked him out."

"Of course we did," Ed answered. "And his e-record looks clean."

"Too clean," Mike remarked.

"What auction house is he with?"

"Churchills," they said in unison.

I raised an eyebrow. "Of England?"

Both women nodded.

"They've been around a long time, guys," I said.

"*They* have," Ed said, "but Shatts hasn't. He's a freelancer...been on their broker list for less than a year."

"How about before that?"

The twins shook their heads.

"Did you try contacting Churchills?"

"Sure," Mike answered. "But they wouldn't release any personal info. We were thinking maybe you could dig up something on him."

I looked at the two doubtfully but catching disappointment in their eyes, blurted out, "Why not?" trying to sound more confident than I felt. "It might be the perfect case to get my feet wet."

That evening, I spent several hours searching the Web for anything on the *Sitting Tiso* and or Mr. Benny Shatts. Like the twins, I failed to turn up much. As I sat there thinking about my next move, Blue joined me in the art studio.

"Hey, bud," I said as he leapt to my lap and nuzzled me with his jaw. "Come up here to give me inspiration?" In answer, the cat lifted his head, inviting me to scratch the downy fur on his neck. I complied, and after working the area thoroughly, was allowed to massage ears, and the bridge of his nose, before he jumped down and walked slowly out of the room.

As his sinewy feline form disappeared, an idea hit me. Turning back to the computer, I massaged my fingers together before typing in the search phrase, "Japanese Historical Museums". Several sites appeared on-screen. It took the good part of an hour to scroll through their inventory. All owned pieces from the Kamakura period, but there was no mention of the *Sitting Tiso*.

I was about to exit the final screen when a subheading near the bottom caught my attention. My cursor found the line that read "Missing/Stolen" and when I clicked on it, the page that came up made me smile.

My man Tiso topped off a short list. Seems he'd been stolen from the Tokyo Museum of Art History back in 1939 and has been missing ever since. An accompanying article ticked off details about the rare piece and ended with a promised reward for its safe return. The last sentence warned that it is a crime against the Japanese government to be in illegal possession of this important historical artifact.

Before signing off, I reentered the Churchills website. The *Sitting Tiso* was not listed in their inventory. Apparently, Benny Shatts was hawking more than Churchills' standard inventory and using the firm's good name to lure fat cat buyers.

I woke early the following day, did some laps in the pool, showered, and then settled myself at the computer. Linking up with the salon's main frame, I accessed my client files. Mikala LeMeux's home number was listed, so I placed the call.

"Max, darling," growled Mikala in a voice shaded by thirty years of cigarette smoke. "How the hell are you?"

"Fine, Mikala. Thanks. And you?"

"Tired. Running roughshod over my good-for-nothing corporate board takes all my energy."

"Give it up," I joked. "You have plenty of money."

"And do what?"

"Indulge yourself."

"I already do that, as you well know. And I'm only ten years older than you, mister. I'll retire when you retire."

"That might be soon, Mikala. I'm not in love with business like you are."

"Hell, I don't love it. I *need* it. It's the only thing I do well."

I was about to bring up Benny Shatts when Mikala proffered an invitation.

"What are your plans for this afternoon, Max?"

"Nothing I can't postpone. Why?"

"I'm throwing a little impromptu get together here at the house. The twins are coming and a couple of others. Care to join us?"

"Do I get a tour of your art collection?"

"Naturally," Mikala assured me. "Nobody escapes without me boring them to tears with that damn collection."

"Then I'll be there. Thank you."

"Come over about three," she said as if it was a command. "We'll open the first bottle of wine and you can tell me why you called."

Mikala's home is in the city of West Bloomfield, an affluent suburb northwest of Detroit, where people with money like to live in gated communities. The residents are predominantly white but a variety of cultures have crept in through the years, giving the expensive vanilla milkshake a little ethnic color and flavor.

Mikala had given me flawless directions, but she had neglected to inform the entrance guard to her private neighborhood that I had been added to the guest list. Even after a call to her home and a recheck of my driver's license, it looked doubtful that the guard would let me pass. Finally after circling the SUV twice and surveying my backseat to make sure I wasn't smuggling in any subdivision terrorists, he reluctantly raised the gate.

A former macaroni manufacturer must have designed the layout for the streets of Mikala's neighborhood. They twisted round and around like a plate of spaghetti. By the time I arrived at the address, I felt vaguely hungry. The house itself was a sprawling, two-story French provincial, a quarter of a mile off the road. When it first came into view, I half expected to see Jed Clampett out shooting squirrels on the vast lawn. Massive double front doors marked the home's entrance. Seconds after using the brass doorknocker, I was ushered inside by a nattily dressed butler.

"Mr. Snow?" the man said. He looked like a young Louie Armstrong. "My name is Lamar."

"Nice to meet you, Lamar."

"Oh it's my pleasure, sir," the man said. "I've heard Madam speak of you many times."

"Any of it good?"

"Mostly good, sir," he remarked, "except when she's having trouble doing her hair in the morning."

I raised my eyebrows and Lamar broke into an infectious laugh.

"But that doesn't happen very often, sir."

"Really, Lamar?"

"Absolutely not," he answered, unable to check his toothy smile. "But when she does get herself all worked up over that one little hair that just won't stay in place, oohh, it's a good thing you can't hear the woman."

Still chuckling, Lamar led me through the home's cavernous interior to an enclosed patio toward the rear. He paused at the entrance, straightened, and did a little servant's cough. "Madam will join you presently, sir," he recited, trying his best to keep a straight face. "She's on a call to Paris and regrets not being present for your arrival."

I winked at the man and stepped into a sunroom the size of a small gymnasium. One side was a workout space containing pool, running track, and a set of balance bars. The other was arranged for entertaining, with an island bar, an elaborate grill that vented out the glass ceiling, and a burnished steel dining set that could easily seat twenty. I stood there, hands in the pockets of my black slacks, marveling at the room's size until the lady of the house interrupted my thoughts.

"Max," Mikala called out as she glided across the marble floor, the hem of her ankle length, electric-blue dress billowing out behind her. "What a pleasure you could come on such short notice."

"You look radiant, Mikala," I said. Pleased by my comment, the slim, fifty-something woman did a quick turn.

"I owe it all to my hairdresser," she replied, primping the soft curls framing her delicate face. "The man works miracles."

"Hardly that, darling," I said. "Let's just say I put the icing on your cake."

Mikala laughed; a sound somewhere between Bea Arthur and Cancer of the throat. "That's why I don't mind you overcharging me, Maxie," she said before heading off to the bar. "You're such a good bullshitter."

I joined her and she displayed two selections of white wine.

"I think I promised we would open the first bottle together," she said. "Which would you prefer?"

I tapped the Talbut Chardonnay, a favorite of mine, and she uncorked it with practiced ease.

"Now," Mikala said as she finished pouring. "What made you call me this morning? Did I miss an appointment?"

"No," I answered raising my glass to her. "I wanted to discuss your pending deal with Benny Shatts."

Mikala took a long drink of her wine, before eyeing me appraisingly. "Sounds like Frick and Frack have been bending your ear."

I shrugged. "They were concerned."

"So they sent you to talk me out of buying from Benny?"

"Not exactly. It's just that they don't trust Shatts and frankly I don't blame them."

"And why is that?" she said over the rim of her glass. "Do you know something about him I don't?"

"Only what I could find on the Internet."

Mikala leaned a hip against the bar and waited.

"Did you know the piece Shatts is trying to sell you is a protected Japanese artifact?"

Mikala poured herself a bit more wine, and then strolled over to the pool. "I'm a collector, Max. Collectors go after the best they can afford."

"Can you afford it?" I asked, joining her poolside. "And I'm not talking money. If the wrong person discovers it's in your possession, you could find yourself in trouble."

Mikala was about to answer when Ed and Mike entered the patio. By their side were two men I didn't know, but from their similar look and body shape, they had to be brothers.

"I appreciate your interest, Max," Mikala said quietly. "But unless you can give me something better, I'm going ahead with the deal."

The foursome walked over to join us.

"Maxie," said Mike. "Mother didn't say you'd be here."

Ed did the introductions. "Max Snow, hairdresser extraordinaire; meet the Grimm brothers. John." She put a hand on the shoulder of the man beside her. "And James."

I shook their hands. "Grimm?" I said. "Any connection to the author of the famous fairytales?"

Mike grinned lustily. "The only tails these boys are connected to are ours."

"Michelle," Mikala said while filling four more glasses. "Don't be so crude. Max doesn't want to hear about your decadent sex life and neither does your mother."

"I don't mind," I said, eyeing the two identical faces. "Gives me something to think about on cold winter nights."

Lamar entered the patio next followed by a short, rail thin man that looked to be somewhere in his late sixties. He wore a western style denim shirt, black jeans, and cowboy boots trimmed in matte silver. Clutched in his boney fingers, was a high-crowned Stetson with a turquoise hatband.

"Max," Ed whispered as Mikala floated across the room to greet her sixth guest. "You're about to meet Benny Shatts."

I gave the newcomer my full attention, instantly understanding why the twins described him as weasely. The man had small, rodent-like eyes set too close together, a long pointed nose that could easily double as a snout, and just to prove God has a sense of humor, an untamed salt-and-pepper mustache stuck out at odd angles.

When Mikala strolled arm and arm with Shatts over to our little party, his head moved in quick jerks from person to person. "Hey, y'all," he said in a nasal pitched southern drawl. "Hope you fine folks are doing well this afternoon."

After lunch we all strolled up to the second floor library and toured Mikala's collection. Our hostess described each piece while Shatts filled in with obscure details. I was impressed with the man's knowledge. As we were exiting the room, Shatts touched my arm and nodded at me to hang back.

"I can tell you're interested in Oriental antiques," he said, grinning.

"Interested, yes. But I'm no collector."

"Well how about we get you started. I've got a line on two Utamaro woodblock prints from the late eighteenth-century. The owner is in a hurry to sell, so I can get you a great deal."

I had gleaned enough information off the Net to know that original Utamaro didn't come cheap and was curious about what he thought was a deal. "How much?"

"My client is asking a hundred and fifty thousand apiece," he said, and then offered the hook. "But I think I can convince her to sell the pair for a quarter-million."

I tried not to look too shocked. "Is that a good price?"

"Oh, the best. The best," he insisted. "Utamaro is hot right now. You couldn't go wrong on an investment like that. Absolutely not."

"What else is available?" I asked, as a scheme to test Shatts's veracity began forming in my mind.

"Well," said Shatts, rubbing his hands together. "I've got an early nineteenth-century hanging scroll by Sengai. The old man had a spontaneous style that would floor you, all full of uneven lines and wild colors."

I nodded like I knew what he was talking about.

"I also represent a six-fold screen by Jakuchu. Mid-1800's ink and color impasto on hand-made paper. It is absolutely beautiful."

"I'm sure it is."

"Mikala tells me your home is a Japanese style pagoda."

"Last time I looked."

"I'd love to see it," Shatts said and pulled a business card from his shirt pocket. "Maybe if I got the feel of the place, I could recommend other pieces."

"What if I wanted something a little more...rare, Benny?" I said, lowering my voice to conspiratorial.

"Like what?" Shatts said as his weasel-like eyes darted quickly across my face.

"Like the *Sitting Tiso* Mikala is interested in."

The lips beneath the whiskers tightened into a thin line. "That type of piece doesn't come on the market very often."

"I'm not surprised," I said. "I understand it was stolen from the Tokyo Museum, and that it's illegal to own it."

Shatts shrugged in answer to my teaser. "All I can say is that the Tiso has been in the possession of several collectors here in the States and I assure you, none of them are in the habit of breaking the law."

"Hey," I said. "I'm not suggesting they are. Like most things worth owning, beauty has its risks and rewards."

"Right. Right," Shatts said as he rocked back on his heels. "That is exactly right."

"Am I also right to say that money talks, Benny?" I asked, throwing in a hook of my own. "What if I wanted to buy the *Sitting Tiso*? Is there still time to get in the running?"

Shatts cocked his head and eyed me like a cat sizing up potential prey. "We're talking about an antique worth 1.5 million dollars. Are you ready to spend that kind of money?"

"The money's no problem," I said, "but let me ask you a question."

Benny's head bobbed like a butcher taking a meat order.

"I understand Mikala is going to trade you quite a bit of her collection for the piece."

"That's correct."

"And then you have to turn those pieces over to realize your profit?"

"Well yes, but..."

I shook my head. "Sounds like a lot of work, Benny. What if I made you a cash offer?"

At the "c" word, Shatts rose up on the toes of his alligator boots. "I have my reputation to consider," he said, pulling nervously at the silver tails of his string tie. "Mikala and I have a verbal agreement."

"How about if I add another hundred-thousand to your commission? Would that convince you to kill the verbal deal?"

The man licked his thin lips hungrily. I could almost see the wheels in his brain doing the numbers. "How long would it take you to come up with the cash?"

"A few days."

Shatts worked his jaw back and forth as if chewing on my proposition. "You have a deal, Max. Come up with 1.5 million by," he glanced at his wristwatch, "this time next Sunday and the Tiso is yours."

"You mean 1.6 don't you, Benny?"

"Yes. Yes, of course. 1.6. Thank y'all for reminding me."

When I left Mikala's home around six, the twins walked me out.

"So, what did you think of Benny Shatts?" Ed asked as they watched me climb inside my truck.

"I think the little rat would sell his mother to the Taliban if the price was right," I said, snapping my seatbelt closed.

"You got that right," Mike agreed. "He's even creepier than I remembered. How are we going to kill his deal with Mom?"

"I've already started that ball rolling," I said and winked at them. "Although Mikala might end up hating me for it."

As I drove off, I went over my hastily thought up plan. True, I had managed to delay Mikala's deal with Shatts, but only for a week. Now I had to come up with a good reason for her not to buy from the little guy.

At home, I fed Blue dinner and afterwards brushed his silky coat; a twice-weekly ritual each of us enjoyed. It had a relaxing effect on me and as an added benefit, cut down on the amount of hairballs he chucked up behind the furniture.

About eight that night, my mother phoned.

"Yo, baby boy. Where the hell have you been? I've been calling all afternoon."

"Never mind where *I've* been, lady. Where are *you?*"

"Oli and I are back in Chicago. He had some business to take care of and I wanted to shop. Right now we're having dinner at the Four Seasons."

"So why call me?" I said; feeling irritated. "Is it fun rubbing Grillo in my face?"

"Oooh. Testy, testy. No. I called to tell you I'd be home tomorrow."

"Yeah?"

"And we need to talk."

"So talk," I said.

"Not now. I want to talk to you in person."

"If it has anything to do with you and Mr. Mafia, I'm *not* interested."

"Yes you are," she cooed in the way she always did after a couple of drinks.

"No, I'm not. The only news I want to hear about you and Grillo is that you're dumping him."

"Not even close," she said, and then hiccupped into the phone. "We'll talk tomorrow. Love you."

The next morning was clear and sunny so I decided to go for a run. I'd been ditching my regular exercise routine lately and paid the price, by losing my breakfast a mile down the road. Ever since Zed left, I wasn't exercising, or eating healthy. And meditation, a daily routine when she was around, had been virtually nonexistent for weeks.

An hour later, I walked in my backdoor—make that stumbled in—and just as I reached for a bottle of water, the phone rang. Jug in hand, I dragged myself into the main living area and looked down at the caller I.D. The readout said "unknown caller". After the fourth ring, my curiosity won out and I picked up.

"Spicy Sam's Pizza Parlor," I said, using a very bad Italian accent. It was the same lame joke my father had used when I was a kid.

There was no immediate response as the caller considered the possibility of a wrong number.

"Is that you, Max?" a male voice said.

"That depends. Who's this?"

"It's Benny. Benny Shatts."

I rolled my eyes and took a long pull from the water bottle. The guy didn't believe in letting any grass grow under his feet. "Hey, Benny. What's up?"

"Thought maybe I could drop by your home tonight," he said, "and show you pictures of the antiques I was talking about."

"Tonight?"

"If that's not a problem."

I would have preferred female company, especially the kind that would be willing to massage the kinks out of my aching muscles. But duty called and I started reciting directions.

At 6:20 pm I heard a knock on my back door. When I opened it, Shatts, dressed in boots, jeans, fringed suede jacket, and a black Stetson, bowed slightly at the waist.

"*Konban wa*, Max-*san*," he said, using the traditional Japanese evening greeting. "The beauty of your house honors the heart and brings joy to the eye."

"Thanks, Benny," I said, returning the bow. "Come on in."

Shatts stepped inside and looked over the almost two thousand square feet of uninterrupted space. The first floor of my home is totally wall-less with different living areas being defined by furniture clusters.

"There are no walls," he said, gazing around in awe. "I've never seen anything like it."

"I don't think there is anything like it," I replied. "Seigo Nakao was the architect and I've read he never designed two houses alike."

"Seigo Nakao did this?" he asked with renewed respect. "I should have recognized his style."

"He built it for a gangster named Johnny Lott about three years ago."

Shatts peeked into the sunroom, a thirty-by-thirty foot half-circle with floor-to-ceiling windows that overlooked an outdoor patio and the lake. "I remember reading about that," he said. "Wasn't Lott shot to death in the driveway?"

"That's what they tell me."

"How long have you owned the house?"

"Just over two years."

"Simply beautiful," Shatts said. "And perfect for the pieces I'm suggesting."

We had a glass of cabernet in the sunroom and Shatts put on the hard sell. When he thought his pitch had succeeded, he leaned back into his chair and smiled confidently. "Well. What do you think?"

"I'll consider the other pieces, Benny. But I definitely want the Tiso."

"You're sure now, that you can come up with 1.6 million by the end of the week?"

"Will you have the Tiso?"

"Oh yes," he said excitedly. "It's practically in my possession already."

"Then the money is as good as there too," I said, curious as to where he might keep such an expensive work of art.

Ten minutes later, Shatts peeked at his watch and stood. "I hate to drink and run," he said, as I escorted him to the door, "but I have another appointment. I'll contact you near the end of the week to set up a delivery time."

From inside the house, I watched Shatts climb into a silver Lincoln Continental. When he was halfway down the drive, I grabbed my keys, jumped into the Lexus, and sped off after him. He caught the main road to the I-96 and thirty minutes later exited at Northwestern Highway. After a right on Franklin Road, he headed north and to my great surprise, turned into the parking lot of Grillo

Beauty Supply. I zipped into the driveway of the dark office building next door, looped around the far side, and killed the engine.

My heart thumped hard against my chest as I jogged to the rear of the building to peek around the corner. The Lincoln was there, with Shatts still behind the wheel. I could see his rodent-like face illuminated by the parking lot security lights. A cell phone was pressed to his ear. Judging by his angry gesticulations, it must have been a pretty edgy conversation. A moment later, he exited the car, squared the Stetson on his head like a gunfighter readying for a showdown, and walked briskly to the entrance.

I crept along the rear of the neighboring building, trying my best to blend into the shadowy landscape. It was hard to tell what was going down but one thing was certain, Shatts wasn't visiting GBS to buy beauty supplies. The hair on his head was so sparse, a single bottle of shampoo would last him a year.

When the door to Grillo's building opened, Candy Sprinkles stepped out and the two stood talking. I couldn't hear a word but the conversation didn't look friendly. Candy, dressed in jeans, white turtleneck, and running shoes had fists planted firmly on her hips, while Shatts paced back and forth like a caged tiger. The scene ended when the obviously pissed off man threw up his arms as if in defeat and stalked back to his car. His engine caught, the headlights flashed, and he sped off in a burst of squealing tires.

My first inclination was to follow, but when Candy didn't immediately go back inside, I decided to stick around. She pulled a cell phone from her back pocket and I duck-walked through the dense assortment of shrubs hoping to eavesdrop on the conversation. A few yards ahead there was a shuffling sound in the bushes. I glanced over to see the biggest, ugliest possum I had ever had the displeasure of laying eyes on. The animal was over three feet long from snout to its rat-like tail, and he didn't look happy to see me. In fact, as my eyes adjusted more to the darkness, I could see it was baring its pointed yellow teeth.

I started to back away but the fat little bugger lunged in my direction, causing me to trip and fall into the shrub behind me. It was a barberry and sharp thorns poked into me from every direction. Sensing his advantage, the possum snarled ferociously and chomped down on the toe of my boot. I freaked, and after rolling painfully out of the bush, scuttled back on one leg in an attempt to dislodge the determined creature.

Drawn by the commotion, Candy followed her ears, cell phone in one hand, a small, chrome revolver now in the other. Before she could get close enough to eyeball me, I gave the possum a stiff kick in the ribs that sent it scurrying in her direction. She took one look at the butt-ugly animal charging out of the bushes and to my relief, bolted back into the building.

The minute she disappeared inside, I took off in the opposite direction. When I reached my truck, I slapped it in reverse, did a k-turn on the wide drive and within moments, I was back on Franklin Road cruising south.

At home, I brewed up a decaf espresso, settled onto the couch, and wondered for the umpteenth time why Benny Shatts had visited GBS. The man was obviously loathed by Candy. Her body language during their confrontation was pure—die a thousand deaths you little sleazebag. Olympio Grillo, on the other hand, seemed the more likely visitee. I had no trouble imagining him and Shatts partnered up in a variety of unsavory business deals.

The next morning, I woke to the sound of a phone ringing in my ear. Raising my lids to half-mast, I looked around and groaned when I realized I had slept another night on the couch. Used to be I could only sleep in my waterbed, but that was before Zed exited my life. Without her next to me, the bed didn't seem half as comfortable.

The phone on the coffee table kept up its demanding din, so I plucked it up and croaked out a hello.

"Still in bed?" Marie said sprightly. "It's after nine you know."

"It's also my day off, you know," I returned gruffly.

"You're always in a bad mood lately," she said. "What's the problem?"

I mumbled something about her and Grillo but she ignored it.

"Oli and I just picked up breakfast for the three of us," Marie announced. "And we're on our way over. You get to supply the coffee."

"I don't want that man in my house, Marie," I growled. "If you show up with him, I'm not coming to the door."

"No problem," she said breezily. "I'll use my key. See you in about twenty five minutes."

She disconnected and I sat there staring at the phone. "Damn the woman!" I said to Blue, who had awakened at the other end of the couch and was stretching his back legs one at a time. "What the hell doesn't she understand about the word no?"

Blue didn't say anything; he only yawned and trotted off to his feeding station in the kitchen. The cat didn't give a dog's ass who came to the house, as long as his food bowl was filled twice a day.

"You're not going to like Grillo," I said as I opened a can of Ocean Fish Feast and served it up to my howling feline master. "He's probably the kind of guy that hates cats."

I showered and was in the middle of my shave, when I heard my mom's voice calling from the main floor.

"Maxie? We're here. You got that coffee brewing?"

"It's all ready," I yelled back. "Be down in a minute."

When I walked into the kitchen, Grillo was grating a block of Swiss cheese into a frothy egg mixture. Thick slices of bacon were sizzling in a pan on the stove and Marie was slipping a-half-dozen fresh croissants into the oven to warm.

"Max," Grillo said, offering me a hand to shake. "Good to see you again. Hope you don't mind me using your kitchen."

"Max doesn't mind at all," Marie said, while she stood on her tiptoes and kissed Grillo on the cheek. "He's almost as good a cook as you are, Oli."

Ten minutes later, we were seated at the dining room table, eating the best scrambled eggs I had ever tasted. I would have said so too but I resented discovering that Grillo had yet another talent to add to the list. If I found out he was an artist or could do hair, I might run screaming into the lake.

"Maxie," Mom said, as if on cue. "How do you like my haircut?"

I looked up from my plate and noticed for the first time that her hair had been neatly trimmed.

"Oli did it," she said, beaming at the man. "Isn't he wonderful?"

I cut my eyes to Grillo, who waved away the compliment. "I had a yen to be a hairstylist when I was in my late teens," he said. "But my dad nixed the idea."

I scooped up another mouthful of eggs and chewed resentfully.

"Not that I come anywhere close to your abilities," he said. "You gave Marie a beautiful haircut. I just followed your lines."

I grunted and went on eating. It was becoming more and more difficult not to like the man. If it wasn't for the Mafia connection, I might have tried a little harder. He was obviously making Marie happy. She was practically glowing.

We finished the meal and were enjoying a second cup of coffee when Blue walked over, no doubt drawn by the smell of bacon. Grillo noticed him immediately, and put a hand out for him to sniff.

"Hey there, kitty," he said as Blue jumped up on his lap. "Aren't you the friendly one?"

I could hear the feline traitor's purr from across the table. So much for my Grillo-the-cat-hater theory.

"He's an Oriental, isn't he?" Grillo asked.

I nodded.

"What's his name?"

"Blue."

"I can see why," Grillo said and ran a palm down the cat's sleek backside. "Just look at those handsome blue highlights."

"If he's bothering you," I said, "just push him off."

"Not at all," he said. "I love cats. I've got four Persians back in Chicago that I miss terribly."

"They're beauties too," Marie chimed in after topping off Grillo's coffee cup. "I met them when we visited Oli's parents."

I steeled myself with a long slug of java and looked directly at Grillo. "What kind of business is your *Family* in these days?"

Marie kicked me under the table.

"We've diversified our interests in the last few years," Grillo said, unruffled by my obvious innuendo. "But in the main we do trucking, import, export, and we own several office buildings in Chicago and Arizona."

"What?" I said, unable to stop myself. "No cement works? How do you make shoes for your victims?"

Grillo flashed me an indulgent grin and continued to pet Blue. "Like I told your mother, Max, that kind of rough stuff only happens in the *Godfather* movies. The Mafia is strictly a business entity these days."

I glanced at Marie. If looks could kill, I'd be six feet under.

"Ignore my not so subtle son, Oli. He hangs out with cops, and mistrusts everyone."

"No, no," Grillo said. "That's quite all right. The Mafia has an unfortunate reputation that I can't say isn't well deserved."

"He doesn't have to be rude about it though," Marie said, while raking me with hard eyes once more. "And if he does it again, I'm going to spank him."

Her rebuke reminded me of Riff's warning not to reveal what I knew about Grillo. "Marie is right, Olympio. Sorry if I offended you."

"No offense taken, Max. Your concern for Marie is admirable."

We were all silent for a beat until Marie asked if anyone wanted more to eat. Both Grillo and I shook our heads.

"What I would like," Grillo said, "is to check out the lake."

"Sure," said Marie. "I'll get my coat."

"I'd like to have a private conversation with Max, honey," Grillo said, patting her hand. "How about if you clean up while he and I take a walk?"

Mom agreed reluctantly and after giving me a "behave yourself or else" look, she walked to the kitchen and started loading the dishwasher.

I grabbed a coat, led Grillo through the sunroom and down to the patio overlooking Cradle Lake. It was sunny and fairly warm for early January. The temperature this winter had yet to drop below fifty degrees.

"Big lake," said Grillo as his eyes scanned the open expanse of gently rolling water. "Is it any good for sailing?"

I nodded. "The wind is generally from the west, so it's an easy ride home."

"I love to sail," Grillo said. "But it's usually on Lake Michigan."

"What kind of boat do you have?" I asked.

"A twenty-eight-foot Sun Odyssey."

"Big boat," I commented.

"On *that* lake," he said. "I wouldn't go out in anything smaller."

"How many crew members does it take to sail something like that?"

"With experienced people, two. Three or four when the water is rough. You've already met one of my crew."

I gave him a blank stare but then remembered Candy Sprinkles had talked about sailing on the Great Lakes. "You mean Candy?"

Grillo pulled a big, fat Cuban from an inside pocket of his overcoat and took his time lighting it. "She's as good on a boat as any man."

I wasn't sure what to say at that point since I had no way of knowing how much Candy had told Grillo about our night together.

"I heard you two had a good time when you came to dinner," Grillo said.

I couldn't tell if he was baiting me or what. The look on his face was still friendly. "I found Candy fascinating," I said. "A sweet lady and an excellent cook."

"She is that," Grillo said as he puffed on the cigar and shaded his eyes against the sunlight. "She also fucks like a five-hundred dollar whore. Wouldn't you agree?"

Grillo turned back in my direction when I didn't answer. "Don't sweat it, Max. Candy is not my girlfriend. She beds who she wants."

I could feel my heart beat and despite the pleasant temperature, cold sweat dampened my palms. "It wasn't planned, Olympio. We drank too much wine."

He held up a hand. "Like I said, don't sweat it. If I was pissed, you'd be at the bottom of this lake right now wearing a pair of those cement shoes you mentioned."

"Thought you said the rough stuff was all in the past."

"I lied," he said, while inspecting the cigar in his hand. "Marie doesn't need to know everything. She's safer that way."

"What's *that* supposed to mean?"

"Exactly what it sounds like. I have a great affection for your mother and I wouldn't want anything to happen to her."

I stared at Grillo, trying to figure out if the comment was a threat.

"You seem like a no nonsense guy, Max," Grillo said, after relighting the cigar. "Pretty feisty too for a hairdresser."

"Feisty?"

Grillo grinned. "I understand you own a gun."

"Marie tell you that?"

"She didn't have to. My research people uncovered pretty much everything about you."

"Oh yeah?" I said, annoyed but curious to hear more. "Like what?"

"Like you've got a license to carry," he said, as if reading off a list. "Take Claritin for your allergies. Have a touch of arthritis. You won twelve million in the lotto. Retired, but came back into the business with your little friend that got herself murdered. And you're living in the house that Johnny Lott had built for himself."

I shrugged, like the litany of personal facts was no big deal. "Tell me something that isn't common knowledge and I might be impressed."

"Okay," Grillo said, smiling confidently. "You're in love with a beautiful woman from Belize. Her name is Zed. She's six-foot-two, black hair, black eyes, and built like a brick shithouse."

"Anybody who knows me knows that." I said. "Try again."

"Your girlfriend was trained in the healing arts by a native medicine man. She's been living in America for ten years and right now she's back in Belize, shacked up with her ex-lover."

I turned from him and walked down to the lake's edge. Grillo was too good. I didn't want him to see how shook I was about the ex-lover comment.

"There's a lot more," Grillo said when he joined me. "But I'll just skip to the meat. I know about you finding Lott's four-million dollar stash in your house."

I tried to look calm when I faced him but didn't think I pulled it off.

"Lott and I were good friends," Grillo said, grinning in triumph. "We shared many secrets."

"You couldn't know anything about me finding money in the house," I said, trying a bluff, "because it's not true."

"Sure it is," he said, waving to Marie who was observing us through the sunroom door. "I told you before; it's my business to learn all about my customers."

"I hate people nosing around in my life, Grillo, but I guess since you're the big Mafia man, there ain't a damn thing I can do about it."

"Not much," he answered. "But I didn't tell you all that to make you mad."

"Oh, really? Then why?"

Grillo took a long drag on his cigar, then let the smoke curl out slowly. "You've heard the expression 'knowledge is power'?"

I stayed silent.

"Well I'm all about gathering knowledge," he continued. "When I've got enough, I sell, trade, or use it to motivate people to my way of thinking."

"And what do you hope to get from me?"

"I want you to become a customer of GBS."

I shook my head. "This is not about me dealing your beauty products."

His eyes narrowed in reluctant respect. "You're a sharp man, Max."

"Yeah. I'm also feisty. Now what do you want?"

"I explained your value to me the first time we met."

I rolled my eyes. "If you mean that 'you own a high profile salon in an affluent mall and sell a lot of product' crap, I'm not buying it."

He smiled indulgently. "Large amounts of money move through your salon every day, correct?"

"Yeah? So?" I said, getting impatient for the bottom line.

"So I'd like you to move some of *my* money along with it."

There it was and it wasn't even close to what I had expected. "Are you talking about laundering Mafia money through my salon?"

"Exactly," said Grillo before tossing his barely smoked fifty-dollar cigar in the lake. "What do you think?"

I was too pissed to restrain my tongue. "That you picked the wrong guy. And that your research people should have tipped you off."

"Nevertheless," he said, stepping into my personal space. "When I want something, I get it."

"Not this time," I said, angered by the threat.

The gray eyes turned stormy as he fingered the lapels of my jacket. "I can make you do anything I want," he said softly. "And what I want...is for your salon to become my laundry."

"Then you'd better off me or buy me out, because that's the only way it's going to happen."

Grillo's expression softened. He backed up a pace. "I don't want to use force, Max, but I'll do what's necessary to secure your cooperation."

"Like what?"

"Like I might tell some folks Lott owed money to, that you're sitting on his four-million. Or maybe I'll whisper it to his crazed widow, who would cut your dick off and stick it up your ass if she discovered you were holding out on her."

"There *is* no four-million," I insisted but he ignored the comment.

"I could easily contract a hit on your girlfriend."

I tried to laugh that one off, but it came out pretty lame. "Zed would spot them before they even got close."

"Maybe," he said, cocking his head. "But you can't be sure, can you?"

"You would do that, huh? Have someone murdered to get your way?"

"And sleep like a baby," he said, laying his cheek against folded hands.

"What's to stop me from going to the cops?"

Grillo looked up and down the empty beach. "Lack of witnesses?"

"I could spill the whole thing to Marie."

Grillo rocked a shoulder. "She told me how you feel about us seeing each other. It would sound like you were blowing smoke up her ass."

He was probably right about Marie. Even when she's not in love, it's like talking to the wall. As far as Zed's safety is concerned, murder in a remote place like Belize, might be easier than I thought.

"I don't need your answer now," Grillo said, clapping a hand on my shoulder. "I'll be in Italy for the next week or so. We can talk again when I get back."

"Going to pay your respects to the Don?" I asked sarcastically.

"Not this trip," he said. "A friend of mine arranged an audience with the Pope."

"*The* Pope?"

Grillo nodded. "I was...instrumental in getting several churches built in Peru and Bolivia. In appreciation, His Eminence invited us to visit the Vatican."

"Us?" I asked, afraid of what his answer would be.

"Yes," said Grillo. "Marie and I. That's what we came over to tell you."

Chapter 5

▼

The happy couple left for Italy the very next day and although Marie would have expected me to call and say I had arrived safely at my destination, she didn't operate under the same constraints. If the tables were turned, she'd track me down like a bloodhound and give me the old "mothers have rights children don't" speech I'd heard all my life.

Knowing Marie's penchant for altercations, I had kept Grillo's threats to myself. It would be just like the quick-tempered woman to confront him at an inopportune time, and I'd be thousands of miles away with no chance to help.

That evening, Blue and I were sitting on the couch watching *Felix the Cat* cartoons on our new 55" plasma TV. Personally, I could have gone with a smaller size, but knew if I had; the voice in my head would have nagged the shit out of me. It liked everything big and expensive. If I didn't put the brakes on occasionally, I'd end up in the poor house.

Felix and the Professor's genius nephew Poindexter had just landed on the moon in their homemade flying saucer when Blue cocked his head toward the phone sitting on the coffee table. Half a second later, it signaled a call.

"This is Max."

"Hey," two female voices said in unison. "It's us."

"Ladies," I said, muting the TV's sound. "What's up?"

"We called to make sure you were on the job," Mike said.

"Yeah", Ed said. "What are you doing home? You should be out there detecting for us."

"Even Sherlock Holmes took breaks," I said. "And Blue eats the house plants if I don't show my face around here once and a while."

"How *is* that sexy little kitty?" Mike growled.

"Blue is the man," Ed chimed in. "Next life, I want to be she-cat to his he-cat."

"Forget it," Mike teased. "Blue and I have like, a cosmic connection. If anyone's going to cat around in the next life with that bad boy pussy, it's moi."

"Huh," Ed said. "You freakin' wish. It is so about Blue and me."

"Hello," I sang. "If you two called to talk to the cat, I can put him on."

"Oh, oh," said Mike, "I think Maxie's jealous."

"I *am* not."

"Well you shouldn't be," Ed cooed. "You're every bit as sexy as your cat."

"You certainly are," agreed Mike. "It's just that Blue is so…strokeable. And the way he looks at me with those big green eyes is to die for."

"I know what you mean, sister," Ed gushed. "It's like he's trying to see into my soul."

"What he's trying to see into," I said, "are your pockets. You might be hiding treats."

"We *are* hiding treats," Mike teased.

"Yeah," Ed chimed. "But we're willing to share—especially with you."

"Um…you two want to check your hormones for a minute and tell me why you called?"

"We want to know what you're doing about Shatts," Mike said. "His deal with mom is coming up."

"If push comes to shove," I said, "I'll buy the Tiso myself."

"What?" the two voices chorused.

"Benny and I worked a deal. I come up with the price plus commission by the end of the week and he sells to me."

"We couldn't ask you to do that, Max," Mike said.

"No," Ed said. "We couldn't."

"You didn't ask," I assured them. "I thought it up on my own."

"But all that money," Ed said.

"I've got it. And if the Japanese government isn't willing to return my investment, I'll sell it to somebody who is."

"We are definitely going to have to reward you for your noble efforts, Sir Max," Mike teased. "How would you like two willing handmaidens to warm your bed tonight?"

"Sounds cozy, ladies," I said, feeling the pull of the wild side. "It really does. But I'm afraid I'll have to take a raincheck."

At the salon two days later, during a break between clients, I was skimming through the morning paper when a story about a deadly hit-and-run in the city of Southfield caught my eye. The piece, barely three inches long, was enough to tell me neither Mikala nor I would be completing any deals with Benny Shatts. The antique dealer had been run over in the parking lot of his apartment house, and was now a guest at the Oakland County morgue.

"Anything wrong, boss?" asked Trish White, a young shampoo assistant sitting across from me. "You have an odd look on your face."

I gazed at her pale, fairy-like features framed by a thick curtain of black hair, streaked electric-blue. "Not really, Trish," I said. "An acquaintance of mine was killed in an accident last night and I was wondering how to tell some mutual friends what happened."

"Bummer," Trish said; her brown eyes wide with concern. "Seems like a lot of people are dying these days."

I didn't ask what she meant by that. Ms. White was doing the "Goth" thing. Her interpretation of the style was to dress in black, do her face up like a vampire, and discuss the dark side like other people did the weather.

Back in my studio, I dialed Mike and Ed's number but only reached their answering machine. I left a message and was in my car when the twins returned the call. Each was on a separate hand set. They had twin phones installed in every room of their house.

"Can you believe it, Maxie?" Ed said.

"About Shatts?"

"Yeah," Mike kidded. "*You* didn't bump him off, did you?"

"My hands are clean, ladies, and so are my tires."

"What do you think happened?" asked Mike.

"Ditto," Ed put in. "Neither of us liked the little nerd but we didn't want him dead."

"Your guess is as good as mine," I said. "Hopefully I'll get some details from a friend who works for the Southfield P.D."

"You mean Linda Riff?" Ed asked.

"Of course he does," Mike said. "She was the babe Max was boinking before he met Zed."

"Excuse me," I said. "I do not boink women. I make love to them. And that's the last time I'm telling you guys anything about my sex life."

"Why?" Mike teased. "We tell you everything about ours."

"Clients are supposed to confess all to their stylist," I said. "Not the other way around."

"But it's *your* sex life we're interested in," Ed said. "We already know about each other's."

"Well, lots of luck from here on in. Your memories are too good."

"The offer still holds for you to become part of our sex life," Mike purred. "Then we can all keep quiet about it."

"Excellent idea," Ed put in. "Now there's a secret worth keeping."

"Gotta go now, ladies," I said, determined to resist the siren song of the whore.

"Chicken?" Ed challenged.

"Yeah," Mike said, following her sister's lead. "Afraid of double trouble?"

"You bet your sweet butts I am," I said, and severed the connection before I could reconsider.

At seven that night, I thought about Riff and wondered if she was feeling sociable. When she didn't answer her home phone, I dialed her work number.

"This is Lieutenant Riff," she answered in her official cop voice. "How can I help you?"

"You could come by my house and have dinner with me tonight."

"Tell me what you're cooking and maybe I will."

"How about loin lamb chops, dilled baby redskins, a spinach salad with warm bacon dressing, and a loaf of fresh baked rye?"

"Tempting," Riff said. "What's for dessert?"

"An apple pie from Pickadilly."

"The kind with the French cream on the bottom?"

"Yup."

"And the apples that stay firm until they melt in your mouth?"

"Uh huh."

"Be there in an hour."

When I heard Riff's car pull up to the back door, I slid the chops under the broiler. She used her own key and stood at the door stomping her feet.

"Shit," she said, slipping out of her coat, and rubbing her hands together. "I think winter's finally here."

"Cozy up to the fire, Lieutenant," I said, thinking there weren't many women who could make jeans and a simple white v-neck sweater look as tantalizing. "I'm just finishing up dinner."

As soon as everything was ready, I called Riff to the table in the sunroom. I set out plates and silverware, positioning the salad bowl between us.

"Hope you don't mind sharing," I said as she sat across from me. "I read somewhere that it makes a meal more intimate."

"Plus," she said, after spearing a forkful of spinach, "we get out of washing a second bowl."

When she finished her dinner—including two pieces of pie—Riff pushed the chair back and unsnapped the top button of her jeans. "Whew," she said patting her stomach. "I've got to get me a man who can cook like this. How come you're not fat as a pig?"

"Because I'm tortured by the mad physical trainer twice a week," I said. Riff and I work out together at the Farmington YMCA Tuesdays and Fridays, where she prods my ego into keeping up with her. "And I punish myself by running around the lake if I indulge in too many mega-carbs."

We sat in companionable silence for the next several minutes, sipping our wine, and thinking our own thoughts. The friendship we shared had evolved over the years to one that doesn't need constant chatter.

Yawning, Riff drained what was left of the wine into our glasses and met my eyes. "Have you heard from Zed?"

I shook my head. "Not for three weeks."

She held my gaze. "You thinking she's not coming back?"

"To tell the truth," I said on a sigh, "I don't know what to think anymore."

After loading the dishwasher, I joined Riff on the couch. She held the TV remote and was watching the Lions' game without sound. Settling in beside her I propped my feet on the glass coffee table.

"So," I said, trying to sound casual. "Tell me about Benny Shatts."

"Ahhh shit," she said without taking her eyes off the TV. "I knew this dinner had a catch."

"There's no catch. I just wondered what happened."

Riff shifted her gaze from the TV screen to me. "Now why would you be wondering about a thing like that? Did you know the guy?"

I nodded. "Met him at a client's house. He was trying to sell me some Japanese antiques."

"When was the last time you saw him?"

"Three nights ago."

"Where?"

"Right here."

"Why?"

"I just told you. He was trying to sell me some antiques."

"Since when do you go in for antiques?"

I was reluctant to tell Riff about working for the twins. As far as she was concerned, amateurs should stay out of criminal investigations. "I was invited to see Mikala LeMeux's collection and decided to start one of my own."

Riff stared unblinkingly and I felt my cheeks flush.

"Yeah, right. And the Lions are going to take the Superbowl this season."

"What *did* happen to Shatts?"

Riff pointed at the TV screen and mouthed a silent curse. The Lions had just fumbled the ball on the Rams' ten-yard line and the opposition had run it back unopposed. "Do you believe these Bozos?" she said, snapping off the power. "Jesus!"

"About Shatts?" I said, snatching the remote from her hand before she could hurl it across the room. "You were going to tell me about how he died."

"I wasn't going to tell you anything," she said, leaning back against the plush silk cushions. "You asked me."

"Okay. So I asked. Are you going to tell me or what?"

"As of now, it looks like a hit."

"What makes you think that?" I asked.

"Because nobody runs a guy over by accident and then comes back to finish the job."

"He was run over twice?"

"Twice is the M.E.'s opinion," Riff said. "But Shatts looked like a pancake. Must have been a truck or a heavy SUV that whacked him."

"Why would anybody do that?"

"You tell me."

"I have no idea. The guy was a little creepy but that's no reason to kill him."

"What do you mean, creepy?"

"You know...sleazy...like a used car salesman in the movies."

"Let me get this straight," Riff said, holding up a palm. "You thought Shatts was creepy-slash-sleazy but you were going to do business with him?"

"I..."

"Don't bullshit me, Max. I can tell by your face there's more to the story."

I scanned my brain deciding how much to tell her, then cleared my throat. "Have I mentioned the conjoined twin clients I do?"

Riff nodded.

"Well they approached me about investigating Shatts."

"Why you?"

"I might have mentioned I was taking the P.I. course."

Riff rolled her eyes. "Have you even completed like one lesson yet?"

"I've looked the book over."

"Well then," she snorted. "That explains why they'd come to you instead of hiring a professional."

"You can be such a smart ass cop sometimes, you know that?"

"And you can be such a dumb ass 'I looked the freakin' book over and now I'm ready to rock' P.I. wannabe."

"I never told them I was a P.I. Only that I'd see what I could find out."

"And what was that?"

"That Shatts worked for Churchills as an independent broker, although I suspect he only used that as a front to sell high end, possibly illegal-to-own, antiques."

"He didn't actually sell for Churchills?" Riff asked.

"He might have, but he had his own deals going on the side."

"Like?"

"Like he was trying to sell Mikala LeMeux a wood sculpture from the Japanese Kamakura period. A piece called the *Sitting Tiso*."

"The Kamakura," Riff said. "That would be thirteenth-century."

I raised an eyebrow.

"My first degree is in Art History, in case you forgot," she said.

"Apparently."

"How much money are we talking about?" Riff asked.

"A million-five."

Now it was Riff's turn to raise an eyebrow. "Why so pricey?"

"Age has a lot to do with it," I said. "But I suspect it's because our man Tiso was stolen from the Tokyo Museum in 1939." I related the story I got off the Internet.

"That would add to its value," Riff commented. "But isn't it illegal to own that kind of thing?"

"That's what it said on the museum website, but I'm not sure."

Riff held out her wine glass and I refilled it from a fresh bottle of Zinfandel. She removed her shoes, then resettled against the cushions. With her legs tucked up beside her and the firelight catching the violet flecks in her blue eyes, she looked incredibly sexy.

"I know what you're thinking," she said.

"Oh really?"

"You're thinking about trying to get in my pants."

I drew her foot into my lap and slowly massaged the toes one at a time. "Can you blame me?" I said as I worked the heel of my palm up and down the bottom of her foot. "The food, the wine, the firelight."

Riff pulled her foot away and tucked it into the back of the cushions. "That feels too good," she said. "I can't think straight when you're touching me like that. And besides, I thought you wanted to know what happened to Benny Shatts."

"So what happened?" I asked, feeling hopeful at the sight of erect nipples beneath her tee-shirt.

Riff crossed an arm over her breasts and shook her head playfully. "As far as we can tell, he was leaving his apartment when he got tagged."

"Any witnesses?"

"Nada. We talked to everyone in the building. No one admitted to seeing anything."

"Nobody heard anything either, I suppose."

"No," Riff said, "but it was after two am when it happened."

"How can you be sure Shatts was *leaving* his apartment? Maybe he was coming home."

"We checked his answering machine," she explained. "He got a call at 1:35 am from some woman who told him to meet her in an hour at the 7-Eleven down the road."

"Did he have caller ID?"

"Yeah. The call was made from a phone booth in the 7-Eleven parking lot."

"Talk to anyone in the store?"

Riff nodded. "Night clerk said he saw a black Porsche Boxter pull up to the booth at approximately one thirty. It stayed a few minutes, and then took off."

"Was it a hard top or convertible?" I was thinking about the black Boxter I'd seen parked behind Grillo's office building the night I had dinner with Candy.

"I don't know," Riff answered. "Why?"

I shrugged. "No reason. Just trying to get all the facts. Did the caller say anything else?"

Riff eyed me. "Something about having what Shatts wanted. We figured it was sex or drugs. You got any reason to think otherwise?"

I didn't answer immediately, which was the wrong thing to do with the quick-witted woman.

"What do you know about this, Max?"

"Only what you told me," I said after deciding it wasn't the best time to reveal all. I didn't want to throw suspicion on Candy by mentioning she might own a black Boxter. Or that when Shatts was arguing with her the other night, he seemed to want something she was determined not to give him.

"What kind of car do your twin friends drive?" Riff asked.

"I'm not sure. But I assume it's something with a bench seat since they're connected at the shoulder. What are you suggesting?"

"I'm not suggesting anything. I'm trying to guess what you're not telling me."

"There's nothing to tell."

Riff looked skeptical but didn't push it. "I'd like to talk to these women. Any objections?"

"None that I can think of. Except..."

"Except what?"

I wrapped my hand around her right ankle, drew it back into my lap and started massaging her toes. "They might kid you about being my lover. They're kind of ballsy like that."

"You *told* them we were lovers?" Riff asked as she offered the second foot for attention. "Do you always brag about your sexual conquests to clients?"

"Absolutely not," I said, working my way along the muscles of her feet. "But those two have a way of worming things out of me."

"I'll bet," Riff said, scooting down the couch and draping her calves over my thighs. "Do the legs next. I think I'm getting a Charley horse from standing on my feet all day."

I slid a hand up the back of her pant leg and kneaded the firm calf muscles.

"Mmmm," she said. "That is so good, Snowman. Yeah...yeah, right there. Feel the knot in that muscle? Work that."

I increased the pressure and was again rewarded with the sight of erect nipples beneath her tee.

"Like that?"

"Harder," she ordered, staring slitty-eyed at me. "Squeeze right there."

I complied, kneading the stressed muscle until I felt it suddenly release against my fingers.

"Damn," she said, sighing deeply and resting her weight on me. "That was almost as good as sex."

"Oh, I don't know," I said, reaching for the tab on her zipper and tugging it down an inch at a time. "Give me half a chance and I think I can do even better."

To my delight, she allowed me to strip off her jeans and kiss my way slowly up one silky inner thigh. When I reached my target, then paused, her eyes locked onto mine.

"Don't you dare stop there," she hissed, "or I'll write your ass a ticket for loitering in an erogenous zone."

The next morning, as I watched Riff's red Mustang disappear down the drive, I had a light feeling in my heart. Sure I had gained another point on my whore-meter but I consoled myself by remembering Grillo's taunts about Zed being shacked up with her old boyfriend.

On impulse, I picked up the phone and called Grillo's office. With Shatts dead, my work for the twins was basically over but I wanted to satisfy my curiosity about a few details—not the least of which was when Grillo and my mom planned to return from Italy. Candy answered and after some brief small talk about her trip, I invited her to lunch.

It was 12:40 when I joined Candy at Maria's, an upscale Italian place on Northwestern Highway, a few miles north of her office. When I arrived, Candy was already seated at a table slightly apart from the noisy lunch crowd. Dressed in a blue-green DKNY business suit, the same shade as her eyes, and with that tousled blonde hair falling helter-skelter around her face, she looked totally edible.

"Max. What a pleasure to see you again."

"The pleasure is all mine," I said, taking the hand she offered. "Thanks for agreeing to meet me on such short notice."

"Is this a good restaurant?" Candy asked.

"Best Italian in the area. I'm surprised your boss never brought you here."

Candy started to comment when a short, pudgy waiter with a hairless pate and droopy walrus mustache swept up to the table.

"Hello, Mr. Max," he said, sounding as if he'd taken lessons in gay-speak since the day he was born. "You are looking so handsome today."

"Thank you, Patrick. How's life treating you?"

"Just marvelous now that Tom and I are back together. I don't know what you said to him, but it worked wonders!"

"I just told him the truth, Patrick. That there aren't many good men in the world like you, so he'd better hold on tight."

"Oh he is, he is," Patrick said, going slightly pink. "Thank you so much."

After I introduced Candy, Patrick insisted on ordering for us. When he whisked off to the kitchen, she gave me an inquiring look.

"I've been cutting his boyfriend's hair for years," I said in explanation.

"Did you really save their relationship?"

I shrugged. "It's not like I'm Ann Landers or anything. Sometimes an empathetic ear lets people come up with their own solutions."

Candy propped an elbow on the table and laid her chin on a palm. "Your work must be fascinating."

"It can be. At times I feel like a cross between a bartender and a priest."

She laughed lightly. "The bartender part I can buy. But I'm kind of struggling with the priest thing."

"Hey, I wanted to be a priest when I was in fourth grade."

"Well I for one am glad you abandoned the calling."

Our eyes met, and Lord, give me strength; I read sweet invitation there.

"So," she said. "Why did you ask me to lunch?"

"For a couple of reasons. One of which is that I happen to enjoy your company."

"Why thank you, kind sir. What's the other?"

"I wanted to ask some questions."

"Ply me with good wine, and you can ask me anything."

Candy gazed at me with those sea-green eyes, and although I felt my will to confront her ebb, I pushed ahead. "How long have you been with Olympio?"

"Depends on what you mean by been with."

I must have looked confused because she immediately offered an explanation.

"I met him seven years ago. We dated for a while, for two years actually. But I couldn't take the competition."

"You mean other women?"

Candy nodded. "And the occasional man."

I was taking a drink of water during her revelation and nearly choked on a piece of ice.

"Don't hurt yourself, Max. Some of us are lucky enough to enjoy both."

"Meaning you're into women?" I asked, trying to sound casual.

She stared directly at me. "A woman naturally knows what a woman likes."

"Now you're trying to make me feel inadequate," I joked.

"You shouldn't," Candy said, running polished nails down the back of my hand. "I actually prefer men. And you are one of my favorites."

"And you, Ms. Sprinkles, are an excellent liar."

Candy laughed. "I get plenty of practice working for Olympio. But I wasn't lying just now."

I swallowed hard and tried to ignore the familiar call of the wild. "So, after you stopped being his girlfriend, you became…?"

"I'm not sure what you'd call it, but girl Friday comes close. I take care of his personal business, track his investments, hire people, fire people. I'm also the CEO of Grillo Beauty Supply."

Before I could respond, Patrick returned to our table. With a flourish, he set out appetizer plates, two small salads, a serving dish filled with steaming calamari, and a bottle of Chianti. After displaying the label—Antinori 1997—he popped the cork and poured a small sample. I did the taste thing and when I nodded, he filled our glasses.

"The calamari is excellent today," he said, flashing Candy a toothy grin. "I had the chef give you a little extra. Enjoy."

When he left, I raised my wine glass in Candy's direction. "To the most attractive CEO I've ever had the pleasure to lunch with."

Candy tapped her glass against mine. "The position is in name only, I assure you, but the job comes with great perks."

I sipped my wine and met her eyes. "Do you know that Olympio wants me to launder Mafia money through my salon?"

"Yes," she said without the slightest hesitation.

"Do you also know he threatened me and my girlfriend if I refuse?"

She nodded.

"And you're okay with that? I mean, working for a guy who uses violence to get his way?"

Candy paused a moment before answering. "I know you'd like me to say I'm not, but I want to be honest."

"Please do."

"The answer is yes…and no. I don't always approve of Olympio's methods, but I've been around him too long to pretend I'm totally put off. Does that shock you?"

"A little."

Candy picked up a piece of calamari with her fingers, popped it into her mouth, then licked the saucy tips clean. "Enough that you don't want to have lunch with me?"

"I wish you wouldn't do that," I said, staring at her. "It makes me lose my train of thought."

"Sorry. I'll try to behave."

"Shit," I said, shaking my head. "Now I'm not sure I want you to."

"No, really," she said, folding her hands like a schoolgirl and resting them on the table in front of her. "What else would you like to know?"

I ate some calamari and wiped my mouth with a napkin. "Do you know a man named Benny Shatts?"

If Candy was surprised by the question, she showed no sign. "I did say I'd be honest, didn't I?"

"You did."

"Then, yes. I know Shatts."

"How is he connected with Olympio?"

"I didn't say he was."

"Then you're saying he's not?"

The luscious mouth pulled up at the corners. "I think I'll plead the fifth on that one."

"What?"

"I refuse to answer on the grounds that it might incriminate you."

I nodded. "Okay. How about this one? Do you know Shatts is dead?"

"No," she said. "Can you hum a few bars?"

"Funny lady," I said and we both laughed. "Here's an easier one. Do you always carry a gun?"

"Yes. Don't you?"

"No."

"Well you should," she said, spearing the last piece of calamari with her fork. "Detroit is a dangerous town."

"Tell me about it. I grew up there. Ready for another question?"

"I love this. It's like playing *Who Wants to be a Millionaire* without the lifelines. Shoot."

"What kind of car do you drive?"

"A Porsche Boxter."

"What color?"

"Black."

"Hardtop or...?"

"Ragtop," Candy said before I could continue. "It's eight months old and fully loaded. Want a ride somewhere?"

"No. I was just wondering what a woman like you would drive."

Patrick returned with our entrée, removed the used plates, set down new ones, and placed a platter of cheese-encrusted ravioli between us. "*Quattro Formagi*," he said, sniffing the tempting aroma. "Best in the state."

Patrick departed and I served the ravioli.

"I'm betting that question about my car was more than curiosity," Candy said.

"No," I lied. "I spotted the Boxter in the parking lot of your office and wondered if it belonged to you or Grillo."

Candy seemed unsatisfied with my answer but to my great relief, she didn't pursue it.

After lunch we walked to her car where she gave me a long, amorous kiss.

"How about coming back to my apartment?" she said, against my cheek.

I was tempted, make that extremely tempted, but when I visualized my whore-meter inching up, I declined.

Candy shrugged and unlocked her car.

"By the way," I said as she slid onto the driver's seat and cranked the engine. "When are the lovebirds returning from Europe?"

She pulled a palm pilot from her bag and flipped it open. "Day after tomorrow. At…" she tapped the screen. "Four-thirty."

"Are you meeting them?" I asked.

"No. I'm off to Chicago for several days. I arranged for a limo to pick them up."

Chapter 6

▼

Marie finally called that night and confirmed what Candy had told me about their arrival back in Michigan. When I asked if she was having a good time, she sighed deeply. "It's been wonderful."

"Did you really get to meet the Pope?"

"Sure did. We had tea with him at the Vatican."

"What did you talk about?"

"Hell if I know. He and Oli spoke in Italian most of the time. But he smiled at me a lot."

"When you get back here, we need to have a serious talk about Grillo, Mom. He's not as reformed as he claims to be."

Static crackled across the phone line. When it cleared, I thought I heard Marie say something about marriage.

"Who's getting married?" I asked. But the heavy static returned and I lost her.

The day Mom was scheduled to arrive came and went. I called her house for two days after that, but only got the sound of the ringing telephone. Marie didn't own an answering machine. Her opinion was that if someone needed to talk with her, they'd call back. She also refused to carry a cell phone. Her rationale? They are a government plot to record everybody's conversations.

I tried Candy at GBS but she was still in Chicago. Next I considered phoning the airlines, but had no idea which one Grillo and Marie might be traveling on. By the third day, I was getting a little panicky and decided it was time to call Riff. The phone was in my hands, when I heard a knock on my back door. I opened it to find Marie and Grillo standing on the stoop.

Ignoring the man, I focused my anger on Marie. "Where the hell have you been?! You were supposed to be home two days ago."

"We stopped in London on our way back."

"To do what?" I snapped. "Have lunch with the friggin' Queen?"

"What is your problem?" Marie said, pushing past me. "You need to start taking Paxil or something."

"What I need is a little respect and courtesy," I seethed through clenched teeth. "Why didn't you call and say you had changed your plans? Did it ever occur to you I might get worried?"

"It's my fault, Max," Grillo said, closing the door behind him. "I wanted your mom to meet a priest friend of mine in London and it took longer than I thought to get the marriage license."

At his words, incredulity replaced anger and I glared at Marie. "Please tell me you didn't marry this guy."

She smiled and held up her left hand. There was a diamond on her third finger as big as a marble.

I gaped at her dumbfounded. "What the hell is the matter with you?" I finally managed to sputter. "Don't you have any self control? You know nothing about this man."

Grillo stepped up and placed his arm protectively around Marie. "It's what we both wanted, Max. We're too old for long engagements."

"You," I snarled, facing him, "have been bullshitting this crazy woman from day one. If you had any balls at all, you'll tell her what you really are."

"Don't you speak to my husband like that!" Marie said, her eyes narrowed and steaming with anger. "And as for that crazy crack, the apple don't fall far from the tree, buster."

Grillo stepped between us. "It's okay, honey. This is a surprise for Max. He needs to adjust."

"What I need," I exploded and stomped to the door, "is for you to get the fuck out of my house. Now!"

"He's not going anywhere without me," Marie insisted.

I swung the door wide and jerked my thumb outside. "Fine. Then you can leave too."

Later that night, I was lying in bed staring at the dark ceiling when the phone rang. Before picking up, I glanced at the caller ID. My mom's name and number glowed electric green in the darkness. I snatched it up, ready to apologize, but when I said hello, Grillo's voice spoke in my ear.

"Glad you're still awake. Can we talk?"

"I have nothing to say to you."

"Oh I think you do. I think you'd love to tell me to go fuck myself."

"Now that you mention it, the thought has crossed my mind a few hundred times."

Grillo chuckled. "You've got a bad attitude, Max. Someday it's going to get you in trouble."

"Is there a point to this call?"

"Just trying to make peace in the family. You upset your mother tonight. I was hoping we could work out our problems and be pals."

"Sorry. It's hard to warm up to someone who wants to involve me in crime and threatens my friends."

"Okay. So we got off to a bad start."

"Is that what *you* call it?"

"Believe it or not, Max, I'm a nice guy once you get to know me."

"Uh huh."

"Marie thinks I am."

"She's impulsive and easily impressed."

"And I don't impress you?"

"Actually you do."

"But…"

"But you're a liar, an extortionist, and probably a murderer. Is that the kind of man you'd want *your* mother to marry?"

"Actually my mom married a man exactly like that. He's also loving, caring, and a good provider. Aren't those things you want for Marie?"

"Absolutely. I just have a hard time picturing them coming from you."

"Hey," he said and chuckled. "I respect your honesty."

"A pity I can't return the compliment."

Grillo laughed again. "You're a pistol, Max."

Yeah, I thought. Too bad I'm not pointed upside your head. "Since you're in such a talkative mood, tell me about Benny Shatts."

"Tell you what?"

"What's your connection to him?"

"We were partners in the antique business. He sold them and I stole them back."

I took a moment to consider that, so Grillo filled the silence.

"The Asian antiques market is hot right now. I own a few very rare pieces. Benny finds collectors, makes the sale, recons the placement, and I arrange to steal it back."

"That is so shitty."

"Maybe. But I sold one particular piece three times last year, to the tune of five-and-a-half million."

"The insurance companies gotta be seeing a pattern."

"I don't see how. The pieces are never insured."

"People pay over a million dollars for an antique and don't insure it?"

"These pieces are technically illegal to own. So there's no insurance, no police report when it's stolen, and I take only cash or trade."

It was a sweet setup, but I wasn't about to admit that. "Why tell me all this?"

"Because you asked and because there's nothing you can do with the information."

"Mind telling me something else then?"

"Like what?"

"Were you responsible for Shatts's murder?"

"No. You were."

"Excuse me?"

"You signaled the hit when you followed him to my office."

Grillo's words were like a quick shot to the gut. My playing amateur detective had cost a man his life. "Did Candy tell you I was there?"

"She didn't even know."

"Then how?"

"In my line of work, round-the-clock security is a given. You were made before you ever got out of your truck that night."

"So you had a man killed because I followed him?"

"That's not the only reason. I told Benny never to come to the office without being invited."

"How dare you play God with people's lives."

"I never thought about it like that," he said, sounding almost happy about my accusation. "Olympio Grillo, God's proxy on earth. Has a nice ring, don't you think?"

"You're a sick bastard."

"No. I'm a good businessman. Loose cannons cause problems."

"If you have trouble with independent thinkers, you married the wrong woman. Are you going to put a contract out on Marie when she steps out of line?"

He didn't answer and his silence hung heavy between us.

"Hurt Marie or Zed, Grillo, and there won't be enough security in the world to save your ass from me."

"Tougher people than you have tried, Max. But I'm still here."

Chapter 7

After Grillo's call, sleep was out of the question so I made my way down the dark stairs. My idea was to do some laps in the pool; drain off the anger and frustration. But when I looked out and saw a layer of snow blanketing the patio, I decided to boil out my troubles in the hot tub.

A thousand thoughts competed for my attention. Chief among them was what to do about Marie and Grillo. "How could she have married that bastard?" I asked the empty room. "Things would be so much easier if…" I stopped mid-sentence, realizing that wasn't true. Grillo had targeted me and my salon before he even met Marie.

I shifted position and let one of the powerful tub-jets massage the base of my neck. "Tell Marie what's going on," said a familiar voice inside my head. "She's an intelligent woman. She'll listen."

"No, she won't," I said out loud. "She doesn't hear shit when she doesn't want to."

"Take everything to Riff," the voice suggested.

I shook my head. "Too risky. Grillo's people might be watching."

"You're saying somebody is following you?"

I shrugged. "Haven't noticed anybody, but I wouldn't put it past Grillo to hire a shadow."

"His threats could be a bluff," the voice said. "And he *does* want your cooperation."

"What if they're not?" I said. "Someone could get hurt."

"You could do what Grillo wants; make it easy on yourself."

"Yeah, right," I thought before sliding beneath the bubbles. Involvement in a felony isn't exactly my idea of easy.

At noon the next day I was filling in for Gwen at the reception desk when four tuxedoed waiters wheeled carts stacked with covered serving plates through the salon's open double doors.

"Mr. Snow?" asked a tall, stiff shouldered man who seemed to be directing the others.

"That would be me."

"Where should we set up?"

"Set up what?"

"Lunch for twenty."

Several of the staff filed into the reception area, no doubt drawn by the delicious aromas coming from the steaming carts.

"I didn't order lunch," I said as the headwaiter handed me a snow-white greeting card. Embossed on the front was a set of wedding bells. Inside was a handwritten note from Grillo and Marie that read "Please allow us to share the joy of our union with you and your staff."

I toyed with the thought of refusing but could see that would be a disaster. Resignedly I led a parade of waiters, food, and staff to the break room.

Lunch consisted of stuffed Cornish game hens, a mixed green salad with raspberry vinaigrette, herb-roasted Yukon Gold potatoes, and for dessert, chocolate Crème Brulee. When everyone had finished, the headwaiter pulled back the white skirt on his serving cart to reveal twelve slim silver boxes, approximately the size of a legal envelope.

"A gift from Mr. and Mrs. Grillo," he announced while handing one to each of the stylists.

Inside was a pair of New Cosmos Hikaris, the Rolls Royce of hairstyling scissors, and by the looks on their stunned faces, the staff was elated. Olympio Grillo, master of manipulation. Now he would be everyone's pal and I'd have a hard time convincing people he was trouble.

As if on cue, Grillo and Marie entered the room to a chorus of thank-yous and congratulations. The hubbub settled down when the stylists drifted out and the three of us were left alone.

"Sorry about last night," I said, directing the comment to Marie. "I was worried when you didn't return on time. Guess I got carried away."

Grillo stood quietly for a moment, and then excused himself, saying something about hitting the bathroom. As the door closed behind him, I hugged Marie.

"Does this mean you approve of my marriage?" she asked, holding me at arm's length.

I shook my head.

"Why not?" she said, readying for a confrontation.

"I'd try to explain but you're too far out in the love zone to listen."

"Try me."

I eyed her doubtfully but tested the waters. "Grillo is not what he's pretending to be, Mom."

"Oh really," she said, her brown eyes flashing. "Then what is he?"

"I can't say now."

Marie glared and raised a single eyebrow. It was a look I knew all too well.

"I can't," I insisted, "because I don't want you to confront him."

"About what!?"

I shook my head. "Just be careful, okay?"

"You actually think I'm in danger?" she said, sounding incredulous.

Before I could answer, Grillo stepped back into the room.

"We have a present for you too, Max," he said, handing me a manila envelope. "Check this out."

I sat down at the table and removed the stack of papers. The first page laid out a business proposal detailing my partnership in a chain of hair salons, all using the name Maxie's.

"Now before you say no," Grillo said, "hear me out."

I looked at him with all the skepticism I could muster.

"This would be an opportunity for you and Marie to become very wealthy," Grillo said quickly.

"I'm already wealthy," I returned. "And I'm no business man. Handling one salon is enough hassle for me."

"You would be a partner in name only," Grillo reassured me.

I looked over at Marie and read encouragement in her eyes.

"This would be a different kind of salon," Grillo went on. "We would locate them in major malls with most of the space being used to sell product. The salons would be in the back. Something small but classy, maybe three or four chairs."

"It's been done," I said. "There's one in practically every mall."

"One is the key word," Grillo explained. "They have no competition. We'll do it better and blow them out of the water."

I shook my head. "Thanks for the offer but I have zero desire to go into business with you."

Grillo seemed undeterred. "There would be no risk involved on your part, Max."

"Yeah, right."

"It's true," he insisted. "The corporation will be owned by you and Marie on paper but under the mothership of Grillo Beauty Supply."

"I said I'm no business man, Olympio. I didn't say I was stupid."

"I wouldn't be talking to you if I thought you were, Max. But I can't see why you're objecting."

Marie stood and paced the room. She had been uncharacteristically quiet.

"If you don't want to do this for yourself," Grillo encouraged, "think about Marie. Wouldn't it be nice to know she's financially secure?"

"She has money," I said. "Her last husband left her a bundle."

"Most of that was lost when the market took its last nosedive," Grillo said. "Her portfolio was tech-heavy and the rest was invested in two dot-coms that went belly up."

I looked at Marie and she nodded.

"Well I've got enough money for both of us," I said. "I'll take care of you."

"I don't want to be taken care of," she protested. "I want to earn my own way. I also want something to do."

"Like what?"

"Like helping manage the chain of salons."

"You don't know what you're asking, Mom."

"I'm asking for a chance to be self-sufficient," Marie insisted.

"What the hell are you talking about? Your husband here is worth millions."

"But *I'm* not," she said.

I shook my head. "I'll back you in any business you'd like to start, but I'm not selling my soul to the Mafia. And neither are you."

Grillo took Marie aside and whispered something in her ear. She looked doubtful but after a few moments, left the room. When the door closed behind her, I got up to leave too, but Grillo restrained me with a hand on my arm.

"Max, listen to me."

"Forget it, Grillo. I'm not playing the patsy so you can make more money."

"It's not only for me. I want to do this for your mom."

"Do what? Make her a criminal?"

"As far as Marie is concerned, this will be a legitimate business. She'll never know what's going on."

"But I will," I said. "And if she gets access to the business records, she'll figure it out too. The woman is no dummy."

"I know that."

"You do, huh?" I said. "And when she confronts you with the truth, what then?"

For a fraction of a second, Grillo was speechless.

"She won't find out," he said finally. "But if she does and wants to call it quits, I'll let her."

"Sorry, I'm not going to allow you to involve my mom in a felony."

At my last words, Grillo's eyes narrowed. "You will join me in this business venture, Max, or I swear your girlfriend will be dead by the end of the week." He reached in his coat pocket, pulled out a photo envelope, and tossed it onto the table. "Take a look."

I peeled back the gummed flap and slid out several overexposed prints. All were shots of Zed, some from the front, some from the back. In two, there was a handsome, dark skinned man by her side and they were holding hands. I looked from the pictures to Grillo, who wore a smirk of satisfaction.

"The photographer could use some lessons in lighting and exposure times, but I think he caught Zed's true vulnerability. Wouldn't you agree?"

My hands were shaking when I dropped the pictures back on the table. Grillo picked them up and returned them to his coat pocket.

"A phone call is all it would take, Max. You're already responsible for one death. Care to make it two?"

I lunged at him, and when my hands circled his neck, we tumbled to the floor with me on top. Grillo might have been gray-haired and fifteen years my senior, but when I swung a fist at his face, he caught it with one hand, wrapped the other around my forearm and tossed me over his head like a ragdoll. I hit the wall with a thud that knocked the wind out of me, and lay there watching tiny white lights do the Hustle before my eyes. Without a word, Grillo stood, dusted off a pant leg, and offered me his hand. I brushed it aside and struggled to a seated position.

"Your choice isn't a hard one, Max," he said. "Join me and make yourself a nice pile of change or your girlfriend dies."

I was on my feet when Marie stuck her head in the break room. She looked hopeful but I shook my head and turned away.

Grillo laughed and patted me on the back like we were old pals. "Max needs some time to think it over, honey. Let's not push him."

Chapter 8

▼

Feeling the need to get the hell out of there, I told Gwen to cancel my remaining appointments for that afternoon. As I walked through the salon, every stylist I passed voiced approval of Grillo, mentioning how happy I must be that he and Marie had tied the knot. I acknowledged their comments with a nod but kept silent.

My insides were shaking as I hoofed it to the SUV. A combo of fear and impotence can usually do that to me, and I had just received a bellyful. When the whole Grillo thing began, I had asked myself why he would go through so much trouble to blackmail me. In a good year, my salon sold maybe two hundred thousand in hair products; a decent amount, but hardly worth Mafia interest. Now I knew. If Grillo could somehow force me to front for a chain of product-heavy salons, he'd be in a position to launder millions. His reason for wanting such an uncooperative partner remained a mystery.

Lost in the zone, I walked past my truck. After backtracking, I beeped the door open and fired up the engine. The day was as cold as the proverbial witch's tit, so I flipped on the seat heater. When the first trickle of warmth began to toast my buns, I pulled out of the mall lot.

With my brain set on automatic pilot, I merged into the eastbound I-96 traffic, settling into the center lane. My halfhearted plan was to visit Riff and confess my troubles, but as I neared the exit to her office, I abandoned the idea.

Forty minutes later, I walked in my back door and headed directly to the phone on the kitchen wall. I needed to talk to Zed, but when I dialed the number she'd given as her contact in Belize, I wasn't really expecting an answer. I had already tried to phone her a dozen times, without success. But on the tenth faint ring, someone actually did pick up.

"Holla," said a voice almost lost in a sea of static.

"Hello?" I said, still shocked that the call had gone through. "My name is Max Snow. I am trying to contact Zed."

Dead silence met my statement and I wondered if we had lost the connection.

"Hello? Hello? Can you hear me?"

A string of heated Spanish cut in and out of the rolling static. Before I could say another word, a forceful disconnect stung my ear.

"Same to you, Pedro," I growled, slamming the handset down on the receiver.

Blue wandered into the kitchen at that moment and looked up questioningly.

"Ah, some bozo down south was giving me shit," I said, lifting the cat to my chest. "One call in twelve goes through and I get Mr. Fists Across the Border."

The cat purred and bumped the top of his head against my chin. He was after strokes, not attitude. As I scratched in all his favorite places, a new idea surfaced. If I couldn't contact Zed by phone, I would damn well fly down to Belize and warn her personally.

"Forget it," the little voice in my head snapped. "Grillo would figure out where you went before you got there and order the hit."

I thought about that and decided it was a real good possibility. "So what do *you* suggest?"

"Send somebody else down there."

"Like who?"

"I could tell you," the voice said, "but I refuse to do all the thinking around here."

"You are me, you stupid shit, so just spit it out!"

"I might be part of you," the voice protested, "probably the best part, so I demand some respect. And while we're on the subject, I'm tired of that little voice crap. What if I started calling you little Max?"

My eyes rolled to the top of my head. "What would you like to be called? Mr. Know-it-all?"

"That handle would fit, but I want a cool name."

"Like what? I'm afraid to ask."

"Like Tonto."

"*Tonto*?! As in the Lone Ranger's sidekick?"

"Yeah. What do you think?"

"I think if people ever found out I named my brain, they'd put me in a rubber room."

"Who's going to know?"

I breathed out an—ah, what the hell—sigh of resignation. Some men name their pecker. Why not a name for my brain?

"I'm uncomfortable with that particular analogy," said you know who.

"Too bad," I shot back. "I'm the boss. You're only the sidekick. Now, who do you suggest we send to Belize?"

"Think about it, Max. Who could probably leave immediately, knows what Zed looks like, and wouldn't ask too many questions?"

I considered the three-pronged description and like magic, a still of a horsy-faced man flashed on my mental screen. "Kenny Dougland?"

"Halleluiah," said the smart-ass voice that now had a name. "He got it on the first try."

Kenny Dougland is a mentally challenged, forty-five-year old who does busboy duties at one of the mall restaurants. We met in the coffee shop months ago, and because I was buzzed on too much caffeine, I invited him to visit the salon. He took the invitation and ran with it, stopping by my private studio several times a day, and deciding we were best buds. Kenny shares space at a group home in the city of Southfield, and suffers—or enjoys—depending on your perspective, what is commonly called a split personality. When he's in what I think of as his wackier mode—you have to get to know him to really tell them apart—he exhibits a strong, often eerily accurate, psychic power.

I looked up his home number, dialed, and crossed my fingers. An answering machine clicked on after the fifth ring and the theme song from *The Simpsons* filled my ear.

"Hi. This is Kenny," my friend shouted over the music. "If I'm not home, call me at work or at my folks' house."

He gave both numbers. After striking out at his place of employment, I called his parents' home, located at the opposite end of Cradle Lake. When a man answered, I identified myself and asked if Kenny was there.

"Yes," the man said stiffly. "Kenneth is visiting this afternoon but he is presently napping. Is it important that you speak to him, Mr. Snow?"

"Kind of, yeah."

"Then I shall awaken him. Please hold the line."

After a short wait, a sleepy sounding Kenny came to the phone. I made arrangements to pick him up, and thirty minutes later, we were standing in my kitchen holding mugs of hot chocolate.

"You got any of those little marshmallows?" Kenny said, eyeing his cup. "My mom always puts little marshmallows in my hot chocolate."

"Sorry, dude. I'm fresh out of the little guys. How about a regular sized one?"

Kenny frowned like he couldn't quite grasp the concept, but when I produced the bag, he held out his cup.

"Cool," he said, poking the snow white puffball with an index finger. "I never thought of putting a big one in there."

As he sipped around the marshmallow island, Kenny glanced at my home's spacious first level. He was so fixated on checking the place out that I had to take him on a tour before he could concentrate on what I was asking him to do.

Back in the kitchen, I made him a second cup of cocoa, popped in another marshmallow, and we got down to business. "I need you to do me a big favor, K-man."

Kenny looked out at me expectantly from beneath the bill of his ever present pink cap. "Are we working on a new case?"

"Not exactly," I said but when his smile faded, I changed tact. "Well yeah, actually I am. Could you help me out?"

Kenny nodded enthusiastically and leaned forward.

"Do you remember Zed?" I asked.

"You mean the tall woman who looks like Xena, the Warrior Princess?"

"That's right. What I need you to do is take a message…"

"She's your girlfriend, right?" Kenny broke in.

"Right, she's my girlfr…"

"The one who helped your mom and me save you from that trash eater at the mall?"

Kenny, Zed, and Marie had indeed rescued my butt from being crunched in one of the mall's giant trash compactors. How I happened to find myself there is a whole different story.

"She's the one," I said, stopping to wait for his next interruption. When it didn't come, I laid out the idea of him going to Belize.

"Belize?" Kenny said, sipping his hot chocolate and looking thoughtful. "Is that in Florida?"

"Right coast, wrong continent, man. Belize is at the butt end of Central America."

Kenny's expressive features morphed to confused.

"It would be a long trip. Think you can handle it?"

"I guess so," Kenny said. "But how am I going to get there?"

"Fly. What else?"

The man's liquid brown eyes widened. "You mean in a plane?"

"That's what most people fly in," I said. "Will this be your first time up?"

"Yeah," Kenny said while nodding vigorously. "But I've watched the movie *Airplane!* thirteen times."

"Then you've earned your wings, dude. My travel agent will get you rolling."

"Is she coming with me?" Kenny asked.

"Who?"

"Your travel agent."

"No," I said, but when he looked disappointed, I offered an alternative. "Would you like to take somebody along?"

"I could take my roommate, Josh. I don't think he's ever been to Belize."

"Cool," I said. "Think he would want to go?"

"Are there any women there?"

"In Belize? Sure. Why?"

"Because Josh is a babe magnet."

I smiled. "A babe magnet? He wouldn't think of putting the moves on Zed, would he?"

"He might," Kenny said seriously. "But she's a little tall for Josh."

"How tall is he?"

Kenny, who stands approximately 5'9", held out his hand to indicate the height of his shoulder, so on a good day, Josh could only be about five feet tall.

"Well if Josh *does* decide to go with you," I said, "tell him Zed's off limits."

"I'll tell him," Kenny said. "But I can't promise anything. Women love this guy."

On our way back to Kenny's parents' house, I told him to pack for the trip like it was summer.

"But it's winter," he exclaimed.

"Not down there, man. You're going to the Equator."

"The Equator?" Kenny said, sounding confused again. "I thought you said we were going to Belize."

I told Kenny to call as soon as he talked to his roommate about the trip. He got back with me about five to confirm that Josh, the babe magnet, had agreed to go along. I managed to snag my travel agent before she left the office and with her usual speed and efficiency—I love travel agents! They take all the hassle and anxiety out of going places—she had the boys good to go the following day. They would leave out of Detroit Metro, make a connection in Dallas, fly to Belize, then take a ninety-minute boat ride to Zed's home island, Blackbird Cay.

After arranging with Kenny for a pickup the next morning, I spent some time compiling any information I thought my messengers could use. It included the phone number Zed had given me, everything I knew about Blackbird Cay, and the names of two of her friends that live there. After that, I scanned the only photo I had of Zed, made copies of everything, then put together a package for each man. By midnight I was dog-tired—sorry, Blue—and moments after crawling into bed, I was sound asleep.

I met Josh, last name Jackson, the following day when I picked up the boys at their apartment. Josh really did turn out to be approximately five-feet tall, and although he claimed to be thirty-seven, his diminutive stature and delicate bone structure made him look more like a teenager. If he was mentally handicapped, I couldn't tell. Mostly he was a nonstop talker who voiced an opinion about anything and everything.

Inside the airport, I got to see our ladies' man in action. Josh hit on practically every female we passed, including a soldier standing guard near a metal detector. Thankfully, no one took offense, although the soldier did shift her M-16 from shoulder to shoulder a little more than seemed necessary.

On the drive home, my cell phone buzzed. When I answered, Marie started talking without any preliminaries.

"So what have you decided?"

"About what?"

"You know what, and I want an answer today."

"Too bad, because you're not going to get one. I need time to think."

"About what? Oli is offering you the opportunity of a lifetime."

"Uh huh," I said, knowing the doubt in my voice would piss her off.

"If I could reach through this phone, young man, I'd slap some sense into you."

"Well, lucky me."

"You won't be, if you make the wrong decision."

I laughed. "If that's a threat, lady, your husband already beat you to it."

"Olympio has never threatened you, if that's what you're implying."

"Whatever."

"You were a stubborn little shit as a child," Marie bristled. "And you haven't changed a lick."

"I'm a chip off the old block, no doubt about it."

There was total silence for several seconds, and I could almost feel her hot anger radiating through the phone line.

"Look, Mom," I said, knowing I had played her long enough. "I haven't said no yet. But managing a chain of hair salons isn't something I'd take on without a ton of consideration, and neither should you."

"Well Oli wants to get moving on this."

"Like I care what Grillo wants. If it wasn't for your butt being into this thing, I'd tell him to take a flying leap."

"I wouldn't do that if I were you."

"Why? Think he might get pushy if I disturb his timetable?"

"*He* might not," Marie hissed. "But *I* will."

"I'm kind of big to put over your knee."

"You'll never be that big, mister. And don't you forget it."

Chapter 9

A fervent wish that my life wouldn't get any more complicated crashed when I pulled into my drive and spotted a woman sitting cross-legged on the back porch. She was dressed in a light-blue parka with the hood pulled up, faded jeans, and black high-tops. I parked directly in front of her and when she pushed back the hood, I experienced an "oh my God" sensation in the pit of my stomach. It was my ex-wife, Susan Brady, whom I hadn't seen in almost a decade. We had divorced when she made the choice to study Zen Buddhism in Japan.

Susan stood as I exited the truck. I was pleased to see that the ten years she'd spent in the East had been good to her. The pretty, boyish face looked thinner, as did the six-foot frame that once had the power to drive me to distraction. The slight appearance was exaggerated by her new look, shaved to the bone haircut ala all good Buddhist nuns, plus the fact that the clothing she wore was several sizes too big.

My delight in seeing her again must have been obvious because she matched the smile on my face, joined her hands in the traditional Japanese greeting, then bowed low at the waist. I returned her bow and she threw her arms around my neck. When we parted, both of us brushed away tears.

"Your house is beautiful, Max," she said as I unlocked the door and invited her inside. "I see you haven't lost your taste for Asian style."

"Thanks," I said, eyeing her outfit and hair-free scalp. "I see you haven't either."

Susan looked down at her simple attire as if noticing it for the first time. "Actually, this is pretty snazzy for me. In the *zendo* I wear a sack dress and palm sandals."

"How spiritual," I said and we both laughed.

"Look at you," she said, fingering the lapels of my dark plum, calf's leather bomber. "All Norm Thompson-ed out and living in a million dollar pagoda."

I shrugged at the left-handed compliment and for some reason, felt a little self-conscious.

"They both look great on you," Susan said, patting my cheek. "Not everyone is crazy enough to take a vow of poverty like me."

"What's up with that, anyway? Does being poor somehow get you a closer seat to God?"

Susan's smile was as warm as ever. "My meditation improves with everything I let go of. So in a way, yes."

I cranked up the double-sided fireplace, threw several fat pillows near the hearth and invited her to get warm while I made tea. When I carried out the steaming cups on a glass tray, Blue was sitting in Susan's lap getting his ears massaged.

"So tell me," I said, sitting beside her and looking into the wide, golden-brown eyes. "What brings you to America and my humble home?"

Susan sipped lightly at the tea. Through the steam, her face looked delicate and sad. "Did you know my father died last year?"

"I heard he was sick," I said as a sense of loss squeezed my chest. "But I didn't know the big lug took off."

"He thought the world of you, Max," Susan said as a single tear slid down each cheek. "I'm not sure he ever forgave me for divorcing you."

"Oh yes he did," I assured her. "We met for lunch a couple of times during your first year in Japan. Tom told me he respected your decision and admired the strength it took to make it."

Susan's answering smile told me she was grateful for that information. I guess it is hard, even for a Buddhist nun, to let go of everything.

"Dad left me his house and the surrounding acreage in Webberville," she said. "I've come home to start my own monastery."

"Can you do that?"

"Sure," she said, running a palm over her bald head. "I'm fully ordained."

I gazed at her in amazement and shook my head. "Now that must have been a tough go for a smart-ass *gaijin* like you."

"You wouldn't believe how tough," Susan said, sipping her tea. "Now I've come home to teach you poor confused Americans how to give up your decadent lifestyle."

I raised an eyebrow. "You've been hangin' in the temple too long, sweetheart. The only thing Americans want to give up is not giving anything up."

Susan laughed. "Buddhists really aren't much different. The Zen master who taught me loves double-shot lattés, Big Macs, and *People* magazine. He's also obsessed with Internet chat rooms."

"If you've taken a vow of poverty," I said, reaching over to scratch Blue's head, "where will you get the money to start a monastery?"

"Dad's house is totally paid for, and I leased the surrounding acreage to some local soybean farmers. The rent will take care of the taxes and give me a small income until we're up and running. After that, we'll hold retreat weekends and bring in guest speakers."

"Ambitious plans."

"Talk about ambitious," Susan said. "I hear you own a salon in the Rolling Pines Mall."

I shrugged again and shook my head. "A friend asked me to finance the business with some of my lottery winnings. I got stuck running the place when she died a couple months ago."

"I heard you won the lottery."

"Yeah. How about that."

"How much?"

"Twelve million, but since I took the cash payoff, I got six, minus taxes."

"Wow," Susan said, shaking her head in disbelief. "If I'd hung in there, I'd be a rich suburban housewife now."

We talked for several hours that night, each of us detailing the ups and downs of the last ten years. About midnight, I walked Susan up to the guest room and told her to make herself at home.

Half-an-hour later I was drifting off to sleep when I heard my bedroom door open. Susan entered wearing the oversized tee I had given her to sleep in, and stopped at the foot of my bed.

"I was crazy enough to take a vow of chastity," she said, grinning. "But it's been so long since I've been held by a man. Would you mind?"

I flipped back the covers and she snuggled in beside me.

"Thanks, Maxie," she whispered, lying her head in the crook of my arm. "This feels just like old times."

I awoke the next morning to the smell of sausage frying, followed my nose to the kitchen and found Susan cooking breakfast. I poured my first coffee of the day before giving her a quick hug. "What's up with this?" I said, glancing in the pan. "I thought all Buddhists were vegetarians."

"The dead animals are for you," Susan said. "I had a bowl of oatmeal several hours ago."

"Several hours ago? What time did you get up?"

"I usually begin my morning meditation at four, but I was so comfortable in your bed, I indulged myself and got up at four-thirty."

"How decadent," I said, topping my cup. "I must be a bad influence on you."

"You always were," Susan said, as she plated the sausage and eggs and placed them on the kitchen table. "Why stop now?"

During breakfast Susan asked if she could stay with me while her house was being renovated.

"Be my guest," I said. "Stay as long as you need to."

"You don't have a woman in your life? Someone that might object to my being here?"

Over my third cup of coffee, I told her about Zed and how I had come to fall in love with the mysterious Medicine woman from Central America.

"Where is she now?" Susan asked.

"Back in Belize."

She looked at me expectantly.

"Said she needed to take care of some things down there."

"How long has she been gone?"

"Too long."

She gazed at me from under lowered brows and shook her head. "It's your own fault, you know."

"How's that?"

"You insist on falling for independent women."

I nodded. "It's my cross to bear, all right. But I have no regrets."

"And you're not down in Belize with her, because...?"

I shrugged. "Because she asked me not to?"

On the evening of Susan's third day with me, we had just finished dinner when there was a knock on the back door. I opened it to find Marie and Grillo standing side by side.

"Whose beat up old Beetle is that parked in your drive?" Marie asked as she bustled into the room.

"That would be mine," Susan answered and Marie turned toward the voice.

"Holy shit. Is it really you, Susan?"

"In the flesh, Marie. How are you?"

Grillo followed my mom inside and I made the introductions.

"*Konban wah*," Grillo said, bowing slightly. "So you're the Buddhist nun in the family."

"Guilty as charged," Susan said. "Do you speak Japanese?"

"*Sukoshi*," he answered. "I spent a summer at *Zenenji* Temple in Kyoto when I was in my late thirties. I was the first *gaijin* ever permitted to take part in an *O-Zesshin* there."

Marie gave me a quizzical look and I explained that an *O-Zesshin* is kind of like a meditation marathon, *sukoshi* means a bit, and *gaijin* is the Japanese term for foreigner.

"Really," Susan said, sounding impressed. "Did you have an interview with the Master?"

"Several," Grillo replied. "He assigned *mu* as my *koan*, and it practically drove me crazy."

While Grillo and Susan swapped stories about their experiences in Japan, Marie dragged me into a corner of the kitchen.

"What the hell is she doing here?"

I explained about Susan starting a monastery and that she'd be staying with me for a while.

"Sounds cozy," Marie snipped. "But I don't think Zed would like it."

"I think you're wrong."

"Well then, I don't like it."

"Oh really?" I said, glancing over at Grillo. "Guess we can all make poor judgment calls occasionally."

I watched as hot anger flashed in her eyes.

"When are you going to get over your jealousy, Max?"

"Jealousy?"

"You heard me. You can't stand the fact that I am happy with Olympio."

"That is such a crock," I whispered. "I'm happy you've found someone, but why did it have to be him?"

"Because I fell in love, that's..."

"The man is not what he's pretending to be, Mom," I said, cutting her off abruptly. "Get your head out of your crotch for crissake."

Marie's eyes hardened again but before she could say anything, Grillo called to her from across the room.

"We have to leave now, Marie. Our dinner reservations are for eight."

I kissed my mom's cheek before she could back away. "Sorry. Guess neither of us wants the other to run our lives."

When they had gone, Susan and I finished cleaning up the dishes. "Olympio seems nice," she said as she dried her hands on a towel. "But I think your mom still hates me."

"You're dead wrong on the first call, Sister Susan. And Marie doesn't hate you. She only thinks you're a whacko."

Chapter 10

The next morning I was paying bills online when Susan handed me the cell phone.

"Long distance," she said. "Thought you might want to take it."

A feeling of hope filled my heart as I put the phone to my ear. "Zed?" I asked almost breathlessly.

"Holla, Max," she said in her creamy South American accent. "Long time."

"Too long," I replied. "How are you?"

"Good, although I miss you."

I felt my throat tighten. "Ah...same here."

Susan sensed it was time to depart and left the room.

"Guess who I found on my doorstep this morning?" Zed asked.

"The Blue Fairy?"

"Close," she said. "Only there were two of them."

"How are my messengers anyway?"

"Travel weary, but fine," she answered. "I read your letter."

I had sent a letter with Kenny detailing what was going on, and warning Zed about Grillo's hit man. "Please be careful," I said. "These people are professional killers."

"I had already spotted them before your boys showed up."

"There's more than one?"

"Yes, two. They are staying at different motels and pretending not to know each other."

"But how..."

"They were hard to miss on the Cay, especially the guy with the camera."

"Where are they now?"

"Some friends of mine are talking them into leaving the country as we speak."

I felt an immense sense of relief, and a little silly for not trusting Zed's instincts.

"Sounds like you have trouble up your way," she said. "Can you handle it alone?"

"Things just got easier, but I could use help. You planning to come back anytime soon?"

The prolonged silence told me the answer before she could.

"I am not sure when I will be able to return," she said. "There are still things I have to do here."

I thought about Grillo's taunt that Zed was shacked up with her old boyfriend. The memory made me more afraid of losing her, than jealous. "You *are* coming back though, right?"

"I will be back," she said.

I could only hope she meant it.

"The woman who answered the phone sounded nice," Zed teased. "New maid?"

I explained about Susan's return from Japan and how she happened to be staying with me.

"I will look forward to meeting her," Zed replied. "Maybe we can take some meditation classes at her monastery."

The words about our future lightened my heart. "I have kind of been ignoring my spiritual side since you left. Don't think I'm eating right either. I miss your cooking."

"And I miss yours. I have been craving your grilled Rainbow Trout."

We talked until the phone line suddenly filled with static.

"I will be sending Kenny and the human hormone back tomorrow," Zed shouted above the noise. "They will arrive in Detroit about seven on Continental Flight 1952. I will email you if they do not take off for some reason."

"You've got access to email?"

"For a short while, anyway."

"Well how about writing and telling me what's going on?"

There was a loud pop of static and Zed's voice became a fading whisper. "I am not sure what's going on myself, but I will try."

Susan made dinner for us several nights in a row. Since her cuisine style was all about veggies, rice and legumes, I was feeling good about my eating, but more than a little gassy. With her encouragement, I started meditating again, but frowned on getting up at four o'clock. Seven seemed a much more civilized hour to empty my brain.

To return the favor, I started Susan swimming and lifting free-weights twice a day. She was, in my opinion, underweight for a woman of her stature, so after each of our workouts, I'd reward us with cookies, or thick wedges of chocolate cake. We continued to share my bed, but because of her vow of chastity, sex was out, which was cool with me. I appreciated her warm company and it was nice to share a relationship with a woman that didn't kick up my whore-meter.

Grillo must have gotten the word that his men in Blackbird Cay had been invited off the island. He called soon after Kenny and Josh arrived home, trying to make it sound like it was his idea to pull the hit team.

"I want to apologize for threatening your girlfriend, Max. Marie told me last night that Zed saved both your lives a while back."

My eyes rolled so far skyward, I almost fell over. "Well, thanks, Olympio. That's real decent of you."

"I never would have really hurt her. It was just my way of motivating you to do something good for yourself."

I didn't say anything, because the only response I could think of was to laugh, or call him a liar.

"Marie is anxious for your decision on the salons. I think she'll make a crackerjack general manager."

"Let me repeat myself, Olympio. Your wife is no dummy. She'll catch on to your scheme as soon as she sees the books."

"I've taken steps to assure that won't happen," Grillo said. "Marie has agreed that with all her other duties, the financial aspects of the business will be in the exclusive care of the company CPA."

I should have known Grillo would find a way to cover his ass. If he could keep Marie busy enough, she might never realize a crime was taking place. I could tell her, of course, and already had in a roundabout way. She was either ignoring the facts, or hoping none of this was true.

"So you've got nothing to lose by throwing in with me," Grillo added.

My laugh sounded cynical even to me. "You insult my intelligence with that bullshit, Olympio. It's obvious what my liabilities would be if I agreed to your deal."

"The monetary rewards are just as sweet."

"Not to me," I retorted. "I've got plenty of money."

"I wouldn't be too sure about that," Grillo said. "I've had my people check out your financial situation down to the penny. You're not worth as much as you might think."

"Yeah, right."

"It's true. You want the breakdown?"

I didn't say yes, but he gave it to me anyway.

"Your cash payout in the lottery after taxes was less than five million. You picked up Johnny Lott's house for 2.5, added the flanking lots, put in your pool, bought some nice rides, a couple of boats, and you invested almost half-a-mil into the salon."

"You're forgetting the four million dollar stash you say I found in my house."

"Marie told me you gave Zed a million for pulling your ass out of the fire, seeded another three hundred thou around the zoo when Andra's murderer drilled you up on the water tower. And you spend money like a drunken sailor."

"My salon makes money."

"Not so far," he said smugly. "You're too generous to your employees so at best you've broken even."

While I ran Grillo's figures through my stunned brain, he continued his snow job.

"All I'm asking is to use your name and squeaky clean IRS record for four years," he said, trying his best to sound reasonable. "For that privilege, I'll pay both you and Marie a tax free half-million a year. At the end of that time, you can walk away or stay in, whatever you like."

I knew it would be a mistake to accept his offer. Nobody walked away after being involved with the Mafia. They might get blown away, but walk away? I don't think so.

"What if I just told you no; that I wasn't interested?"

"No is not an option," Grillo replied calmly. "Negotiate any other part of our deal if you must, but you *will* come in with me."

"You really get off on controlling people, don't you?"

"Life is a game, Max. I'm a winner because I set the rules."

Before I could think of a retort, Grillo issued an ultimatum.

"Bottom line, Maxie. You have twenty-four hours to tell me what I want to hear."

"And if I don't?"

"I've already said what I might do if you force my hand. Expect any one of them."

He rang off and I glanced at the digital clock. It was 7:17.

I didn't hit dreamland at all that night, and although Susan stayed beside me, her sleep was restless and fitful. I was just dozing off when she got up for her morning meditation. Seeing that I was awake, she invited me to join her. I declined, saying I was going to try to sleep for a few hours.

During breakfast later that morning, I asked about her plans for the day.

"Some friends from the temple in Ann Arbor are going to help redo the hardwood floors at my house. It will probably take most of the day."

"Need any help?"

"Not really. There will be six of us and that's more than enough."

Susan left for Webberville twenty minutes later, and for a while I prowled the first floor trying to decide what to do. The stupid part of my brain said I should take the Mafia's money and hope for the best. The not so stupid part understood that to do so would be like whacking myself in the head with a can of super-hold hairspray for the next four years.

Later that day Susan called to say she'd be spending the night in Ann Arbor with her friends. And although I'd miss her comforting presence in bed, at least she'd be out of harm's way if Grillo made good on his threat.

At 7:20 pm I had just finished the dinner dishes when the phone rang. I walked into the living area and saw Olympio Grillo's name and phone number glowing green on the caller-ID. After four rings, the answering machine clicked on, but before it could begin its recorded message, I picked up the receiver.

"Yeah."

"Good evening, Max. I trust you dined well."

"I thought it over," I blurted out before I could stop myself. "And I've decided to decline your offer."

There was silence for several seconds and I pictured Grillo fielding the rejection.

"You're sure about that? Your mother will be very disappointed."

"I am," I said before I lost my nerve. A moment later there was a click and the dial tone buzzed my ear.

At eight, the phone rang again. The caller-ID announced the number as unlisted so I let the machine answer it.

"Max? This is Loretta Lott. If you're there, pick up."

The name and recognition of the voice made my palms go instantly clammy.

"A little bird just told me you found money in your house that belongs to me."

I stared dumbly at the phone. My caller was Johnny Lott's widow, an attractive, intelligent, but equally unpredictable, French hellcat, and probably the most dangerous woman I knew. Loretta joined my client list six months before Lott got whacked. I had purchased my home from her. And after literally stumbling onto the four million her late husband stashed behind a false wall in the master bedroom, I had neglected to cut her in.

"Phone me tonight, Cherie." It sounded like an order. "If you don't, I'll catch up with you at the salon tomorrow."

She ticked off her home number and by the time the line disconnected, my head was cradled in my hands.

"Shiiit!" I hissed, sinking down into the deep cushioned couch behind me. "Anyone but her, God. Please let it be anyone but Loretta Lott."

I sat there a moment, hoping God would deliver a miracle, but knowing how the Big Guy loves a good joke, didn't actually expect him to. The way I figure it, Mr. G. is up there watching us all on his billion channel big-screen TV, and when he gets bored—sure he gets bored—think about it—he hits a button marked "DO SOMETHING WEIRD TO THIS ONE" on his universal remote.

The something weird in this case was not only the femme fatale Loretta Lott, but her current live-in boyfriend and mob hit man, Josef Gunner. Alone, Loretta was scary as hell. Paired with bad boy Gunner, it would be like facing Jack the Ripper and Lizzie Borden on crack. True to her word, Loretta called me at the salon the next afternoon. She made no direct threats, except to inform me she would be stopping by my house that evening to talk. The tone in her voice told me it would be a big mistake not to be there.

When I arrived home that night I found a note taped to the stair banister. It was written in Susan's familiar scrawl, and informed me that she would once again be spending the evening with her Ann Arbor friends.

About eight, there was a sharp knock on my back door. I opened it to find Loretta Lott, flanked by the handsome, sharp-featured Gunner, and a tall skinny guy with big ears who reminded me of the punk Sidney Greenstreet sent to tail Bogart in *The Maltese Falcon*. The two men brushed passed me, gave the first floor the once over, and then the thin man jabbed the barrel of a gun against my neck. Gunner patted me down. After pulling the .40 caliber Sig from beneath my shirt, he nodded at Loretta who stepped inside.

"Packing heat, Max?" she said as she flipped her long dark hair behind her shoulders. "You're not afraid of me, are you?"

"Not of you, exactly," I said. "But I kind of figured you'd bring company."

Loretta cut her eyes to the right and the two men backed off. She dropped her silver-fox coat on a kitchen chair and like she still owned the place, strolled leisurely into the main room. She wore a snug leather mini that showed off the heart-shaped curves of her ass, a deeply v-ed aquamarine sweater that did the same for her ample chest, and a pair of towering black pumps, with double rhinestone ankle straps, that under other circumstances could make me drool like a baby.

Skirting the men, I followed reluctantly behind her. When she stopped beside the fireplace and turned to face me, a look of amusement etched her perfectly tanned and very French features.

"How you can stand living in this fucking warehouse?" she asked. "It is even worse than I remember."

I sat on the couch opposite her, trying not to look as nervous as I felt.

"Something bothering you, Cherie?"

I glanced back at the boys in the kitchen, and then returned my gaze to her face. "It isn't every day that people push their way into my home at gunpoint. So yeah, I guess you could say I'm a bit edgy."

"Ignore my little guard dogs," she said. "They will stay put, until I call them to heel."

"How comforting."

Loretta sat on the raised fireplace hearth directly across from me. When she saw my eyes dart between her legs, she spread them several inches wider.

"Enjoying the view?"

"Looks tasty," I said, thinking a little flirtation might soften up her mood.

Her response was a predatory smile that made my gonads disappear. "You are much braver than I gave you credit for, Maxie. Perhaps if you survive the evening, I will allow you to make love to me."

When I didn't immediately respond to her dubious offer, she leaned back against the stone fireplace and laughed softly.

"Why are you here, Loretta?" I said, feeling some of my fear ebb toward anger.

"To retrieve what belongs to me, Cherie. But I have already told you that."

I tried my best to look innocent. "If Johnny left anything valuable in the house, I haven't found it."

Loretta crossed one leg over the other, inspecting her glistening ankle straps in the firelight. "I am sorry, Max, but I do not believe you."

I shrugged. "The only thing I've found since I've been here is a Buddha shrine hidden behind a wall in the bedroom."

"The master bedroom?"

"Yeah."

"Anything inside?"

"A statue of the Buddha that you're welcome to have if you'd like. A handgun that I gave to a cop friend of mine, and a Kevlar vest."

Loretta looked unconvinced. "Show me."

As we moved to ascend the staircase, Gunner trotted forward. "Stay, my darling," she said, tracing his jaw with a jewel studded fingernail. "If I need you, I will call."

"But Loretta," the man protested. It was the first time he had actually spoken. "He might have another gun stashed somewhere."

Loretta looked at me. "Do you own another weapon, Max?"

I shook my head.

"There, you see, dear, sweet, Gunner." She brushed her hand across his cheek. "Mommy is in no danger."

At the entrance to my bedroom, I paused and turned to her. "Your boyfriend doesn't seem like the kind who enjoys a short leash. What gives?"

Loretta glanced around at the room's decor disapprovingly before she answered my question. "Desire for pussy can enslave almost any man, Max. And mine is tres sweet."

I reserved comment. It seemed the safest thing to do.

Loretta followed me to the heavily textured wall and watched as I pushed back the hidden panel. When we stepped inside, overhead lights came on automatically. Set against the far wall was a waist-high, carved marble altar. On top sat a twelve-inch jade green statue of the Laughing Buddha.

"Is the Buddha jade?" Loretta asked.

I shook my head doubtfully. I'd become fond of the little green guy and didn't want to lose him. "Never had it appraised."

"You found Johnny's gun in here?"

"Yeah. And a Kevlar vest."

"Nothing else?"

"No."

"Strange," she said. "This is exactly the kind of place Johnny would use to hide cash."

"Well I didn't find any."

Loretta seemed unconvinced as she brushed past me and walked out of the bedroom. After peeking into the art studio and the spare bedroom, she led the way back downstairs.

When we reached the main floor, the thin man circled behind me and Gunner approached from the front.

"Gentlemen," Loretta said casually. "Mr. Snow has been lying to me. Please persuade him that it is best to always tell the truth."

Before I could react, my arms were pulled in a vise-like grip behind my back. Gunner connected a quick right jab to the center of my gut, and the unexpected punch stunned me like a mule kick. If I wasn't being propped up, I would have gratefully folded to the floor.

"Again," Loretta said. When Gunner's fist connected with my jaw, my head snapped back like a Pez dispenser.

Gunner's third and fourth blows struck me full in the chest. As my arms were suddenly released, the hard stone floor rose up to smack me in the face.

"I suspected all along that Johnny was stashing cash," Loretta said as Gunner hoisted my limp body and held me in place. "Do yourself a favor, Max. Hand it over."

Loretta's face suddenly swam out of focus, but a sharp slap from her open hand brought my attention back.

"Stay awake, Cherie," she said, cupping my chin, "or I will let my friends hurt you again."

Although I wanted dearly to sink into blissful unconsciousness, I forced my eyes to remain open.

"Where is my money?"

My mouth opened several times but I could produce no words. Behind me, the men laughed, obviously enjoying the hell out of my pain.

Loretta brought her face an inch away from mine. "Tell me," she cooed. "And we will leave you in peace."

I could feel my consciousness melting like grease on a hot griddle. Why I fought to remain awake, I couldn't say. The trio was not about to stop until they got what they came for.

"There is no money," I finally managed to say, but the moment the last word left my lips, Loretta slapped me again.

My stunned brain entered a kind of self-protective trance, and although the men shook me roughly, I could no longer keep my eyes open.

As if in a dream, I felt my heels being dragged across the stone floor. The next thing I knew, I was freefalling through space. A moment later, the chlorine-laced water of the sunroom hot tub was rushing into my nose and open mouth. I was hauled up in a quick jerk, but only long enough to suck in a mouthful of air before being forced back under. By the time I was pulled from the steaming water and dumped on the granite tile, I felt deader than dead.

Water streamed from my mouth and nose. When I finally managed to raise my head, I saw Olympio Grillo standing in the doorway. He had a large chrome-plated revolver in his right hand, and its wide barrel was pointed directly at Loretta.

"Tell your friends to take their guns out nice and slow, Loretta," he said. "And toss them over by the wall."

The two men did as he directed. "Now," Grillo said as he stepped inside the room and approached the little group. "I hope you have a damn good reason for harassing my son-in-law."

The startled woman forced a nervous smile. "Olympio. How nice to see you again."

Grillo acknowledged the greeting with a nod, but his gun never left its target.

"Max found money in the house that belongs to me," she said. "We were just...persuading him to return it."

Grillo eyed me and shook his head. "You don't look too good, Maxie. I suggest you give the nice lady what she wants."

I glared at him. It was obvious even in my dazed mental state that the bastard had set this whole thing up. Now he was pretending to save me.

"Surely that money isn't worth losing your life over," he said in a concerned, fatherly-like tone. "Think about what that would do to your mother."

His taunts only served to strengthen my resolve. "There is no goddamn money."

Grillo spread his arms. "Marie told me how you found Lott's half-million dollar stash in the shrine room, Max. Just give it up, and these good people will go away."

As I struggled to my feet, Loretta smiled in triumph and greedy anticipation.

"Take the advice of your father-in-law, mon ami," she said. "He is an intelligent man."

I lowered myself unsteadily into a chair beside the dining table. "Search the freakin' house if you want, bitch. There is no money."

"I'm sorry, Max," Grillo said as he stepped sideways to the built-in bookcase on his right, "but your mother would never forgive me if I let these people kill you." Switching the pistol to his left hand, he touched a familiar spot below the lowest shelf. With an audible click, a three-foot-wide panel beneath it folded away from the wall. Reaching in, Grillo withdrew a beat up brown leather gym bag and nodded at Loretta. "I believe this is what you're after."

With intensity etched on her expressive features, Loretta took the bag Grillo offered and set it on the table beside me. When she popped it open, we both stared at the banded packs of thousand dollar bills filling the case.

Loretta lifted a single pack and fanned through it. Convinced it was real; she crooked a finger at Gunner and said it was time to leave. "I realize this little incident will cost me my favorite hairdresser, Cherie but it could not be helped." She looked at Grillo, who still had his gun trained on her. "We are free to leave, yes?"

Grillo nodded but when both men started off for their weapons in opposite directions; he cocked back the hammer of his pistol. "One at a time, please," he said, looking at Gunner. "You first. Pick it up nice and slow and drop it in your back pocket."

Gunner did as he was told, but didn't look happy about it. The thin man followed suit, and after seeing the trio out the back door, Grillo returned to the sunroom and sat across the table from me.

"You set that whole thing up didn't you, Grillo?"

He couldn't help smiling in self-satisfaction. "Worked pretty good, huh?"

"Where did the money in the bag come from?" I asked.

"Your first year's salary."

"What?"

"Your first year's salary as my partner will reflect the deduction."

Understanding dawned and I shook my head. "How did you know about the space behind the bookshelf?"

"Marie showed me how it worked the first time we visited."

"How did you get in to make the plant?"

"I borrowed her key."

"And the alarm?"

"I brought a friend along," Grillo explained. "Security systems R-him, if you follow me."

I did. "And the point of all this?"

"To help you understand who holds the advantage in our little game of wills."

I stood and walked back into the house with Grillo following close behind. When I reached the kitchen table, I picked up my gun, cocked the hammer and pointed it at him.

"Thinking of shooting me?"

"Give me a reason not to."

"Because your mom wouldn't like it, and you'd be in deep shit with the law."

"The cops wouldn't care if I blew you away, Olympio. You're nothing but a pain in the ass to them."

"True," Grillo admitted. "But my *Family* would take a different view."

I understood him only too well. My life wouldn't be worth dog shit if the Mafia drew a target on my back. "You can continue your little games, Grillo," I said, keeping the gun trained on him. "But I'm not going to give you what you want."

Grillo's expression darkened but he quickly regained his composure. "Then I guess I have to try harder to convince you."

Chapter 11

▼

Grillo called early the next evening. When I didn't tell him what he wanted to hear, he hung up on me. His lack of any argument was scarier then if he had bitched up a storm.

Again I thought about taking the whole mess to Riff. As a cop she'd be very interested, but her help would be constrained by a lot of legal shmegal got-to-do-things-by-the-book bullshit, so I passed.

Early the next morning, I awoke to the sound of the telephone beside my bed. As I groped in the dark for the handset, my eye caught the digital readout on the clock. It was 6:48. The caller was a man I had never met, but someone Susan had mentioned often during her stay with me. His name is Koji, and he is one of the friends from Ann Arbor helping to get her house together.

"Mr. Snow? Can you hear me?" he asked. "This cell phone has a bad battery."

"You're coming through loud and clear, Koji," I said, rallying my attention. "What can I do for you?"

"Is Susan with you?"

The unexpected question made me sit up. "No. Why? Is there a problem?"

"I'm not sure. We were at Susan's house last night when two men came to the door. They said you had been seriously injured in a car accident and they would take her to see you."

At his words, the anxiety tickling my senses suddenly morphed into high gear. "Did you see these men, Koji?"

"Not their faces. Susan talked to them at the door and then they waited for her in the car."

"What were they driving?"

"A late model Mercedes sedan. Dark color, maybe blue or black. It had an antenna on the trunk."

I made a mental note of his description.

"Were you in an accident, Mr. Snow?"

"No, Koji, I wasn't. And please call me Max."

"Then who were those men Susan left with? And where is she now?"

I felt anger clamp around my gut. Grillo had to be behind Susan's disappearance. Who else would want to snatch her?

"Are you still there, Max?"

"Yeah. Sorry."

"Do you think Susan is in danger?"

"I'm not sure."

"Well what should we do?" Koji asked. "Call the police?"

My brain moved at warp-speed. If Koji told his story to the cops, they'd come directly to me. And if Grillo found out, Susan might suffer. I needed time to do some checking. "Why don't we wait a while, Koji," I said, trying to sound reasonable. "The police won't do anything until Susan is missing for more than twenty four hours anyway."

Koji's silence told me he wasn't exactly thrilled with my suggestion.

"Give me your number," I said before he could protest. "I'll call as soon as I hear anything."

Immediately after disconnecting, I dialed Grillo's office. Candy Sprinkles picked up on the second ring.

"Max. How are you?"

"Pissed," I said. "Put Grillo on the line."

"He flew to Chicago this morning. Is there a problem?"

"You know damn well there is, lady. Grillo snatched my ex-wife last night and I want her back."

"I assure you, Max..."

"No, let me assure you, Ms. Sprinkles. And you can tell your boss the same thing. If any harm comes to Susan, it will be the last friend of mine your organization fucks with." Max Snow, virtuoso of the vacant threat.

Down in the kitchen, I made a pot of coffee and paced the floor. Somehow I had to get Susan away from Grillo, which would be a neat trick since I had no idea where she was. The phone rang, interrupting my thoughts, and I plucked it off the wall. "Yeah?"

"Max? Olympio."

"You son of a bitch…"

"Hey," he said over me, "good morning to you, too."

"If I had you here, Grillo, I'd strangle your ass."

My caller chuckled. "You've already tried that, remember?"

I winced at the memory. "Fine, next time I'll just shoot you."

"I don't think so," Grillo replied. "Not when I've got something you want."

"Let Susan go."

"Sure. As soon as you sign on as my partner."

"No!"

"Then your ex gets her next spin on the karmic wheel."

"You'd actually kill her to force my hand?"

"I actually would."

"You're a slime-bucket, Grillo."

"Maybe so, but your mommy loves me."

"Not after I tell her what you've done."

"But you're not going to tell her. Not if you want to keep Susan alive."

When I didn't comment, Grillo made his final threat. "I've got business in Chicago for the next couple of days, Max. Be ready to join my team when I get back."

Chapter 12

Grillo disconnected, and after dropping limply into a nearby chair, my head fell against the cushioned back. "Susan!" I shouted to the empty house. "I am so sorry. I'll get you back. I promise."

"How?" asked the voice in my head. "You don't even know where she is."

"If Grillo's got her, he's keeping her close. And that means she's at the GBS building."

"You can't be sure of that," the voice returned.

"I can't be sure of anything," I said. "But it's all I've got, so that's where I'll start."

"And what do you propose we do, knock on the door and ask Candy to return her?"

"I'll do whatever I have to," I said. "Now stop nagging and let me think."

Fifteen minutes later I reluctantly dialed the phone number of the last person in the world I wanted to ask for help, but the only one I knew who might be able to get me inside Grillo's building and out again. My old friend Bobby Deegan had been a delinquent in his teens, a soldier in his early twenties and a Detroit cop until the age of thirty-five. Kicked off the force for excessive brutality, he did an about face and became a hit man for the mob. My reason for not wanting to seek his assistance? The ruthless bastard had tried to kill me less than two months ago. Ironically it was over the same four million Loretta Lott came after.

Swallowing my pride, I called Bobby's phone number. After several rings, an answering machine clicked on.

"Yo," said the familiar deadpan voice. "This is Bobby. I either don't want to talk to anyone right now, or I'm out. Leave a message if you must."

I hung up and dialed his cell phone.

"Maxie," Bobby said, sounding pleased to hear from me. "Long time, man."

"Not long enough," I said before I could stop myself. "How are you, Bobby?"

"Not bad. Not bad. But since you refused to turn over my four million, I've had to go back to work."

"It *isn't* your four million."

"It isn't *yours* either," he insisted.

"Finders keepers, pal. And I guess some people are never satisfied."

"What's that supposed to mean?"

"It means I could have sent your ass to prison for trying to off me but I didn't, did I?"

"Big deal," he said. "Working for a living is just about prison."

I had a sudden urge to abandon my idea of asking Bobby for help. Before I could speak up, his cynical laugh threaded through the earpiece.

"I can hear your brain battling with itself from here, Maxie. Why not just tell me what you want."

I blew out a long breath and explained my desire to snatch Susan back from Grillo. When I stopped talking, Bobby chuckled again.

"You do get yourself involved with some badass people, don't you?"

"No shit," I said. "Look who I'm on the phone with."

We both laughed at that one.

"I've met Grillo," Bobby said, "but I don't know much about him. Does his thing mostly in Chicago, correct?"

"That's my understanding."

"Must be expanding his range."

"I don't care if he launches it into freakin' outer space. I just want Susan back."

"Good luck, buddy-boy," Bobby said.

"How much to get you to help me?" I asked.

"Too much. I'm not looking to make enemies with Grillo or the rest of his *Family*."

"You owe me, Bobby."

There was silence for a beat.

"What if your ex isn't in Grillo's building?"

"She is," I insisted. "She has to be."

"Why does she have to be?"

"Because Grillo's a cocky bastard, that's why."

"Meaning?"

"Meaning, he'd think GBS would be the safest spot to hold her."

Bobby chewed on my assumption before spitting it back at me. "Right or wrong, it'll cost you a hundred grand for my help."

"What?!" I said as Grillo's review of my financial situation skittered through my mind. "I'll give you fifty."

"A hundred, man, or do it yourself."

"Maybe I will." I could almost see Bobby smiling at my toothless bluff. "Okay. A hundred."

"In advance."

I wanted to argue, but there wasn't time. Grillo could return from Chicago unexpectedly. Koji could go to the cops. "It has to be tonight then."

"Fine with me," Bobby said. "But let's do a drive-by this afternoon. Pick you up in an hour."

I walked out to the garage, pulled a large black suitcase from behind a dusty workbench, and popped the twin locks. After counting out Bobby's payoff, I split the hefty bundle in two and tucked twenty-five-thousand in each of my front pockets. He'd get the remaining fifty G's if he actually returned this evening to help me.

I was looking out the kitchen window at a heavy, lead-gray sky when an old pickup truck came chugging toward the house. It was baby-poop brown between the rust and crust; the poster child for all smog emitting, gas guzzling, pieces of junk still on the road. I swear I'd seen its twin just last week in that classic film *Ma and Pa Kettle at Home*.

The thing bumped to a stop outside my back door, causing ancient brakes to screech like a banshee. When Bobby flashed the peace sign from behind a grimy window, I could only shake my head in reluctant respect. The man was totally down with his profession.

Snagging a coat, I walked out in time to see Bobby, dressed in dingy coveralls, a matching baseball cap, and mirrored aviators, round the side of my garage. He was dragging a trio of twelve foot two-by-fours; leftovers from last year's dock expansion project. When he reached the truck-bed and tossed them inside, a shower of dry rust coated the drive.

"We're going to borrow these," Bobby said. "It will make the old girl look like she's still on the job."

I gave the ancient truck another once over, not willing to bet it could make it back down the drive. "This piece of shit doesn't need a job. What it needs is the scrap heap."

Bobby laughed while sliding behind the wheel. I circled around to the passenger door. When it refused to budge, Bobby kicked it open with both feet.

"What?" he said, watching me as I climbed onto the tattered, grease-stained seat and gave him the eye. "This is a classic."

"Sure it is," I responded as he handed me a black stocking cap and a second pair of mirrored sunglasses. "A classic piece of garbage."

When I donned the cap and glasses, Bobby looked at me appraisingly.

"Got my money?"

"Half of it," I said, digging the cash from my pockets and handing it to him. "You'll get the rest tonight when we're inside the building."

Bobby fanned out the money, sniffed it like he could actually smell the ink, and grinned. "I can live with that."

Fifty minutes later we reached the GBS building. When Bobby pulled around back and spotted the construction rubble stacked near the building's main entrance, he whooped in delight. "Fuckin' eh, man!" he said, elbowing me in the arm. "Just what the doctor ordered."

With the rear end bouncing on spent shocks and rusty springs, he backed the truck up to the rubbish pile. I made a move to get out but he stopped me.

"You stay," he ordered, handing me a clipboard. "Pretend you're doing something useful while I look around."

Exiting the truck, Bobby started sorting through the discarded rubble like a junkman on a mission. Occasionally he'd examine a piece of metal or plastic, mumble something to himself, and toss it into the back of the truck. Five minutes later, he returned to the cab.

"See anything interesting?" I asked, anxious for his report.

Bobby flashed his signature crooked grin and nodded at the windshield. "There are at least a dozen security cameras," he said before cranking the engine over. "Half of them are filming us as we speak. Grillo is either very careful or very paranoid."

My eyes searched the surrounding lot for the twelve-plus cameras Bobby claimed to have made. I spotted a trio of them immediately, their lenses pointed directly at us, affixed to lamp poles surrounding the lot.

"Can you still get us inside?"

"Hey," he said while shifting into first gear and letting the truck roll forward. "Pay me enough and I can get you into Fort Knox."

Halfway around the building Bobby stopped, threw the truck into park, and walked to the rear of the bed. He made a big deal about rearranging the two-by-fours and I suspected something important had caught his attention.

"What's up?" I asked when he slid back inside.

"See that security box above the side door?"

"Yeah."

"Decoy. The real control panel is back where we were, behind the air conditioning unit."

"How do you know that one's not the fake?"

Bobby winked and we started down the drive. "Trade secret, dude."

Bobby dropped me off at home, promising to return at about six. When he roared back up the driveway in a low-slung, black-on-black Firebird, I knew our adventure that night would be just as unpredictable.

"Christ," I said after sliding in beside him and eyeing the sleek, jet-black jumpsuit he wore. "Am I underdressed or what?"

He turned in his seat, giving my outfit of jeans, boots, and black motorcycle leather a glance. His comment was one I didn't expect.

"You carrying?"

I gave him a blank look, thinking my best bet was to play dumb. "You mean my gun?"

"No," he said, turning onto the lake's ring road, "your f'ng American Express card."

Smiling sheepishly, I laid an elbow against the gun in my waistband. "You didn't tell me to bring it."

"Didn't tell you to take a piss before we left either," he said. "Thought you'd figure it out for yourself."

Thirty minutes later, as we exited at Northwestern Highway, Bobby slapped me hard on the knee. "Almost there, dude," he said. "Hope you took care of me in your will."

"You get it all, man," I said, pointing out a cop car parked on our shoulder of the road. "Who else would I leave it to?"

A quarter of a mile from GBS, we pulled into the driveway of a dark office building and parked in the rear lot. Before popping his door, Bobby disconnected what looked like a TV remote from a charger beneath the dash.

"What's that?" I asked as it disappeared into his breast pocket.

"Magic wand," he said, grinning impishly. "Guaranteed to make shit happen."

We exited the car and headed for the tangle of woods backing the lot. Once inside the tree line, I asked where we were going.

"An old railroad track parallels this row of office buildings," Bobby explained. "We'll follow it to Grillo's place."

Behind GBS, we both squatted down and peered through the leafless trees.

"Looks like Candy's home," I said, nodding at the brightly lit third story windows.

"So what?" Bobby said. "You afraid of her?"

"Hell yes, I am. She's Grillo's right hand, and she carries a nasty little revolver."

"Broads aren't my problem," Bobby said. "If she gets in the way, I'll deal with her."

"I don't want Candy hurt."

"I'm not going to hurt anyone," he said, "unless it's absolutely necessary."

"Make sure it isn't."

He only stared at me.

"As soon as we get near the parking lot, I'm going to put the surveillance cameras out of commission," he explained. "After that, we have maybe five minutes to get into the building before the security troops arrive."

"Won't they know something's up?"

Bobby shook his head and pulled the remote from his breast pocket. "When this little baby scrambles the video signal, it will appear like a glitch in the system. Of course the security boys will check around, but by that time, we'll be inside."

"You hope."

"Hey, we could turn around and go home. I'd be happy earning fifty G's for doing nothing."

I bit down hard on my lower lip and shook my head.

"Cool," Bobby said and clapped me on the back. "Then let's do it."

My insides quivered like a plucked bowstring as I followed Bobby through the trees. When we reached the edge of the lot, he put an arm across my chest, pointing out a Chevy Tahoe idling ten yards to our right.

"We've got company," he said.

I craned my neck to see the truck. There were two men sitting in the front seat. "Now what?"

Reaching into a pocket of his overalls, Bobby produced a thick, greasy rag. "I should charge you extra for this, man, but I'm feeling generous."

As I watched, Bobby picked his way through the bare trees, emerging directly behind the truck. From my vantage point, I could see he was using the rag to stuff the tailpipe. In less than two minutes, the truck stalled and after an unsuccessful attempt to restart the engine, the driver got out and lifted the hood. I held my breath, watching as Bobby crawled along the driver's side. When the man's legs were within reach, the guy folded to the ground like a wet towel. Bobby tucked himself beneath the truck at that point. Moments after the second man got out to investigate, he went down too.

"What did you do to them?" I asked after watching Bobby drag the limp bodies into the woods and scuttle back to my side.

In answer, he held up a nasty looking stun gun. "Wired this baby myself. They'll be out for a long time."

I started to move forward but he stopped me and pointed an index finger directly above us. Mounted on the nearest tree trunk, twenty feet up, a security camera was slowly panning the lot.

"When I zap the cameras, head straight for the air conditioning unit. I'll dummy down the security system and we'll slip inside."

"Suppose Candy spots us."

Bobby's eyes flicked up to the third floor windows. "That's what makes this thing fun, Maxie. The mystery, the suspense, the possibility of getting our asses shot off."

To my amazement, everything went exactly as Bobby had described. Three minutes later, we were inside the dimly lit first floor offices.

"The next call is yours, buddy," he whispered. "Where's the ex?"

I considered the possibilities and what I knew about the building. "Grillo's apartment."

"Why not the second floor?"

"That's the warehouse level. Too many employees coming and going."

Entering the stairwell, we started the climb to the third floor. As we did, a door opened above us, and footsteps pounded on the stairs. Retreating, the two of us ducked behind the metal stairway. When the feet hit concrete, I peeked around to see Candy—cell phone in one hand, revolver in the other—push through the door to the office.

Bobby nudged me. "It's now or never, dude."

At the top of the stairs, Grillo's apartment door was wide open. After stepping inside without being challenged, a hunch propelled me down the hallway toward the guest bedroom. Opening the door cautiously, I spotted Susan lying still on a bed. When I started for her, Bobby restrained me with a hand on my shoulder.

"Time to settle your bill, Maxie."

I glared at him like he was insane. "What the hell are you talking about? Help me get her out of here."

Bobby shook his head. "That wasn't part of our deal. My money, if you please."

Pissed, but not wanting to waste time, I fumbled in my pocket and handed him the cash.

"See you in church," he said, and doing a backward skip, disappeared out the door.

I ran to Susan, pulled her into a seated position and shook her by the shoulders. "Susan," I whispered. "Come on, honey. Wake up."

After another hard shake produced no response, I decided she must be drugged. Taking hold of her arms; I maneuvered the limp body across my shoulder. By the time I swung around to leave, the lady of the house had returned and was standing in the doorway, her gun pointing directly at me.

"You are inventive as a lover, Maxie," she said, shaking her head. "But I never would have imagined you capable of this."

I smiled weakly and adjusted Susan's body on my shoulder. "Thanks. Uh, you wouldn't want to reward my efforts by letting us go, would you?"

"Sorry. Now put the lady back down on the bed and we'll figure out what to do with you."

When I made no move to comply, Candy cocked her revolver. The thing looked a hell of a lot bigger pointed in my direction.

"You're very gallant, Max, but if you don't do as I ask in the next three seconds, I will shoot. Trust me on this one."

Heaving a defeated sigh, I turned back to the bed, but before I could lower Susan, there was a dull thud behind me as Candy's body slumped to the floor. I twisted around to see Bobby, stun gun in hand, beaming a Cheshire Cat grin.

"Surprise!" he said, throwing me a two-finger salute. "Didn't think I'd abandon one of my oldest and dearest friends, did you?"

Chapter 13

Getting out of the building, with the security force patrolling the area, proved a lot hairier than getting in, but with Bobby's expertise and the help of his stun gun, we somehow managed. On the drive home, he advised me to find somewhere else to stay that night. I agreed, and after he helped me transfer the still unconscious Susan to the backseat of my Lexus, we shook hands.

"Thanks, Bobby. I owe you one."

He shook his head and flashed the crooked grin. "I'd say we're even, old buddy. But next time..."

"There won't be a next time," I assured him, but he laughed and clopped me on the shoulder.

"My Spider Man senses tell me you're full of crapola, dude. Good thing too, because I can always use the money."

He peeled off down the driveway, and I slipped inside the house. After putting out extra food and water for Blue, I rejoined the snoring Susan, then blasted out of there.

Twenty minutes later I pulled into the lot of a familiar red-roofed two-story motel. The night clerk manning the desk, a tall thin black man with a Clark Gable type mustache, was reading a paperback when I entered the office. Spotting me, he set it aside, stood and smoothed invisible wrinkles from his company tie.

"Good evening," he said. "Checking in?"

"I am if there's anything available on the ground floor."

The clerk, Jeffery according to his name tag, flicked his eyes up and down, tripping my gay-dar.

"I'm sure I can find you something," he said. "Although you look in good enough shape to climb a few stairs."

I smiled politely and took out my MasterCard. "It's my friend in the truck. She's kind of sleepy, and I don't want her to make the climb."

The fact that my friend was female never fazed the man who was now leaning forward against the counter and eyeing me like I was a ballpark frank.

"Need help with your bags?" he asked.

"Thanks," I said, then signed the credit card slip he slid across the counter. "I'm sure I can manage."

His sunny expression never wavered. In fact, at my refusal of his offer, he turned up the wattage on his enthusiastic smile. "Well if you need anything during the night...and I do mean anything...don't hesitate to ask."

Braking to a stop in front of Room 101, I stepped out into the cool evening and opened the back door. As I did, Sleeping Beauty suddenly sat up.

"*Ko Ban Wah*, Maxie-*san*," she said, giving me a dopey smile. "Where are we?"

"At a motel," I said, steadying her when she listed too far to the left. "Think you can you walk?"

Leaning forward, Susan squinted out the windshield, and after rolling her head back to meet my eyes, shook a limp finger at me. "You weren't thinking of trying to take advantage of me in there, were you?"

"You have my word of honor. Now come on." I helped her out of the Lexus and she leaned heavily against me.

"On second thought," she said and planted a wet kiss on my cheek. "Go ahead. I ain't been laid in a coon's age."

Swaying in place, she took a step and toppled forward. I shot out a hand, caught the waistband of her jeans and pulled her upright.

"Not here," she said when I got her back on her feet. "Wait till we get inside."

An elderly couple emerged from a room two doors down. When the man caught sight of us, he gave me a thumbs up.

"Those were the days, weren't they, Murt?" he said, nudging his obviously disapproving wife in the ribs. "Seems like only yesterday."

Inside the room, I lowered Susan onto the bed where she immediately fell back to sleep. I sat down beside her, put my head between my legs, and gave in to the wave of nausea demanding to be recognized. I stayed in that position until the sharp peal of the bedside phone sent truckloads of "run or die!" adrenalin knifing through my veins. When my trembling fingers finally managed to lift the receiver, I put it to my ear without a word.

"Mr. Snow? This is Jeffery at the front desk. Is everything in your room satisfactory?"

"So far as I can tell, Jeffery. What's up?"

"I go on break soon."

"Yeah."

"And I'd be happy to deliver extra towels, or turn down your bed, or perform any other little service Mrs. Snow would…if she wasn't so sleepy."

I shook my head, amazed by the man's persistence. "I'll tell you what you *can* do, Jeffery," I said, thinking to use the man as an early warning system in case Grillo did actually show up.

"Anything."

"If someone besides the cops or the current President asks if I'm checked in here…"

"Yes?"

"I'd like you to lie, and say you've never heard of me."

There was a pregnant pause.

"Uh…sure," he said. "I can do that."

"I'll touch base with you tomorrow," I said conspiratorially, and thinking it might build the mystery for him, cradled the handset without another word.

A few minutes later, I stripped Susan of shoes and jeans, tucking her beneath the covers. In the bathroom, I used the complimentary toothbrush, peed, and then crawled in beside her. She woke, but only long enough to scoot closer, and lay her head on my shoulder.

Too keyed up to follow Susan's lead, I let my brain wander; a dangerous thing to do when it's rife with anger and a desire for revenge, but something had to be done about Grillo. A couple of choices immediately came to mind. One, I could agree to handcuff myself to the creep for the rest of my life. Or two, I could dust off my gun and shoot the son of a bitch. Yow! I thought as I pushed door number two closed, locking it tight. Better not to go there.

Uninvited, the voice in my head put in its two cents. "Grillo would kill you in a heartbeat, chief. Better him than us."

"Yeah, well…" I mumbled.

"Yeah, well," it said, mimicking my non-committal intonation. "You are such a wimp."

"Screw you, big mouth," I protested. "I'm no killer and unless you want to join me in jail for twenty to life, or be hunted down by the Mafia for doing one of its boys, I suggest you help me think of an alternative plan."

We were both silent for a beat.

"Well if we're not going to snuff him," the voice said, "how about we lose him somehow."

"How?"

"I don't know. Kidnap his ass and ship him off somewhere?"

"Yeah, right."

"You got a better suggestion?"

"No."

"Well then think about that one. There has to be a way."

For the next hour or so I lay in the dark considering different ways to snatch Grillo and ship him out of the country. Some of my ideas were so lame they made me laugh out loud. When Susan stirred beside me and started mumbling something in Japanese, my mind shifted to another track. What if I informed the Japanese government that Grillo had the *Sitting Tiso*? Would they arrest him and put him in jail? Nah. Most likely he'd get a slap on the hands and I'd be in more trouble than ever.

As I was dozing off, an idea slipped through the strands of sleep, and my eyes popped open. It was a long shot, like most of my best ideas, but if Susan was willing to help, it had possibilities.

The next morning at nine I was awakened by the beep of my cell phone on the nightstand. The readout told me it was my mom calling, so I punched connect and put it to my ear. "Hey."

"Just what the hell is going on, buster?"

"Good morning, Mother," I said, feeling rested and in the mood to tweak her a little. "Hope you're having a blessed day so far."

"I'll give you a frickin' blessed day. What the hell did you do to piss Olympio off?"

"What do you mean?"

"He flew back from Chicago unexpectedly last night and hasn't stopped bitching since."

"What's his problem?"

"He won't tell me, but it has something to do with you and Susan."

"Well I can't imagine…"

"Don't bullshit me, Max," she said, cutting me off. "What's going on?"

Susan sat up behind me and I put a finger to my lips. "The only thing going on is that Susan convinced me to agree to Olympio's business offer."

There was a pause while Marie considered the statement. "Really?"

"Really. There are a few details I need to go over with him, but basically I'm ready to sign."

"What did she say to change your mind?"

"Does it matter?"

"No, but..."

"Look, Mom, I just woke up and nature's calling. Tell your husband we can talk this afternoon."

"At your house?"

"No," I said. "I have some running around to do. Have him buzz me on my cell phone."

I disconnected and turned to a bleary-eyed Susan. Before she could ask, I laid out the story of her kidnapping, her rescue, and how we ended up at the motel. When I finished, she sighed heavily, leaning back against the pillows.

"Sorry to cause you so much trouble, Maxie," she said, running a hand over the stubble on her scalp. "I can't believe I was dumb enough to get in that car."

"It's me who should apologize, babe. Grillo threatened to do something like that. I just figured you'd be safe with your friends."

An hour later we checked out of the motel and stopped at a Big Boy in the next town for breakfast. After our waitress had come and gone, I looked into Susan's eyes across the table. "So you're really okay?"

She nodded as her hand stroked the arm where the drug had been injected. "A little hung over maybe. How about you?"

I waved away the question. "I'm a man, babe."

Susan laughed. "That's true, but I love you anyway."

"Good thing, too," I said, "because I need to ask a big favor."

"How could I refuse my knight in shining armor? Ask away."

I leaned back in the booth and gave her my serious expression. "You realize Grillo is not going to give up on me."

Susan's lips tightened into a thin line at the suggestion.

"That means I've got to do something about it."

"Like what?"

"Remember telling me about your friends in the Japanese Mafia? The ones that had immigrated to Michigan. What did you call them? The *Yakuza*?"

She nodded.

"And didn't you say that despite being hardcore criminals, most are big supporters of Japanese culture?"

Another nod.

"How do you think they'd feel about Grillo owning the *Sitting Tiso?*"

"They wouldn't like it," she said automatically.

"Would they not like it enough to help us get it away from him and back to Japan?"

Susan looked thoughtful. "They might."

"Now for the big question. Would they be willing to take Grillo along too, and hold him there?"

Susan raised her eyebrows.

"It's the only thing I can think of to get the guy off my back. Either that or I'm going to have to shoot him."

Her eyes searched mine. "You're joking, right?"

"Of course, but that leads us back to my first suggestion."

We were quiet as the waitress delivered coffee for me, hot tea for Susan, and then moved off.

"How long would you want them to hold Grillo?"

I shrugged. "Would you believe…forever?"

Susan took a sip of tea and looked though me.

"So would they do it?"

"We could only ask," she said. "Give me your cell phone."

I handed it to her and after dialing, she pressed the phone to her ear. When someone on the other end answered, Susan spoke for several minutes in Japanese before snapping the phone closed.

"I arranged for a meeting this afternoon," she said.

"Where?"

"A private gym in Southfield. Here's the address." She wrote it down on a napkin and handed it to me. "Drop me off in Webberville. I'll meet you there about three."

Chapter 14

After delivering Susan, I headed home, fed Blue his favorite meal of tuna and green peas; watching in satisfaction as he cleaned his plate, and then each whisker. The familiar ritual had a soothing effect on me. After all I'd been through; I was convinced it's our daily routines that keep us sane.

If I've never described my cat, let me bore you with a few words about this one of a kind feline. Blue is a green-eyed, silver haired Oriental sweetheart that knows when to cuddle and when to leave me alone. A watch cat extraordinaire with a gentle disposition, he sleeps eighteen-hours-a-day and has short bursts of energy that can explode like a volcano in any direction. There are one or two things that bug me about him but nobody's perfect. If he could talk, he'd probably say the same about me.

Around twelve, I called the salon. When Gwen heard my voice, she immediately started griping about the boxes of products that still filled the office.

"Hold on there, Tex," I drawled, attempting to sooth the savage breast with humor. "I got that pesky mystery roped and tied. Take down this number." I recited the address of Grillo's office building. "And arrange for UPS to ship those puppies back over there."

"Finally," Gwen said.

"But not until Friday."

"What?" she snapped. "Why not?"

"I have my reasons, Gwen. Please just do as I ask."

The moment I disconnected from Gwen, the phone signaled another call. It was Olympio Grillo, all upbeat and friendly.

"Maxie," he said, sounding like the consummate CEO. "Marie tells me you're ready to come on board."

"I am if we can agree on two details."

"I'm listening."

"First, the money you're going to pay Mom and me."

"Looking to up the figure?"

"No, your offer is extremely generous."

"Then what?"

"What, is that I don't trust you, so I want the entire four million up front."

There was a long pause.

"Sorry," he finally said, "there is no way I'm going to hand you four million."

"I didn't think you would, so this is what I propose. We pick a local bank, put the cash in a safety deposit box, put that in another box and each of us gets one key."

"Who picks the bank?" he asked.

"Me."

"And why is that?"

"Because for all I know, the club you belong to might own the one you'd pick."

Grillo laughed. "Okay. What's the second thing?"

"I want the *Sitting Tiso*."

"Forget it."

"Consider it a signing bonus."

"No."

I stayed quiet, giving him a chance to reconsider. He and I both knew the potential to launder cash through ten salons for four years far exceeded what the Tiso was worth.

"I'll think about it and get back to you," Grillo said.

"Take your time. I'm in no hurry."

Ten minutes later, Grillo reconnected and agreed to my terms.

That afternoon I pulled into the parking lot of a small, sixties style strip-mall on the northwest corner of Webster and Evergreen in Southfield. The shopping center seemed dated with its faded white aluminum, and crumbling fake brick storefronts. Of the five scruffy looking businesses it housed—gym, party store, shoe repair, clothing resale, and check cashing—the gym, sitting dead-center, was worst of the lot.

Susan's Beetle was nowhere in sight, so I got out, stretched, and approached the door of the gym. A sign taped inside the grimy glass read "Penglai Gym, Members Only". Hanging on a string below it, a note scribbled on a tattered business card read "Closed". Beside the door was a 10' x 10' single pane window. Beyond it, black drapes; their centers, sun-bleached a pukey blue-gray, hid whatever was going on inside. Trying my luck, I knocked hard on the steel-framed glass door. I was about to walk away, when it jerked open.

"Not open to public!" shouted a short Japanese man who although wearing only a pair of navy blue jogging shorts looked fully clothed. Every inch of the man's body, minus hands, feet, neck, and head was covered by an explosion of colorful tattoos; a sure sign to anyone in the know that he was a member of the *Yakuza*.

"Private gym!" he growled angrily. When I didn't step away, he puffed his pecs, causing the face-to-face dragons adorning them to rear back and glare out at me.

"My name is Max Snow," I said, a little too loudly. Like most Americans, I automatically think any foreigner can understand English if the decibels are high enough. "I'm supposed to meet Susan Brady here."

The man, who was at least a head shorter, raked me with ferocious black eyes. "Women not allowed in gym!"

I shuffled my feet, not sure what to say when another man joined us at the door. He was tall for a Japanese, powerfully built, and his own detailed body art split down the center of his chest like an unbuttoned frock coat. In contrast to the shorter man, he, at least seemed friendly. After flashing the peace sign, he waved me inside. The moment I stepped through the door, half a dozen tattooed men closed in around me. Not a single one looked happy about my invading their space.

The tall man barked out a short syllable and the men encircling me retreated to their former positions. When he indicated I should move toward the wall, I sidestepped in that direction, bumped into something, and heard that same something crash heavily to the floor. Turning, I felt my lungs stop short at the sight of a wooden Buddha lying face down on the scuffed tile floor. Irate glances met my contrite smile. A set of steel fingers grabbed the base of my neck, Vulcan death grip style. And the next second, my consciousness closed down like the screen on an old fashioned TV.

Sometime later, Susan's face swam into view. She was kneeling on the floor, stroking my forehead, and the brown eyes flashed with both anger and concern. "Are you all right?"

I nodded and pushed myself into a seated position.

"Dammit, Kano!" she said to the tall man who stood at her side. "This is my friend. The one I spoke to you about on the phone. Why did you let your men attack him?"

Kano looked bemused at the stinging reprimand. "But he is unharmed, Susan-*san*. What is the problem?"

Fresh irritation tightened the set of Susan's jaw but before she could speak, I struggled to my feet and stood there swaying slightly. If Kano was the leader of this group, it probably wasn't a good idea to show him disrespect.

"I'm okay, honey," I said, willing myself not to fall over. "Really."

Kano smiled and nodded his approval. "Your friend is wise, Susan. And he is welcome here."

After a hard look from Kano, the man who had challenged me at the door stepped forward and bowed at the waist. He was introduced as Furuna-*san* and when I mimicked his stiff bow, I received grunts of approval from the others.

"You see, Sister Susan," Kano said. "We are all friends now. Please follow me to my office."

Susan and I trailed Kano around exercise mats and weight machines to a tiny office in the back. With a nod, he invited us to sit in the two nylon-laced patio chairs facing a scarred gray metal desk. He settled into an ancient oak high-back behind it.

"What do you think of my American empire, Susan?" he said, indicating the shabby surroundings with a sweep of his hand. "I am really moving up in the world, eh?"

Susan leaned forward and rested her arms on the stained and chipped desktop. "I take it the *Kumicho* sent you to this country against your will."

Kano held out both of his hands and I noticed for the first time, he was missing the pinky on each. "It was that," he said resignedly, "or lose another finger."

"What was your crime this time?" she asked, shaking her head. "Disobedience? Or are you still losing at *Cho Ka Han Ka*?"

Kano threw his head back and laughed. "My soul remains trapped in the bamboo dice cup, Susan-*san*. Perhaps you have not prayed hard enough for my freedom."

Susan took in my confused expression and explained. "My eight fingered friend here," she said, angling her head in Kano's direction, "likes to play the game called *Cho Ka Han Ka*. Think of it as odds or evens. The problem is he always bets more than he owns and never knows when to quit."

I inspected Kano's hands, which were now flat on the desktop. "Somebody cut off your fingers in payment for a gambling debt?"

"Worse than that," Susan answered for Kano. "He cut the damn things off himself."

Kano acknowledged my incredulous expression with a bob of his hairless, bowling ball shaped head. "It is not so bad. Although it is best to drink a great deal of sake beforehand."

"Why do it at all?"

"Because the *Kumicho* was forced to pay my debt," he said matter-of-factly. "Refusing his command would have cost me a hand, or perhaps one of my children."

"The *Kumicho*," Susan cut in, "is like the Don in the Italian Mafia, only much more powerful. If he tells you to jump off Fuji, you ask only if you should take a running start."

Kano laughed again and slapped the desk with his palms. "Susan knows our customs well, Max-*san*. Her heart is truly Japanese."

All in all, the meeting went well. After explaining to our host how Grillo was using the Tiso, he agreed to do as I asked.

"How would you get Grillo back to Japan?" I said. "By ship?"

Kano nodded. "I know a sea captain that owes me a favor." He paused and gave me a piercing look across the desk. "But why do you want the *Yakuza* to imprison this man? Would it not be easier to kill him?"

I glanced the question to Susan who nodded, pressing her hands together as if in prayer.

"Mr. Grillo's karma has been severely compromised by his profit driven actions," she said in her best Buddhist nun's voice. "With your help, the universe may yet offer him a chance to achieve enlightenment."

I nodded agreement, which made the lines around Kano's eyes crinkle in amusement.

"It is my suspicion," Kano said, leaning back in his chair, "that in sparing this man's life, Max hopes to save his own soul. And perhaps yours also, Susan-*san*."

Susan and I drove to my house in separate cars but arrived simultaneously. She let us in. I made tea. After delivering a cup to where she sat enjoying the roaring fireplace, I returned to the kitchen and prepared dinner. Thirty minutes later, I carried a colorful mix of stir-fried veggies over lemon couscous to the enclosed patio, smiling when Susan followed her nose to the table. Settling into the chair I held out for her, she took in the spicy aroma.

"Living with you," she purred, shifting her eyes to my face, "is like being on the tasting panel of the *Iron Chef*."

"Any expertise I possess, I owe to my teacher," I said and bowed. Susan had introduced me to the culinary arts during our marriage. "And I am forever in your debt."

We ate in silence for several minutes, enjoying our food and each other's company.

"So what do you think?" I asked, serving myself more couscous. "Can we trust Kano?"

"No," Susan said. "Members of the *Yakuza* are far from trustworthy. But to back away now would show weakness and perhaps invite chaos."

I thought about my mom possibly being caught in the crossfire of that chaos and hoped I hadn't made a mistake. Picking up my concerned expression, Susan reached across the table to put her hand on mine. "Thinking about Marie?"

I made a face and dropped my fork onto the plate. "Why the hell did she marry that bastard? The woman lives to screw up my life."

Susan raised both eyebrows. "Oh you poor thing. I'm sure Marie couldn't possibly have feelings for that handsome, charming, wealthy man. This whole mess is just a plot to piss you off."

I stuck my tongue out at her while reaching for my wine. "To love," I said, raising the glass in her direction. "The great fucking complicater."

Later that evening, I was heading for the sunroom hot tub when Susan handed me the cell phone.

"Who is it?" I asked, hoping it might be Zed.

"Kano," she said, registering the disappointment in my eyes. "He wants to talk to you."

I took the phone from her and after stepping down into the bubbling water, released the mute button. "*Konban wa*, Kano. What's up?"

"Everything is set, Max-*san*. Your friend and his prize are to return to Japan where both shall remain for the rest of their days."

I looked over at an expectant Susan and nodded. "And that would happen when?"

"The ship they are to travel on leaves in two days," he reported. "I suggest you bring your man to my friend's restaurant tomorrow night."

"A restaurant?" I said. "Isn't that kind of public?"

"There is a private dining area inside. We will complete our business there."

"Should I ask how?"

"Your party will be served a variety of sushi dishes. Among them will be *fugu*, a delicious but potentially fatal form of blowfish. The nerve toxin contained in its body is said to be five hundred times more deadly than that of cyanide."

"I've heard of it," I said. "It's eaten to show bravery. Correct?"

"*Hai*," Kano said. "That is one reason."

"I've also read that several people die from eating *fugu* every year."

"Right again, my friend. The puffer fish is most difficult to prepare correctly."

"So why serve it to *us*?" I asked, wondering if the *Yakuza* thought it would be easier to bump off both Grillo and me at the same time while capturing the Tiso with less hassle.

"Because it is delicious, with a delicate chicken-like flavor, and because it can produce so strong a sense of euphoria in the diner that he or she may be more easily controlled."

"Think I'll pass on the *fugu*," I said. "But thanks for the offer."

Kano chuckled. "I understand your hesitation, Max. But in this case, it will be necessary."

"You're thinking if Susan and I don't eat it, neither will Grillo?"

"From the way you have described this man to me, yes. But there's no need to worry. The chef I have in mind is a master at controlling the poison. For you and Susan, if you choose to bring her, there will be just enough to create an aphrodisiac effect. For Mr. Grillo, enough to make him sleep for a long, long time."

I wasn't really up for a potentially deadly dining experience, but wanted Grillo out of my life so badly that I was willing to try anything. "What restaurant are we talking about?"

"It is called Lotus," he said. "Do you know it?"

"Yeah. I've eaten there a couple of times. They do excellent sushi."

"I shall inform the staff of your compliment," Kano said. "They will be pleased."

"Do that," I said, thinking it was probably a good idea to stroke a *fugu* chef's ego whenever possible.

"Arrive at the restaurant by seven o'clock," Kano said. "My man will be at the door watching for you. Sayonara."

I pushed disconnect. Susan's questioning eyes met mine. "It's set to go down tomorrow night. Care to come along?"

Susan held up a finger and left the room. Returning a few minutes later, she held an open bottle of Zinfandel in one hand; two glasses in the other. In a flash she shucked jeans and sweatshirt, filled both glasses and joined me in the hot tub. "If we're going to go through with this," she said, handing me one of the glasses. "I feel like getting drunk and laid. How about you?"

I smiled thoughtfully then took a long sip of the hearty red wine. "What about your vow of chastity?"

"What about your commitment to Zed?"

I downed the remaining wine in my glass and held it out for a refill. By the time I settled back against the side of the tub, my overactive hormones had already made my choice. "That commitment has been stretched to the limit," I said, stroking the inside of her calf with my foot. "I doubt if another pull would snap it. Besides, I'm ready for something new."

"New?" she asked while scooting to my side. "Have you forgotten we were married for almost a decade?"

"I haven't forgotten," I assured her as a once familiar hand explored the stiffness between my legs. "But you weren't a Buddhist nun then. I've never made it with a member of the clergy before."

"I haven't changed," she said and running an open palm across my chest, tweaked my right nipple hard between her thumb and forefinger.

"Ow!" I said, reaching a hand playfully toward her small but nicely shaped breasts. "How'd you like it if I did that to you?"

Susan pushed her chest forward, flashing a naughty smile.

"Oh yeah," I said, pulling her against me. "I almost forgot. You like that kind of thing."

Two hours later I had just stepped out of the shower when my cell phone rang. Padding barefoot into the bedroom, I snatched it off the bedside table. The digital readout told me it was Marie calling but when I pushed connect, Grillo's deep voice spoke in my ear.

"Once again I want to congratulate you on your decision to join us, Max. You won't regret it."

"Well thanks, Olympio," I said. "I owe it all to your patient persistence. Let's hope I get what I want out of the deal."

"Oh you will," he said, his voice full of misplaced mirth. "I guarantee it."

Grillo's guarantee was far from comforting. The Mafia rarely leaves loose ends behind to blow up in their faces. He was probably already planning where to dump my corpse after the partnership ended.

"How about if we do the bank thing tomorrow morning?" I said, launching into a little duplicity of my own. "And then we can sign the contracts at dinner."

There was a pause. In the silence, my heart thumped my ribs like a battering ram.

"Tomorrow's not a good day," he said. "I have to meet with the staff of GBS at nine, and then fly to Chicago on business. Let's do it the day after."

"No!" I blurted out, then wished I could take back the forceful protest. "I mean I'm ready now. Give me time to think and I might change my mind."

His silence lasted a full twenty seconds.

"Fine," he finally said and I released the breath I'd been holding. "Tomorrow it is. I'll pick you up about ten."

Chapter 15

I slept fitfully that night, when I slept at all. At five, I got out of bed and fixed myself a pot of coffee. Susan was already deep in meditation. I could see her sitting straight-backed through the sunroom door. She had begged out of remaining in bed after we made love, claiming she was going to "sit" until the next evening. "It will bring us luck," was her excuse, but I sensed her troubled mind. A spark we both thought extinguished long ago had been rekindled last night. And like the kids we once were, neither had the slightest idea what to do with it.

About nine that morning, Riff called. "What up, Snowman?"

"Same ol'..., Lieutenant. How about you?"

"Oh a cop's life is full of excitement. I've just spent a blissful hour filling out reports and doing paperwork."

"Beats a gunfight with a desperate criminal."

"I guess," she said, "but not by a hell of a lot. Hey, don't you work anymore? Every time I call the salon, you're not there."

"I'm a lazy shit as you well know, Lieutenant. Three days a week seem like more than enough for me."

"You rich boys get all the perks."

"You should talk, copper. How about that free coffee you guys get at the doughnut shops? Talk about your perks."

We chatted about nothing for several minutes before Riff got to the reason for her call.

"Saw your truck in Southfield yesterday. Felt like slumming, did you?"

"Just had some business to take care of, Lieutenant. It's a free country, you know."

"That gym you were parked in front of is full of trouble, Shamus. It, and the people who hang there, are good things to avoid."

"Thanks for the warning."

Riff's curiosity was palpable across the phone line. "Got anything you want to share with me? You amateur gumshoes are always hot on the trail of trouble."

"Nada."

"Well is there anything you *don't* want to tell me?"

"I'm clean, officer. You can check my record."

"I'm familiar with your record. That's why I'm concerned."

"Well don't be. Nothing's going on."

"Then what were you doing at that gym?"

"Taking judo lessons?"

"Wrong. It's private."

"Okay. Ya got me. I was actually born to Japanese parents, went through extensive plastic surgery to look like a typical white boy, and I've been a *Yakuza* mole in the U.S. for years."

Dead silence greeted my lame attempt at humor.

"The *Yakuza* don't take prisoners, Snowman. I hope the hell you know what you're doing."

"I'm not doing anything," I said, trying to sound sincere. "An old friend of Susan's hangs out there. We stopped by to say hello."

"Liar, liar, pants on fire," she responded.

"It's true."

"Yeah, right."

Later that morning I was cleaning up the kitchen when a new Mercedes S600 pulled up behind my house. Through the mini-blinds I watched Grillo step out, walk to the passenger side and open the door. I expected to see Marie. Instead the tanned, well-turned legs of Candy Sprinkles slid into view.

Both boss and secretary were dressed for business; he, in a perfectly tailored, navy-blue pinstripe, she, in a mini-skirted, winter-white suit that made her look like some corporate angel. I glanced down at my own outfit of Eddie Bauer khakis, Italian loafers and black cashmere pullover. Casual in comparison, but it would have to do.

Was I nervous? Bet on it. But I was also determined to free myself from Grillo's clutches.

I opened the door before they could knock. Candy, who was in the lead, offered her hand. If she was pissed because of the snatch-back, her expression didn't reveal it.

"Good morning, Max," she said, gracing me with a full face smile. "What a lovely home you have."

"Thank you, Candy. You're looking more beautiful than ever."

Grillo pushed his way in and grasped me firmly by the shoulders. "You won't regret joining us, Maxie. And you're about to make your mom one happy lady."

"If not an honest one," I said.

"Don't worry about Marie," he said. "Her work for the salons will be strictly legit."

"That's impossible, Olympio. And because we're about to become partners, I'll say this one more time. Marie is no dummy. She'll figure out what's going on and she won't like it."

"You're absolutely right," Grillo said. "So to clear the air, I explained everything to Marie this morning."

I raised an eyebrow. "And her opinion of your laundry scam?"

"She didn't approve. In fact she threatened to leave me if I went ahead with it."

My heart jumped at the news, but my brain understood that even if Marie did dump Grillo, my troubles with him would be far from over. "But you two worked it out?" I asked.

"I love your mother, Max. She's a wonderful woman. But despite her strong objections, she was willing to listen to reason."

I wasn't buying it. Marie's innate sense of justice wouldn't allow willing involvement in a crime. "So you're telling me she's okay with your game plan?"

Grillo pulled a fat Cuban out of an inner pocket of his coat and popped it in the corner of his mouth. "Not yet," he said, around the chubby cigar. "But she'll come around."

The sound of laughter echoed through the first floor. I turned to see Candy and Susan, sitting on the couch in front of the fireplace, chatting away like old friends.

"I know what you're thinking," Grillo said over my shoulder. "But when we had her, Susan never woke up long enough to eyeball Candy."

I rounded on him, my anger over Susan's kidnapping too fresh to check. "This is all one big fucking game to you, isn't it?"

Grillo's cigar rose with his tight smile. "Hey. Isn't everything?"

Ten minutes later, Grillo, Candy and I left to take care of the bank business. After a short discussion, we decided on a branch of National City, directly across the street from Rolling Pines Mall.

Inside the bank, we filled out the required forms. A teller escorted us into the safety deposit box area. Grillo explained our desire for a box that would fit inside another. If the woman attending us thought the request odd, she didn't let on. When we were alone, Grillo set the briefcase he carried on the wood table and popped the locks. Inside were eight fat bundles of crisp, new five-thousand-dollar bills.

"Is it all there?" I asked, staring in awe at the tightly packed cash.

"All but the five-hundred grand I paid to save your ass from Loretta Lott."

I picked up one of the hefty bundles, then slid a single bill from the middle. "You don't mind if I let the bank take a look at this, do you?"

Grillo shrugged. "If it will make you happy."

I left the room and stood in line for a teller. When it was my turn, I handed him the bill. "See anything wrong with this?"

The man examined the bill, front and back. "Looks good to me. But hold on a second."

He walked two windows over and handed the bill to an older black woman. After giving the five thousand a thorough going over, she nodded once and handed it back.

"It's the real McCoy," the teller said as he laid the bill in my hand. "Any reason to suspect it isn't?"

"Not really. I'm just the paranoid type."

On the way back to my house I suggested to Grillo that we dine at Lotus that night. "My treat. We can sign the contracts after dinner."

"No," Grillo said. "I'm grilling lamb chops tonight. If you want to join us for dinner, come by my place about eight."

His flat refusal constricted my stomach. "But," I said, scrambling for an objection. "I've already reserved the restaurant's private dining room."

"So cancel," said the Mafia lieutenant who was used to having his orders obeyed without question.

"I don't want to cancel," I protested. "I'm in the mood for sushi, and the atmosphere at Lotus would be more appropriate for exchanging the Tiso."

Candy, who was at the wheel of the big Mercedes, eyed me in the mirror. The expression on her face said, don't push it, but I stood my ground.

"I ordered something special for us," I said, fleshing out the bluff. "So I had to pay in advance."

Grillo turned in the passenger seat and looked at me. "Like what?"

"*Fugu*. Have you ever had it?"

"I have," Grillo replied—and as if he had every right—reached over and cupped Candy's breast. "*Fugu* can be a potent aphrodisiac. Makes this fine wench cum like a volcano. Doesn't it, babe?"

Candy's smile in the mirror never reached her eyes. "That's right. Too bad I'm busy tonight."

Grillo shifted his attention to her. "Busy doing what?"

"Preparing for the meeting we were supposed to have this morning," she said. "As CEO, I *do* have responsibilities."

Grillo laughed and tugged at one of the blonde curls framing Candy's face. "Ain't this woman the shit, Maxie? Takes care of my business like she owns it."

"She's the shit, all right," I agreed. Once again Candy met my eyes in the mirror. "Maybe I'll try and steal her away from you someday."

"No need to do that, partner," Grillo said. "When you sign those contracts tonight, we'll all be one big happy family."

When Grillo dropped me off at home, Susan met me at the door. She wore a knee-length, bronze caftan that made the soft color in her eyes glow provocatively.

"How did it go?" she asked.

"Pretty good. The money's in the bank. Grillo's agreed to meet at Lotus for dinner tonight."

"What about the Tiso?"

"He says he'll bring it with him."

"And if he doesn't?"

"Then we're screwed, babe," I said, shaking my head. "I don't think we'll get a second shot at this guy."

While swimming laps in the pool to drain off my excess energy, I thought about how Grillo's sudden disappearance might affect Marie. There was no doubt my fiercely protective mother would resent his involving me in a crime. His comment about her eventually coming around to the idea was dead off the mark.

A light snow had started to fall as I climbed out of the pool and padded into the sunroom. Susan was meditating in her favorite spot beside the hot tub. As I neared, one eye opened and her Buddha-smile widened.

"Feeling better?" she asked.

I nodded, then knelt to massage her neck. She leaned forward with the pressure. When I hit just the right spot, Susan moaned softly.

"How's the work going on your house?" I asked.

"Gooood," she said, drawing out the word as I increased the force of the rubdown. "But I'm starting to think that running a monastery isn't the right fit for me."

"What?" I said, pausing and drawing her back by the shoulders. "Why?"

Susan turned her head to look up at me. "I suppose you want me to be honest?"

"I wish you would."

"Well," she said, raising her eyebrows, "I think I might be falling in love."

"With who?"

"Believe it or not, you, and that wasn't in my plan."

Heart pounding, I sat, gazing silently into her golden-brown eyes.

"You said you wanted honesty."

"Trust me," I said, "I'm glad you were. But *that* is a shocker."

"Is it?"

When I didn't answer, Susan smiled lightly. "Maybe it's just being together again after all these years, plus the rescue thing. Women tend to fall for doctors, therapists, and men who risk their lives for them."

I sighed. "Didn't I tell you love was the great fucking complicater?"

She nodded while a tear slid down one cheek.

"When you first left for Japan," I said, taking her hands in mine, "I was totally lost. There wasn't a day I didn't think I had screwed up big time—that somehow I was the cause of our breakup."

"That's not true..." she protested but I cut her off with a shake of my head.

"I know that now. It took a while, too long actually, but I'm kind of slow."

"I'm sorry if you ever thought that for one minute," she said, her eyes brimming with tears.

"It's okay," I said, leaning forward to kiss her on both cheeks. "Really. Once I booted my ego in the ass, I was happy for you. A little jealous too, I have to admit. You seemed to have found something worth committing to and I wasn't even close."

"If this is a brushoff," she said, swiping at an escaping tear, "I wish you'd stop being so damn sweet."

Zed's image came to mind as I gazed into the eyes of my first real love. Would the mysterious Amazon ever return from Belize? She had been gone for so long; I was beginning to doubt it.

"I'd offer a penny for your thoughts," Susan said, bringing me back to the moment. "But I already know what they are."

"Think so, huh?"

"Sure. You're not hard to read."

"That's what Zed always says."

Susan stood and walked to the nearest bank of windows. "I'm sorry, Maxie. I should have kept this to myself. You have more than enough on your plate right now."

I moved over to where she stood and took her in my arms. "It would be so easy to fall in love with you again, Susan. I'm halfway there already, but…"

She put a finger to my lips and shook her head. "I understand."

I couldn't resist the moment. When I kissed her, she pressed herself tightly against me. The next thing I knew we were naked on the floor; me with my body pressed solidly into the cool granite, she on top, her tongue doing a slow-dance with mine. Pushing up on hands and knees, Susan did a deft north to south flip. As her hot, wet mouth captured me, I tugged her hips down to join the feast.

Later, in my bed, after our third go at the brass ring, I gazed up at my panting lover and raised an eyebrow. "Whew! Ride em' cowboy, Sister Susan."

"Tell me about it," she said, wiping her damp forehead with the back of a hand. "Five years of celibacy and I feel like I've reverted to a horny teenager."

"You're as freakin' energetic as one, that's for damn sure. Twice is usually my limit."

"Stop," she said, covering her face with her hands. "You're embarrassing me."

"Oh I bet, 'Ms. think we can do it one more time?'"

Susan's eyes darkened with renewed desire as she reached a hand between my legs. "I can if you can."

"Forget it, girl," I replied, placing my hand over hers. "Three orgasms a day should be enough for any Buddhist nun."

Susan was about to protest when the phone beside the bed rang. I picked it up. At the sound of Grillo's voice, the sex mood was broken.

"Just calling to firm up our plans," Grillo said. "Do you want to ride with me to the restaurant?"

"No. I have to stop by the salon. We'll meet you there at 6:45."

"So, Susan is dining with us?"

"She's looking forward to it. How about Marie?"

There was a five second pause.

"She's not coming," he finally said.

I hadn't really wanted my mom to be there, but Olympio's brief statement, and the lack of any follow up gave me hope that things were falling apart at Chateau Grillo.

"Big surprise," I said, giving him a graceful out. "Marie never *was* into Japanese food."

"You are aware of the inherent dangers of eating *fugu* I presume?" Grillo said, changing the subject.

"I've read about them."

"And you're still willing to risk it?"

"Risk is relative, Olympio. You can pass on the *fugu* if you want."

"No way," he said. "I'm into it. How about your ex?"

"You know how Buddhist nuns are," I said, winking at Susan who was beside me listening to every word. "They're trained to cope with anything the universe throws at them."

"Is something going on between you two?" Grillo asked. "I thought Zed was your main piece of ass."

Susan smirked, waiting for me to answer.

"According to the teachings of the Buddha," I said. "All things are transient."

Chapter 16

Probably because I was anxious to get the whole thing over with; the remainder of the afternoon crawled by. Susan had gone back to meditating. Blue was deep into one of his eighteen hours of sleep that day, so I threw on a jacket and headed down to the lake. Walking along the wet sand, I reviewed the plan to get rid of Grillo. Not long ago I had accused him of playing God with people's lives. Wasn't that exactly what I was about to do?

"This is different," said the voice in my head. "The man will eat you alive if you don't get rid of him."

"I agree," I said out loud. "But does that make it right?"

"Right, shmight! You're saving your ass. There's nothing wrong with that."

"What about Marie?" I protested.

"What *about* her?" the voice said. "Think you won't be doing her a favor at the same time?"

"But she loves the guy. I can tell."

"Not anymore. Not since Grillo admitted what he was all about."

"Oh? Are you a clairvoyant now?"

"Don't be such a dick," the voice said. "You know damn well I'm right."

At six, Susan and I were in my truck and on the road. She had redressed in her bronze caftan, but an added sash gave it the look of an evening gown Holly Golightly might have worn to dinner at 21. I decided to go with my mood; black boots, black slacks, black long-sleeved pullover, and a black car coat. Not exactly what you'd call celebratory colors but if Grillo got wise and I had to run for my life, at least I'd blend into the night.

We pulled into the restaurant parking lot at exactly 6:43. Before we could exit the truck, Grillo slid his big Mercedes in beside us.

"Perfect timing," he said when we exited our vehicles and shook hands. "I like that in a partner."

Grillo had dressed down from that morning's "Joe Banker" look. He was now elegantly casual in gray slacks, black turtleneck and a knee-length leather trench coat. In one hand he carried what looked like a square hatbox, his other clutched a cell phone.

"I hope you're right about the food being good here," he said, dropping the phone into an inside coat pocket. "Because I'm starving."

"I'm sure the chef won't disappoint you," I said, glancing at Susan. "One bite of his sushi and you'll be transported straight to Japan."

Lotus occupies the first level of a ten-story office building. Inside the glass double-doors, a thin Japanese with a waxed mustache and neatly clipped goatee smiled and cocked his head in greeting. I gave him my name. After consulting the guest list on his podium, he bowed to our little group then indicated we should follow.

The spacious restaurant's décor was what you might call Asian minimalist; the walls done in tones of mauve, the black accent pieces deliberately downplayed to invite contemplative dining. Ginger and garlic scented the air. As we snaked through the crowded room toward the *shoji*-screened private dining area near the back, hints of rosemary, thyme, and lemon grass joined the mix. At the entrance, we removed our shoes. When the maitre d' slid back the panel, we filed in, seating ourselves on pillows around a low slung, red lacquered table.

"Interesting," Grillo said, commenting on the room's only decoration; a *raku* glazed pot in the center of the table containing a single bird of paradise.

Following a tap on the screen, a tuxedoed waiter appeared. I tried to hide my surprise when I realized it was Furuna, the short man who had challenged me at the door of the gym. He bowed at the waist, before moving to signal two waiting busboys that entered, set up our table, then exited without a word.

"I will inform the chef of your arrival," Furuna said, smiling at each of us in turn. "May I bring anyone a cocktail from the bar?"

We ordered the house sake-blend all around. After it was served and we were alone once again, Grillo opened the hatbox, lifted out what had to be the *Sitting Tiso*, placing it on the table. The ancient sculpture was as magnificent as its price tag. As I turned it carefully around with a finger, I was amazed that the five-hundred year old dry lacquer facial features could depict such emotion. The mouth was only a slash, the eyes blind, yet together they managed to convey a deep sense of peace and spirituality.

"So this is the man," I said, wondering in the back of my mind if Grillo might try to substitute a copy, but my memory of its picture on the Net was fresh. My gut told me it was the real thing.

"He's awesome," Susan commented. Grillo picked it up and tried to hand it to her, but she declined the offer.

Our dinner that evening was a delectable work of art. After my third cup of sake, I was actually beginning to enjoy Grillo's company. He was a colorful storyteller, keeping us entertained with lively tales of life in the Mafia. Some were funny, some suspenseful, others like scenes straight out of the *Godfather* movies.

Furuna appeared at the door and announced to our little group that the chef would serve the *fugu* personally. When a hairless man walked in, dressed in a chef's toke, carrying three plates of sushi on a silver platter, I was shocked to see that it was Kano. Grillo caught my look of recognition, and his eyes narrowed.

"You two know each other?"

"Kano is an old friend from Japan," Susan said, thinking fast. "Max and I ate here last week and I introduced him."

Grillo eyed Kano's missing fingers as he set a plate of *fugu* before each of us. "Are you a member of the *Yakuza*?"

The question spiked my blood pressure. I glanced quickly at Susan.

"In my youth, I strayed to that path," Kano said in explanation. "Thankfully the loss of fingers does not interfere with the duties of my profession."

"Where were you trained as a chef?" Grillo asked.

Kano's smile was enigmatic. "The Oda School in Tokyo."

"Who was your master?"

"My *sensei* is Lanqi Murimoto," Kano answered.

Grillo looked from Kano to the *fugu* on his plate. I was sure he was going to refuse it.

"You compliment your master with this exquisite offering," Grillo said, bowing his head to show respect. "I have never seen *fugu* presented so artfully."

Kano returned the bow and backed toward the door but as he reached for the handle, it was slammed open. An obviously pissed off Marie stalked in. She wore jeans, boots, a white tee shirt, and motorcycle leather. Her face was sans makeup, the look in her eyes, deadly.

"Don't you dare make any deals with this snake," she said, addressing me but never taking her eyes off Grillo. "He's a goddamn crook and a bully."

Before anyone could respond, Furuna reentered the room flanked by two busboys. Marie cut her eyes to them, then returned her withering gaze to Grillo.

"You didn't sign anything, did you, Max?"

"Marie," Grillo said sharply but I was already up and heading for her.

"Let's talk outside, Mom," I said, but she jerked her arm out of my grasp.

"There's nothing to talk about," she insisted. "You're not going into business with this sewer rat. Period."

Furuna and his men stood patiently waiting for direction. When I tried again to steer Marie out of the room, she jumped back and into the arms of the two busboys who gently but firmly, picked her up and carried her out the rear exit of the private dining room. I followed. In the alley behind the restaurant, they released her and left us alone.

"What the hell's the matter with you?" Marie seethed. "For weeks you've been insisting Olympio is an asshole and when I agree with you..."

"Will you shut up for one second?"

"Don't you tell me to shut up," she said, stretching to her full five feet two inches. "You are not hooking up with that bastard."

I gave her a pained look. "Can you please just trust my judgment for once? I've got a plan to get rid of Grillo for good."

Marie gaped at me open mouthed. "You're not going to kill him, are you?"

I shook my head. "No, but if you don't stop bitching and let me get back inside, you're going to ruin everything."

Marie sputtered something unintelligible while circling me three times. When she finally stopped, she seemed more in control. "All right, go," she said, pointing at the door, "but be friggin' careful, and call me later."

Heading back inside, my heart was pounding so hard I thought it might burst from the effort. I could only hope Grillo was still there. After Marie's performance, he might have decided to split, effectively closing my window of opportunity.

At the front entrance to the private dining room I had my hand on the sliding screen when a voice called out my name. It was high pitched, almost a squeal and could belong to only one person I knew. When it called again, I turned to see Bette, decked out, makeup and all, like a classic, white-faced Geisha, shuffling toward me in an ornate red kimono.

When she reached me, I spread my arms to stop her from entering the private dining room. She took this as an invitation, enveloping me in a full body hug.

"Damn, am I glad you're here," she whispered in my ear, and then nipped at the lobe with her teeth. "My fuckin' date back there is boring me to tears."

I glanced in the direction she indicated, spotting a thin lipped, long necked, anemic looking man standing alone beside a table for two, staring at us. Dressed in tweed pants, a wrinkled white dress shirt, and bow tie, he lacked only the requisite pocket protector full of leaky ink pens to make him a true nerd.

"You're not thinking of taking that poor thing to bed, are you?" I asked.

Bette followed my gaze and gave her escort a finger wave. "Sure. Why not? He's got the price."

I glanced at the guy again, shaking my head. "Because you'd probably kill him. That's why."

Bette held me at arm's length, smiling mischievously. "Flatterer. Care to save his life by taking me home with you?"

"Sorry. I'm here with friends."

Bette looked around me at the screened dining room. "Who you got in there?"

"Nobody you need to meet."

"Is it a woman?" she asked, but before I could answer, Grillo slid open the entrance panel.

"Well, hello there," he said. "And who might you be?"

"The name's Bette," she said as she raked her eyes up and down Grillo's muscular form. "And you?"

"Olympio Grillo," he said, taking the hand she offered. "A pleasure to meet you, Bette. Max has so many interesting women in his life."

Bette looked past Grillo to Susan who was still seated at the table. "Hello, honey," she said and waved. "Please excuse the interruption. Max and I are old friends."

"I'll just bet you are," Susan said. "Max is the friendly type."

Nodding in agreement, Bette, who has her own unique slant on reality, stepped around Grillo and approached the table.

"Geez," she said, scoping out Susan's shaved head. "What happened to your hair, honey? Was it Cancer?"

"No," Susan said. "A Bic razor."

"Get out of here," Bette said. "You shaved it off on purpose?"

"Yep."

"Kind of old to be a skinhead, aren't you?"

"Actually, I'm a Buddhist nun."

"Omigod!" Bette squealed. "You're Max's ex-wife!"

"That would be me."

Bette laughed gaily and sat down beside Susan. "So what was it like being married to Mr. Wonderful?"

Susan looked up at me. "Oh, it had its moments."

"And I bet some of them were in bed, right?" Bette said, elbowing Susan in the side. "Max is a real powerhouse in the sack."

"He is, huh?" Susan said, looking pointedly in my direction.

I sighed and shook my head. "Bette, don't you think your date's getting lonely out there?"

"He'll keep," she said. "I don't go on duty until my clothes come off."

Grillo laughed and put an arm around my shoulder. "Where's Marie?"

"I sent her home."

"And she went quietly?"

I raised an eyebrow. "Marie doesn't do anything quietly, as you must know by now."

"And you're still willing to complete the deal?"

"Hell, yes," I said. "You convinced me with your speech about my waning finances, but don't count on Marie to work with us."

"I think you're right about that," Grillo said. "I also think I'll be in big trouble at home tonight."

"I warned you not to marry her," I said. "The woman is crazy. I've got the psychological scars to prove it."

Furuna joined Grillo and me at the door, eyeing Bette. "Is there a problem, gentlemen?"

Before I could answer, Bette called to me.

"Maxie, do me a favor. Wave my date over here. His name is Bernard."

Chapter 17

Reluctantly I walked over to the man's table and introduced myself. "Hi, ah...Bernard, is it?"

The man nodded repeatedly like one of those bobble-headed dogs people put on the back deck of their car.

"I'm Max Snow."

"Bernard Lunchkin," the man said. The top of his head barely reached my shoulder.

"Bette would like you to join us," I said, nodding at the private dining room.

"I...I..." he stuttered.

"If you'd rather not, I understand."

Bernard looked from the private room to the restaurant's main door, then back at me, obviously deciding whether to make a break for it or join the group of strangers.

I heard the click of wooden sandals and turned to see Bette approaching.

"Come on, Bernie," she said, taking him by the hand. "My friends won't bite."

Inside the room, Bette positioned Bernard between Susan and Grillo, rounded the table, then sat next to me.

"Now this is cozy, right?" she said, beaming a loopy smile. "Boy, girl, boy, girl, boy."

No one said anything so she went right on talking.

"Bernie and me already had our dinner," she said, eyeing the sushi on our plates. "But you know how Chinese food is. You eat, and ten minutes later you're hungry again."

I was about to explain that Lotus is a *Japanese* restaurant when she stretched a hand toward my plate.

"Mind if I taste…"

I pulled the dish out of her reach. "Sorry. This was prepared especially for us."

Furuna, who had been standing in the doorway watching the drama unfold, snapped his fingers. A busboy rushed in with two more set-ups.

"Shall I have the chef prepare two more orders of *fugu*?" Furuna asked.

My headshake was overruled by Bette's verbal assent. Ten minutes later, Furuna returned to serve the newcomers. When he bowed and left the room, Bernard cleared his throat.

"P-people can die from eating the puffer fish," he said, blushing scarlet. "I saw a special about it on the *Discovery Channel*."

Grillo smiled indulgently. "Trust me, young man. When prepared by an experienced chef, the exotic fish is delicious, not deadly."

Bernard's answering smile looked more like a grimace. "Well, I still don't know," he said, poking the sushi with a bony finger. "I have a very delicate intestinal system."

"Bernie," Bette cooed from across the table. "Eat your *fugu* like a good boy and mommy will give you a treat later."

As if the sushi had suddenly become the most appetizing food on the planet, Bernard picked it up, and downed the whole thing in one gulp. Susan caught my eye while we waited for him to keel over. When he didn't, I took a tentative bite, and the remainder of our little party followed my lead.

"Excellent," said Grillo as he wiped his mouth with a snow white napkin. "That touch of wasabi was just the right thing."

"Mmmm. Yeah," Bette agreed. "I could do that all over again. Waiter," she said to Furuna, who was still lingering. "Another round of *fugu* over here."

Furuna stepped into the room and bowed his apology. "This dish is only available upon special request. The chef used what was left on hand to prepare the last two orders."

Bette looked disappointed, but only for a second. "Don't sweat it, dude. Just bring us some sweet-sake for dessert."

Bowing, Furuna left the room, closing the panel behind him.

Bette poured herself a cup of tea, then snatched up the *Sitting Tiso* like it was a blue light special in K-Mart. "This old thing looks pretty crusty. What is it?"

Grillo and I reached out for the sculpture simultaneously.

"It's an antique worth over a million dollars, Bette," I said. "If you drop it, you'll be working that hot little fanny of yours overtime for the rest of your life."

Bette released the Tiso to me. I set it gently on the table.

"Geeeze," Bette said, rolling her eyes at my fervent concern. "It's only money. Am I right?"

Before I could answer, my lips and tongue began to tingle intensely. It was a very weird sensation, although at that moment, not an unpleasant one. I looked over at Susan who must have been experiencing something similar. She had a hand to her mouth and was feeling her bottom lip.

"The tingling you feel is an effect of the *fugu*," Grillo explained without being asked. "A light sense of euphoria should follow. After that, you're going to feel like doing it doggie-style right here on the table."

I looked at him skeptically but damn if he wasn't right. I really *was* beginning to feel euphoric. Kind of like the buzz after a second glass of good wine.

My horny little friend Bette on the other hand, had obviously sailed right through euphoria. She was eyeing my crotch with a look I could only describe as predatory.

"I am *so* hot," she whispered in my ear after leaning close. "Wanna take me home and put out my fire?"

The buzzing sensation in my head had grown almost audible. And as if someone had flipped a switch on my nervous system, my arms and legs suddenly seemed outside my control. When Bette reached a hand between my legs, I was powerless to stop her.

Looking over at Susan, I saw her eyes had turned inward. As I watched, unable to help, she blinked repeatedly several times, swayed in place, then fell over sideways.

Beside her, Grillo didn't look like he was faring much better. His right hand was pressed to the left side of his chest. The handsome face, usually so composed, looked pained, and had turned the color of pickled beets.

Bernard, on the other hand, seemed empowered by the *fugu* toxin. His mousy features had morphed to all hard planes, and the formerly weak eyes were now slits of accusation. When Bette slid a fingertip inside the waistband of my pants, the small man launched himself across the table like a rocket. Barely missing the ancient statue, he slammed me square in the chest with a full-on head butt that sent all three of us crashing to the floor.

A moment later the surrounding scene took on the feel of a silent movie. Everything in view was drained of color. Bette and Bernard moved their mouths as if speaking, but no sound reached my ears. I remember thinking this must be how life looks in the end. Because I was sure it was the end. Sure my worst fear had been realized and the *Yakuza* had poisoned us all. Somehow the finality of it didn't shock me. If this was how death felt, it wasn't so bad. In fact, it was kind of cool.

"Cool for you, maybe," said you-know-who in my head. "But I'm not ready to go. And what about Susan? You're responsible for her death too, you know. Not to mention Bette and nerd-boy. Get your ass up and help them."

"Can't do it," I said, feeling almost giddy. "Would if I could, but I can't."

"Dork!" the voice said in disgust.

"Loser!" I shot back.

"Next life," the voice said. "I call the shots."

"You wish, you little shit," I said just before I passed out. "You freakin' wish."

Chapter 18

I woke from a dreamless sleep the next morning. When my eyes floated open, I saw a vaguely familiar coffee-brown face staring down at me.

"Well, good morning, darlin'. We were wondering when you would rejoin the living."

I gazed around at what was quite obviously a hospital room, before refocusing on the woman's face. "Maggie?"

"Hey," she said smiling broadly, her teeth shining white in contrast to her licorice toned lips. "You remembered my name."

"Am I back at Beaumont?" I asked.

"Right again," Maggie said, as she straightened the sheet covering me.

When the reason I was in the hospital suddenly hit me, I sat up and grabbed the nurse's wrist. "There was a woman named Susan with me last night, and three other people."

Maggie nodded at the bed beside my own and I looked over to see Susan lying there, asleep but alive.

"Two of the others are in the room next door," Maggie said.

"Who?" I asked, still holding her wrist.

"A skinny little white boy and a gal that looks kind of like a cartoon character."

I sighed in relief and sank back onto the bed. "What about the other guy?"

"Sorry," Maggie said, shaking her head. "The man's heart was paralyzed by the poison. He died before they could get him here. Was he family?"

"No," I said as an image of Marie skittered through my mind. "Well, sort of."

Maggie lifted a chart at the foot of my bed and scanned it. "Says here, y'all ate bad fish. What kind was it?"

My stomach lurched at the thought of last night's fateful dinner. "Puffer fish. The Japanese call it *fugu*."

Maggie screwed up her face. "*Fugu*? Wouldn't catch me eating no fish with a name like that."

"Last time for me too, Maggie. I promise."

The door to the room pushed open a moment later and Linda Riff stuck her head in. "Well, well, well," she said, walking to my bedside. "Look what the cat dragged in."

"I plead the fifth," I said, flipping a pillow over my face. "Now go away."

Riff snatched the pillow and tossed it to the foot of the bed. "Fat chance, chum. I've got questions, and you better have some damn good answers."

"Maggie?" I whined at the nurse who was leaning over Susan, checking her pulse. "Isn't there something in my HIPPA rights that protects me from police harassment?"

"Sorry, Mr. Snow. Lieutenant Riff's got special consideration, seeing she carries a gun and all."

"But…" I protested.

"Bye-bye, Maggie," Riff said, over her shoulder. After noting something on Susan's chart, the nurse winked at me before leaving the room.

"Now," Riff said, sitting on the side of my bed and folding her arms. "Let's have it."

I gave her the whole story. Grillo's proposed money laundering scheme, the pressure he had put on me to play ball, and Susan's kidnapping. My cop friend listened patiently but when I finished, she didn't look the least bit satisfied.

"So because Grillo was messing with your life you made a deal with the *Yakuza* to kill him?"

"No!"

"Then, what?"

"I just wanted them to take him back to Japan and keep him there."

Riff shook her head. "I told you that bunch at the gym do *not* take prisoners, didn't I?"

I nodded, feeling a twinge of guilt over Grillo's death.

"You couldn't just come to me, huh?" Riff said. "You had to play amateur detective and risk people's lives."

I bristled at the accusation and came up off the pillow. "Bette and her friend just showed up out of the blue," I shot back. "I didn't invite them there."

"I'll give you that," she said, leaning forward to poke me in the chest with a finger, "but you still put Susan's life on the line."

"Susan knew the score. And if I didn't do something about Grillo, he might have gone after her again."

Riff shook her head without saying a word. She'd never admit it but she knew I was right.

My mind strayed to Kano and I asked her what was going to happen to him.

"Nothing legal, if that's what you mean," Riff said. "He has a license to prepare *fugu*, and shit happens. Although he'll probably be deported back to Japan."

I smiled at that, settling back against the pillow. That son-of-a-gun had engineered this whole thing knowing he'd be sent back to Japan.

"I don't know why you're looking so smug, Snowman," Riff said. "If Grillo's *Family* finds out you had anything to do with his death, you'll be following the bastard to Hell."

Riff left without another word and a few minutes later, Susan woke up. I buzzed the nursing station. After the doctor had come and gone, I explained to her what had happened.

"So Grillo's really dead?" she asked, her expression serious.

"Yeah, babe. Sorry to have involved you in all this."

Susan shook her head. "It's my own fault. I should have known Kano would pull something like that."

I wanted to protest but before I could, there was a knock on the door.

"Come," I said.

Candy Sprinkles walked in looking formal and officious in a tailored, black pantsuit. Her left hand clutched the strap of a sleek Dolce & Gabbana handbag. The right was hidden by a leather trench that draped her forearm. If she was holding a gun under it—and there was a damn good chance she was—visiting hours were about to end.

"I see that both of you survived last night's fish fry," she said, stepping between the beds. "Care to explain why?"

I shrugged. "Don't you know what happened?"

"I know what the cops are saying—that Olympio died from eating poorly prepared *fugu*. My question is—why aren't *you* two dead? Answer carefully. You're already in big trouble."

"With who?" I asked.

"I think you know."

"Have you talked to anyone from that organization about what happened?"

"No, I was waiting to speak with you first."

"Before we get into that," I said, feeling a sense of hopeful relief wash over me, "let me ask a question. Where does Grillo's death leave you?"

"Out in the cold," she said defiantly. "Olympio's brother, Anthony will probably take over the GBS operation and we don't get along too well."

"So what are you going to do?"

"What's it to you?"

"I was thinking that we might make a deal."

Candy's eyes cut sideways to Susan before returning to me. "I'm listening."

"First, let me assure you, I had nothing to do with Grillo's death, and neither did Susan."

Candy did a quick eye roll.

"It's true, I swear."

She folded her arms and waited.

"Does Grillo's death means Marie will inherit his estate?"

"Not all of it," Candy said. "She signed a pre-nup."

I did a palms up.

"According to the agreement I read, Marie ends up with ten million, a penthouse condo in downtown Chicago, and a half-mile of oceanfront property on Maui's Ka'anapali coast. Unless of course his family decides to challenge the will, which is a real good possibility."

"And how about you?" I asked. "What do you get?"

Candy's beautiful mouth tightened at the question. "Not that it's any of your business, but I don't get a goddamn thing!"

I let her statement hang between us for a full ten seconds.

"Okay, Candy, this is my offer. If you can convince whoever needs to believe it, that Grillo decided to take a pass on our proposed partnership, I'll pay you one million dollars."

Candy's eyes narrowed. "What makes you think they'd believe me?"

"Because you were Olympio's girl Friday, and privy to all his business decisions."

She chewed her bottom lip as she mulled over the offer.

"If you can do it," I said, "we'll both be off the hook."

"I'm not on any hook," she protested, although there wasn't much conviction in her voice.

"Wake up, Candy. You're in bed with the devil. And someday one of the *Family* members is going to decide you know too much. A million dollars would go a long way in helping you avoid the flames."

"Two million would go farther," she said, obviously realizing the strong hand she held.

"A million-five," I said. "And that's my last offer."

"Two," Candy countered. "And that's mine."

I glanced at Susan who had her eyes closed and head bowed, like she was meditating.

"You drive a hard bargain, Ms. Sprinkles. But if you can do what I ask, you have a deal."

When Candy left the room, Susan opened her eyes to look over at me. "Where are you going to get two million dollars to pay her off?"

"There's four sitting in a safety deposit box with my name on it."

"But can you get at it without Grillo?"

I beamed at her. "He insisted Candy be named as his proxy on the bank's registration forms. I have no doubt the ever efficient Ms. Sprinkles knows exactly where the key is."

Susan and I were dressed and waiting to be discharged when the door opened again. Marie walked in, looking a little sad, but all in all seemed to be holding up.

"Sorry about Olympio, Mom."

"Save it," she said, waving away the sympathy. "When the bastard slapped me last night, it was all over between us."

"He slapped you?"

"Twice," she said, touching her left cheek with a fingertip. "We were arguing about him pressuring you, when he hit me."

"Did he hurt you?"

"Only my pride," she said. "I thought I could take on anyone..." she stopped and her eyes filled with tears, "but he made me feel like I was past it."

"Yeah right," I said. "You came into that restaurant looking to bust his balls, Marie. And that was *after* he hit you."

Comprehension lifted her shoulders and her spirit caught up quickly. "Fucking eh!" she said, wiping away the tears. "Guess I still got it."

A moment later, Bette came bursting into the room followed by a contrite looking Bernard. When Marie turned to see who it was, she stared wide-eyed at the bedraggled Geisha girl. Bette's exotic makeup job had crashed sometime during the night, and her morning hair looked like a nest full of pissed off snakes.

"What's the matter with the old lady?" Bette asked, directing the question at me. "Hasn't she ever seen a victim of *fugu* poisoning before?"

I could see Marie's back go up at the old lady comment. Before Bette could put her foot any further into her mouth, I introduced them.

The two women took each other's measure, which wasn't hard since they were approximately the same height.

"So you're Maxie's mom," Bette said, sidling over to Marie. "I can see now where he gets his good looks."

Mom brightened at the compliment. For some reason the sight of her grasping Bette's outstretched hand produced an "oh shit!" feeling in the pit of my *fugu* scarred stomach.

"You know, Marie," Bette said, slipping an arm around my mom's shoulders and leaning in to her. "Something tells me that you and I are going to become very good friends."

Chapter 19

I didn't go to Chicago to attend Grillo's funeral. Marie wanted me to, Candy said I should, but I'd had my fill of the Mafia.

Marie must have played the part of grieving widow to perfection, because she returned in the senior Grillo's good graces and on the family's private jet no less. She was convinced Olympio's parents had no problem with her inheriting so much after such a short marriage, but I had my doubts.

Candy Sprinkles, it seems, had played her hand successfully as well. Two weeks had gone by since Grillo's death and no one had showed up to take over his role as extortionist. After a successful trip to the bank to claim the four million, I paid her the agreed amount and hoped to never cross paths with her again.

Did I think because everything seemed to go like clockwork that my butt was in the clear? Not even! I had a nagging fear that the Mafia's Black Hand was hovering over my life, just waiting for the best time to squash me like a bug. My imagination? Maybe so, but at the age of forty-two, I was learning to trust my inner vibes.

Susan continued to stay with me and share my bed, but over breakfast on an unusually sunny March morning, she told me she had decided to move into her finally completed monastery. When I asked why, she shook her head.

"Because I can tell you're still thinking about Zed. And I need to give myself a chance to run the monastery. It's been my dream for a long time."

I wanted to protest, but knew she was right. Both of us had needed the other since the moment she reappeared in my life. But need is not a firm base for a long term relationship. That same night, she packed up her stuff and left.

To occupy my spare time, I threw myself into studying for my P.I. license. The course was challenging, and halfway through, I had just about decided to give it up, when an out of the blue call from a man named John Marsh put me back on track.

"I got your number from a friend who works at the Pinkerton Correspondence School," Marsh said, as way of introduction. "He told me you're doing extremely well in your studies and suggested I contact you."

The flattery caused a grin to spread across my face. "It was nice of your friend to say that, Mr. Marsh, but I'm nowhere near being able to take on a case, if that's the reason for your call."

"Not at all," the man said. "I'm the owner and president of Marsh Investigative Services. Ever hear of it?"

"Not really."

"Our home base is in Ann Arbor," he said. "We handle a variety of investigations throughout the entire Midwest."

The chance to discuss the business with an experienced P.I. was just what I was hoping for, so I jumped at it. "Are you calling to recruit me?"

"I'd like to meet with you some time in the near future and talk about it. Is that possible?"

"Absolutely. Where and when?"

At John Marsh's suggestion, I joined him for dinner the next evening in Ann Arbor. He turned out to be one hell of a nice guy. Claiming to be fifty-six, he looked ten years younger, had a head full of dark brown curls, a solid Dick Tracy jaw, and a mouth full of gleaming white teeth that looked too perfect to be real.

"They're not," he admitted candidly when I got up the nerve to ask about them. "I spent time as a POW in the Middle East, and my guards took great pleasure in removing my teeth one by one."

I winced at the thought.

"They kind of did me a favor though," he said in response to my reaction. "Bad teeth run in my family, so now I've got the best smile of the bunch."

I found John Marsh's casual attitude on life refreshing as hell. He accepted adversity like it was an inevitable part of human existence; a talent I stumbled on occasionally but had difficulty holding on to. Before the dinner was over, I felt I had found a friend. John was totally open about his profession and his personal life. When he told me, after a game of racquetball the next night, that he was gay, I wasn't surprised.

"You weren't checking out my rear end in the shower room were you?" I joked as we stood at the club bar drinking cranberry juice.

"Nah," he said and laughed. "I never was into traveling the ol' dirt road. But the front end looked good."

John Marsh seemed genuinely interested in teaching me the ins and outs of the P.I. business. For the next few weeks he allowed me to tag along on several stakeouts. We worked as a team to locate the errant spouse of a wealthy West Bloomfield matron—hubby had been shacked up with a seventeen-year-old prostitute in a downtown Detroit apartment. We even did personal security for a well known rap star, in town for a concert at the Royal Oak Theater.

A few days after the rapper gig, I called John to suggest lunch but got a recording saying the line was no longer in service. A call to his apartment scored the same message. Plus there was no answer on his cell phone. On a hunch, I called the Ann Arbor Police. After a check, they informed me that John Marsh was not registered in that city as a Private Investigator, and they had no record of a Marsh Investigative Services.

Completely nonplussed, I drove to John's office, found it empty then used my fledgling investigative talents to question people in the neighboring offices. They weren't a lot of help. Not one had seen John move out. The only thing they could tell me was that he had occupied the office for less than a month.

His sudden departure was mystifying to say the least, and I was thinking John may have set the whole thing up to test my ability to locate a missing person, when something happened to make me abandon the theory. In fact, Marsh and the whole P.I. thing were put on indefinite hiatus when a man walked unannounced into my private studio a couple days later, introducing himself as Olympio Grillo's younger brother, Anthony. He was big, like a boxer—size must run in that family—with short dark hair, hazel eyes, and if I was any judge of body language, it certainly wasn't his pleasure to meet me.

"Your receptionist said you weren't with a client. Slow day?"

"N-no," I said, stumbling slightly over the word. The man had an unnerving way of staring without blinking. "My next client is due at five. Is there something I can do for you?"

His eerie eyes still refused to blink as he stared at me. "Yeah. You can tell me why you murdered my brother."

I gulped a lungful of air, and to make a show of not being afraid, forced myself to take a step toward him. "I have no idea what you're talking about. Olympio's death was an accident."

Anthony Grillo's expression of disgust rocked me back on my heels. When he leaned forward menacingly, I caught the flash of a gun-butt beneath his coat.

"You took out Olympio so you wouldn't have to become his partner, Snow. Admit it."

I shook my head. "That's not true."

"What's not true?" Grillo shot back. "That you killed him or that you didn't want to become his partner?"

"Both."

"So you're saying you didn't want out of the laundry scam?"

"No. I mean, yes."

"Yes, what?" he demanded.

"Yes, I wanted Olympio off my case. But, no I didn't kill him."

Anthony Grillo finally allowed his eyes to close. They stayed like that for a good ten seconds. When he opened them again, the pupils had dilated into perfect black holes. "Where is Candy Sprinkles?"

"I don't know."

"You're a fucking liar," he said, pounding the arm of the chair with a beefy fist. "You gave her money to get lost."

"Wrong again," I insisted, but we could both hear the quaver in my voice.

"Afraid of me, hairdresser?"

"Shouldn't I be?"

"Oh yes," he hissed, "you should. Because like the line in the movie goes, 'I'm about to become your worst nightmare'."

"Your brother already beat you to that title," I said, trying my best to sound unfazed, but fazed I certainly was.

"My brother never beat me at anything," Anthony Grillo said. "He thought he could, the stupid fuck. But he was a loser!"

Oh boy! I thought. Nothing like a little sibling rivalry to piss off a crazy man.

There was a soft knock on the door and Gwen stuck her head in. "Your next client's here, Max. Shall I have her shampooed?"

"Stall for a couple minutes," I said. "Mr. Grillo and I are just about to finish our business."

"Grillo?" Gwen said, taking a step inside the studio. "I thought you looked a little like Olympio."

"Gwen," I said sharply, stopping her in her tracks. "Please go back to the desk. I hear the phone ringing."

"I don't hear anything," she protested.

"Well I do. Now go."

Gwen cocked her head and looked at me. "Are you okay? You didn't have any lunch, you know. Maybe you're hungry."

"I'm fine," I said, forcing a smile. "Please leave us alone."

The receptionist nodded curtly and closed the door behind her.

"Smart move, Max. I don't want to hurt anybody I don't have to."

"Look," I said, plucking my cell phone off the station and punching the preset number for mall security. "I don't know where you got the idea that I'm responsible for your brother's death, but you're wrong. And if you don't leave now, Security will escort you out."

A voice answered my call, but before I could speak, Grillo snatched the phone away, snapped it in two like a Popsicle stick, and let the shards of plastic drop to the floor.

"Think a bunch of minimum wage cop-wannabes can protect your ass from me?"

"I don't need protection."

"That's what you think."

Rallying what courage hadn't already abandoned me, I shook my head, walked to the door and swung it open. "Get out."

"Johnny Marsh said you could play tough guy when it suited you."

Recognition of the name stopped me cold.

"That's right," Grillo said, enjoying his successful hit. "Marsh is my loyal ferret, and you, Snow, are way too trusting of strangers."

"If Marsh told you I killed Olympio," I said, trying lamely for cool, "the man is full of shit."

Grillo sneered in triumph. "I don't think so. My man John is a master at digging out the truth."

I mentally reviewed my conversations with Marsh. Sure we had talked about what I'd recently been through with Olympio, but I never admitted anything like that.

There were voices beyond the wall to the reception area and a moment later, Gwen entered the studio followed by two familiar security guards. Both men were almost as big as Grillo. Each of them eyed the mangled cell phone on the floor.

"Did you need Security, Mr. Snow?"

"Do I?" I said, looking at Grillo who shrugged and walked casually out the door.

Chapter 20

Before I left the mall that evening I bought another cell phone. A friendly salesperson helped me keep my original number, and on the way home, I got my first call. It was Anthony Grillo.

"Just thought I'd let you know I was thinking about you, Snow. We'll talk again, real soon," he said before disconnecting.

I gaped at the phone in disbelief. How the hell could he have gotten my number?

"Well, duh," piped in the little voice that always seems to have something to say at times like this. "Think maybe your friend, John Marsh might have given it to him?"

I sighed, tossing the phone onto the passenger seat. "That bastard," I said, feeling disgusted at my naïveté. "He played me like a freaking puppet on a string."

"You got that right, Pinocchio," the voice said. "Get a clue someday, would you?"

By the next morning, my new cell phone had recorded eleven messages from Grillo. Gwen finally stopped feeding me his calls sometime in the afternoon. And back at home, I let my answering machine work its interceptive magic, that is, until I couldn't stand it anymore.

"What the hell do you want from me, Grillo?"

There was dead air on the line for a beat before he spoke. "Only one thing…for you to admit you killed my brother."

I didn't bother denying it again. It seemed like a useless effort.

"I'll have the whole story as soon as I catch up with Candy," he said calmly. "And then your ass is mine."

A click sounded in my ear and the line went dead.

At work the following afternoon Gwen buzzed me in my studio and asked if I would take a call from Chicago.

"Who is it?"

"Olympio Grillo's father."

"Shit," I said, taking a breath before punching up the line. "This is Max Snow."

"Mr. Snow," said a baritone voice. "Salvatore Grillo. I hope I'm not calling at an inconvenient time."

"Not at all, Mr. Grillo. What can I do for you?"

There was a muffled voice in the background. "My wife Sophia and I were disappointed you could not attend Olympio's funeral." His voice cracked on the last word and there was a pause before he resumed. "We would like to invite you to visit us in Chicago. Sophia will prepare dinner, and we can talk."

"I don't know," I said, thinking about Anthony's harassment and wondering if Papa Grillo had put him up to it.

"Please, Mr. Snow. I understand you are busy, but we would like to meet the man Olympio spent his last evening with. It would be a comfort to his mother."

"Sure," I said, thinking it unwise to refuse the polite request. "I'd be happy to."

"How about tomorrow evening? I could send the company jet to pick you up."

"Tomorrow would be fine," I said, but when a mental image of Anthony trying to force me out of the jet in midair popped into my mind, I told him I'd rather drive.

"As you prefer," Salvatore Grillo said. "This is my phone number in case you have trouble finding us. And this is the address."

Marie called immediately after I hung up and I told her about the dinner invitation.

"Are you going?" she asked. I could hear the concern in her voice.

"I don't think it's a good idea not to."

"Yeah, you're probably right. Want company?"

"Thanks. But he didn't say anything about bringing a guest."

My trip to the Windy City was uneventful, except for the brown van that seemed to be trailing me for three out of the five hour drive. It exited off the e-way when I did, stayed just far enough out of range to prevent me from eyeballing the driver, and when I pulled into the entrance of Grillo's swanky subdivision, it continued on down the road.

The uniformed guard at the gated entrance raised a hand when I approached. He looked carefully at my ID. After checking my name off on a clipboard, he waved me through. I arrived at the Grillo home, correction—make that mansion, five minutes later. The multiple-story pink brick manor was twice the size of my own home and surrounded by several acres of well tended landscaping.

The front door opened as I parked on the circular drive, and a short, bony woman, with steel gray hair pulled back in a tight bun, stood waiting at the door. She wore rust colored slacks and a flower print blouse. As I exited my truck, a man dressed in a gray sweatsuit appeared behind her. He was tall, broad shouldered and unmistakably the senior Grillo, with snow-white hair, a matching mustache, and a once muscled body that had gone to fat in old age.

"Mr. Snow?" he said, coming forward. The voice was deeper in person than it was on the phone. "I'm Salvatore Grillo, and this is my wife, Sophia."

"A pleasure," I said, taking the hand Sophia Grillo offered and squeezing it gently. "Please let me express my condolences on the death of your son."

"Thank you," Sophia said, trying unsuccessfully to force a smile. "And thank you for making the long trip to see us."

After shaking hands with Salvatore Grillo, I was ushered inside a large living room done in classic Mediterranean. The walls were painted brick-red, giving everything in the room a warm glow. The furniture was overstuffed and inviting. More than a dozen paintings, all sailboats charging headlong into a raging sea, surrounded us.

"Do you sail?" I asked Papa Grillo as he led the way toward the rear of the house.

"I used to," he said, entering a circular dining room enclosed by a wall of seamless glass overlooking a winter sparse garden. "But I have a bad hip, and for some damn reason, I get seasick every time I go out now."

"You get seasick," Mrs. Grillo said, after inviting me to be seated at a round, cherry-wood table, "because you have an inner ear problem."

"Bah!" Grillo barked while pouring three glasses of dark red wine from a crystal decanter. "Getting old stinks. Take my advice, Mr. Snow, and die before you hit seventy."

"That only gives me twenty-eight more years," I said, before tasting the wine. It was surprisingly light; full of complex fruit flavors. "But I'll try my best. And please, call me Max."

After several minutes of polite conversation, Sophia Grillo excused herself, and went off to check on dinner.

"Eighty-three years old," Grillo said as he watched his wife walk from the room, "and she still insists on cooking every meal."

"Is she any good?" I asked before taking another sip of the excellent wine.

Grillo kissed the tips of his fingers before patting his substantial gut. "Where do you think I picked up these triplets?"

Sophia Grillo proved to be an incredible cook, and I had no doubt she was at least partly responsible for her husband's excessive poundage. Dinner read like a trip through an Italian cookbook, beginning with mushrooms marinated in olive oil, garlic, and peppercorns. This was followed by a flaky chicken-and-egg soup that reminded me of Chinese egg drop, a hearty rice dish cooked with butter and saffron, an eggplant Parmesan that practically melted in my mouth, and for the main course—as if we needed it—braised breast of veal stuffed with spinach and sweetbreads. We finished with a tomato salad dressed with the Grillo's homemade balsamic vinegar and crumbled Gorgonzola.

Over dessert—vanilla *gelato* drizzled with warmed Chambord—the conversation finally turned to their recently deceased son and his last night on the planet. I was in the middle of my well rehearsed story, when I heard a door open and close somewhere. Anthony Grillo walked into the room. The minute he spotted me sitting at the table, his jowly face darkened with anger.

"What the fuck is *he* doing here?" he shouted. "This man killed your son, and you're feeding him *dinner?*"

"Anthony!" Salvatore Grillo bellowed. "Watch your language in front of your mother."

When Anthony screamed something back in Italian, his father glowered at him from his seat at the table. I knew the look. My own father's angry stare had the power to stop a runaway train. Papa Grillo's was no less effective.

Anthony sat down across the table from me, his creepy gray eyes locked onto mine. "What are you doing here, Snow?"

"We invited him," Mrs. Grillo said as she shuffled in from the kitchen with a full plate for her son. "You just eat and be quiet."

I smiled at her then went on relating the tale of Olympio's last night. When I finished, Anthony pointed an accusing finger at me.

"Ask him why four other people ate the same thing as Olympio and all of them survived."

I willed myself to remain calm because I knew my credibility was on the line. "Every one of us was rushed to the hospital that night."

Anthony made a derisive sound and pushed his untouched plate away. "But you're not dead, like my brother, are you?"

"I'm sorry Olympio died," I insisted. "I really am. People take that chance when they eat *fugu*."

"Who suggested having it that night?" Anthony said.

"I did," I admitted. "But it wasn't the first time for Olympio. He told me he had enjoyed it on several occasions."

"Is what he says true, Anthony?" Papa Grillo cut in, his pale eyes wide with surprise. "Had your brother eaten this Japanese poison before?"

Anthony didn't look like he wanted to answer, but under his parent's watchful eyes, he told the truth. "Yeah, we both have, but..."

"You've eaten this poison *too*?" his father roared.

Anthony nodded.

"You have so little respect for your mother? Why not just stab her in the heart?"

At his words, Mrs. Grillo burst into tears and ran from the room.

"Look what you've done!" Salvatore Grillo boomed, pointing at his wife's retreating back.

"It was him," Anthony said, glaring at me. "I'll make the son of a bitch tell the truth."

After reaching behind his back, there was a flash of metal and suddenly a gun was aimed at my face.

"Anthony!" Papa Grillo bellowed. "Give me that gun, now."

Anthony shook his head stiffly, and I felt my eyes widen when he tapped a finger against the trigger.

"I will not say it again, Anthony. Mr. Snow is my guest. His mother is part of this family."

I froze in place, but allowed my eyes to slide from man to man. I couldn't have moved even if I wanted to, which I did, more than anything else in the world.

"He murdered your favorite son, Papa," Anthony spat. "Don't you want to avenge his death?"

"Why would I do *that*?" I said, thinking I'd better speak up or forever hold my peace. "I knew who Olympio represented. Why would I want to risk angering that organization? And he was my mother's husband."

"Olympio told me you hated the fact that he'd married her," Anthony taunted. "Said you kicked him out of your house when you found out about it."

Salvatore Grillo looked at me and raised his bushy eyebrows.

"I was afraid for my mother, yes. I admit it. I didn't want her involved with the Mafia."

"Look at him, Papa" Anthony sneered. "He's so guilty; he's practically pissing himself with fear."

"Maybe if I was holding the gun," I said, "things might be different."

"Maybe," Anthony said. "But we'll never know, will we?"

"Look," I said, turning my attention to the senior Grillo. "I accepted their marriage in the end because I could see Marie loved your son very much."

"And he loved her," a small voice said from the doorway behind us. We all turned to see Sophia Grillo who was pointing a revolver, hammer cocked, at her son. "But you wouldn't know anything about love, would you, Anthony? You only know hate and violence."

"Mama…" the shocked man said but she cut him off with a groan of anguish.

"*You* should have died instead of Olympio," she screamed. "He was good and kind and…"

At his mother's stinging words, Anthony lowered his gun. "The shit is dead," he said, shaking his head in defeat, "and you still love him more than me."

When no one said anything, Anthony stood and walked silently from the room. Seconds later there was the sound of a door slamming closed.

"Sophia," Grillo said as he walked to her and took the gun. "Go sit down."

She did as she was told, joining me at the table.

"I am sorry, Max," he said somberly.

Sofia Grillo nodded but didn't lift her head to look at me.

"It's okay, really. I understand."

"Thank you," Grillo said. "And I assure you that Anthony will not bother you again."

Chapter 21

During the next two days I heard nothing from Anthony Grillo. I wanted to believe he had given up on me. Fat chance. What happened the following morning showed me just how little control Papa Grillo had over his youngest and craziest son.

I was sleeping soundly, dreaming about walking on a deserted beach with a tall dark haired woman when a bloodcurdling scream snapped my eyelids open like gunshots. The clock beside my bed read 6:04 and as my eyes scanned the semi-darkness, I located the source. Blue was sitting tall on his haunches at the end of the bed, head pointed north, screeching like a hungry baby.

"What?" I said, half pissed off, half fearful. In answer, the agile feline leapt to the floor and scowled up at me. "This better be about something more important than breakfast, mister."

Swinging my legs off the side of the bed, I listened to the house noises. Nothing out of the ordinary met my ears but when Blue cried again from somewhere down the hall, I decided it would be a good idea to keep my gun in the bedroom from this day on. Slipping on my robe, I made my way downstairs, retrieved the semiautomatic from the drawer, and had a look around. All doors and windows were locked tight. The security system was armed and ready. When a thorough search turned up no crazed boogiemen with ten-inch fingernails, I traded the gun for a pot of fresh coffee.

Blue entered the kitchen not long after and walked over to his feeding station. When I opened a can of food and spooned it into his dish, he approached cautiously, sniffed twice and shook a paw in disgust.

"You loved this the other day," I shouted as the cat bound across the wide open first level like a deer through a meadow. "And don't think I'm giving you anything else."

Blue paused beneath the entrance to the sunroom and gave me a "yeah, right" look. He knew from experience that if my original choice for his morning meal was rejected, I'd offer up a second to try and tempt him.

Walking into the sunroom with my third cup of coffee, I watched Blue pace back and forth before the bank of windows overlooking the patio. Something outside had snagged his attention, but after peering into the hazy, sunless morning, my human senses declared the scene ordinary. The sight of the pool reminded me that I hadn't done laps in a while, so I shucked my robe, hit the button for the automatic solar cover and followed its progression as it rolled back smoothly. Warm water met cool air, and wisps of steam, wafted by a sudden breeze, danced like mini phantoms across the smooth surface. Something big was floating in the center of the pool. Something human-sized. And immediately after stepping out to get a better look, I pulled a cell phone from my pocket and dialed 911. My second call was to Linda Riff.

The first county sheriff's car arrived in twenty minutes. Two more drove up a few minutes later. By the time the EMT truck finally came around back, the cops had already pulled Candy Sprinkles's body from the pool. She was naked except for a sheer black bra. A bullet hole pierced the center of her forehead. And a thick wad of five-thousand dollar bills was wedged tightly between her teeth.

Riff walked onto the scene just as Candy was being strapped to a gurney. She spotted me being questioned by the sheriff's homicide team; a black woman of about forty and a youngish looking Hispanic guy. She joined us, and after flashing her ID, shot a nasty look in my direction.

"Just can't stick to doing hair, can you?"

"Grillo's brother Anthony did this," I said as the techs wheeled a very dead Candy to the rear of the ambulance and loaded her inside. "He was in the salon the other day, threatening me and asking where he could find Candy."

The two cops locked eyes, but before they could comment, a third joined us. He was big in every direction, with skin the color of toasted almonds, and obviously in command. When I took the hand he offered, it engulfed mine like a catcher's mitt.

"Mr. Snow," he said in a Barry White type baritone, "I'm Inspector Michael Mobley. Looks like you had some trouble here."

All eyes shifted to the ambulance as its engine roared into life. The driver slid the truck in gear, gave a short nod to our little group, checked both his mirrors, then pulled away at a leisurely pace. There was, after all, no need to hurry.

Michael Mobley's liquid brown eyes reclaimed mine as the EMT rounded the side of the house. "Pretty woman."

I nodded. "She used to be."

"What was her name?"

The female deputy offered the Inspector a clipboard with the general facts. Mobley waved it away, before nodding at me to answer.

"Candy Sprinkles."

"Good friend?"

"An...acquaintance."

Mobley did a palms up.

"She was Olympio Grillo's secretary," I said, watching as his expressive eyes acknowledged the now infamous name. "We met several weeks ago at Grillo's residence."

"How do you suppose Ms. Sprinkles got dead and in your pool?"

"How, I don't know, but I've got a good idea who put her there."

Inspector Mobley shifted his substantial bulk and took a step closer to me. The move was intimidating as hell—kind of like having The Incredible Hulk step into your personal space.

I quickly explained Olympio Grillo's attempt to extort my cooperation in a money laundering scheme, his death by *fugu* at the Japanese restaurant, and Anthony's accusation that I had killed him.

"You're running with a rough bunch, Mr. Snow."

"I'm not running with them," I protested. "I'm running away. Problem is they can run just as fast."

At that point, Riff confirmed what she knew of my story. Inspector Mobley's gaze softened slightly but his suspicions remained in gear.

"Do you own a gun, Mr. Snow?"

"Yes," I said. "I keep it in a drawer at the bottom of the stairs."

"May I see it?"

"Sure," I said, leading the little party inside.

At the foot of the stairs, I reached to open the drawer but Mobley put a hand on my arm.

"Allow me." He slid the drawer open and we all looked down at the .40 caliber Sig that lay nestled atop pizza menus and other bits of junk paper. Mobley picked the gun up with two fingers, gave the barrel tip a quick sniff, then returned it to the drawer. "Do you have any others?"

I shook my head.

"What was she killed with?" Riff asked.

"From the size of the hole, I'd say a .22."

My friend's lips tightened visibly at the statement.

"What?" I asked her.

"You don't want to know," she answered, shaking her head.

"The hell I don't. Tell me!"

"When a .22 caliber slug enters the skull, it bounces around like a ping-pong ball chewing up everything in its path."

I winced as my vivid imagination flashed a Pac-Man like scenario onto my mental screen. "God damn that bastard," I hissed and sat down heavily in a nearby chair. "Why did he have to do that?"

All four cops watched me silently. After a short conference, Mobley squatted before my chair.

"We're about done here, Mr. Snow," he said, giving me a half-smile. "You're not planning any trips out of town, are you?"

When I shook my head, Mobley nodded.

"Fine," he said. "We'll be in touch."

He rose like a mountain in front of me, took a step, then turned back. "One last question. Would you have any idea why money was stuffed into the victim's mouth?"

I met his eyes, not sure how much to reveal. If I admitted the cash was part of a Mafia payoff, more questions were sure to follow. "No," I said, hoping he hadn't noticed my hesitation. "I don't."

The cop cocked his head. "You sure about that?"

"Yeah. Why?"

"It seemed like you had something on your mind."

I ran an open palm down my face and looked up at him for a long moment. "I got a lot on my mind, Inspector. It's not every day I find someone dead in my pool."

"I understand," he said, although the wide set brown eyes didn't reflect his words. "Please call me if you think of anything else."

Within ten minutes the homicide investigators had packed up the tools of their trade and left. The team charged with sweeping the woods surrounding my house took off soon after and only Riff and I remained. When she followed me to the kitchen, I poured us each a cup of coffee.

"Thanks for coming," I said, joining her at the glass topped bistro. "I really appreciate it."

Riff nodded but held my eyes for several seconds. "Want to tell me why you lied about that money thing?"

"That depends. Am I talking to Linda Riff, the friend, or Lieutenant Riff, the cop?"

At my answer her lips hitched up in a disgusted sneer. "Do you have any idea how much I hate the fact that you're involved with these ugly people?"

"What?" I shot back defensively. "You think I'm having a good time here?"

Before responding, Riff blew on the steaming coffee in her cup and sipped lightly. "Okay. I'm sorry. Dead people are not high up on the list for me, and that's your fourth stiff in less than six months."

"Keeping count?"

"No, but I'm beginning to think being your friend is dangerous as hell."

"Bail if you want. I'd understand."

Riff shook her head. "Too late, Snowman. I'm in this to the bitter end."

"There's a lovely thought," I said. "But thanks anyway."

"You're welcome. Now what's up with the money?"

I explained about the four million I had reclaimed from the safety deposit box and how I paid Candy half to get me clear of the Mafia's gun sight.

As I finished my story, Riff shook her head. "How the bloody hell do you fall into this shit?"

I shrugged. "Just lucky, I guess."

"That's not the word I'd use for it," she replied. "Does anybody else know about the money?"

"Only Susan."

"You hope. And speaking of Susan, you ought to get on the horn and tell her to watch out for Anthony. Like you said, she could become a target again."

The suggestion stopped me cold and I lifted the cell phone from my pocket. Susan answered on the third ring and when I hung up, Riff eyed me expectantly.

"She's leaving this afternoon for a week in Toronto. Some kind of meditation retreat."

"What about Marie?"

"Last time I heard from her, she was in Traverse City, staying at Chuck and Carolyn's winery. I think she said something about coming home tomorrow."

"Call and tell her to stay for a while."

"Tell her?"

Riff sucked her teeth in frustration. "Ask her then, dammit. Does everybody in your family have to be so freakin' obstinate?"

"What do you mean everybody? There's only the two of us."

"Thank God for small favors," Riff said. "Now call her."

Looking up the number, I called Marie. She resisted the idea of staying put at first, but finally agreed when I promised I would watch my step and call her often. After disconnecting, Riff drained what was left in the coffee pot into our cups. She had a strange look in her eyes, and I thought I knew why.

"I get the feeling you're about to do something noble," I said, "like taking off your police hat to help me with Anthony Grillo."

Riff's eyes narrowed. "I'm thinking about it, but only so I won't have to attend your funeral."

I started to laugh at her joke but the ringing of the phone on the wall cut me off. When I recognized the caller's voice, I bumped Riff's arm. "It's Grillo," I said, with my hand over the mouthpiece. "Grab the other line."

Riff sprinted to the living area and carefully raised the receiver.

"Hope you liked my present."

"What present is that, Anthony?"

He laughed and I didn't like the sound of it. "The one the Man just fished out of your pool."

I stayed silent.

"Candy and I had a long talk before I offed her, Max. She told me everything I needed to know about you."

"Yeah? Like what?"

"Like how you paid her off to convince my father that Olympio had decided to dump you as a partner."

"He did," I said. "That's the reason we met for dinner the night he died."

"Not according to Candy. She said you met for dinner to sign the contracts."

"Well then she lied to you."

"The bitch wasn't about to lie with the barrel of my gun up her cunt."

I grimaced at the thought and a shiver ran the length of my spine. "If Candy confessed that, it was to have the last laugh at your expense, Grillo, so you've still got nothing. And there isn't a chance in hell of your father believing the story."

When Grillo sputtered something unintelligible, I knew my barb had hit home so I tossed another. "Mommy and Daddy know you've lost it, Anthony. They told me at dinner that as soon as possible, they were going to put you away."

"Fuck you," he growled. "My old man will believe me after I tell him what I got from Candy."

"Did you forget that your mother held you at gunpoint the other night, Anthony? All she wanted was an excuse to shoot you down like a dog."

The man exploded in anger and slammed the phone down. Riff and I hung up too but she signaled me to stay where I was. When the phone rang twenty seconds later, I waited through two rings before she nodded at me to pick up.

"Yeah?"

"I'm coming to get you, Snow."

I glanced at Riff who rolled her hand for me to keep it going. "You're a loser, Grillo," I said, thinking fast. "You lost your brother, the respect of your parents, and probably your position in the *Family*. The only thing you do have left is your whacked out brain. Take my advice and put an end to your sorry life."

"I'm going to end a life, all right," he said. "But it won't be mine."

"Oh? What are you going to do?" I said, playing up my role as harasser. "Off another woman? You're a coward, man. A crazy-as-a-shithouse-rat coward and I'm not afraid of you."

The soft click in my ear sounded extremely menacing.

Riff rejoined me in the kitchen, took the phone from my shaking fingers, and sat me down in a chair.

"How'd I do?" I asked in a voice two octaves higher than usual.

"Great," Riff said. "He really hates you now."

"And that's good, right?"

"That, my friend, is perfect."

Chapter 22

I sat there feeling like I had just lit a stick of dynamite at both ends while holding it between my teeth. "So, uh, what do we do now?"

Riff tilted back in her chair. "Now we set a trap for Anthony."

I raised an eyebrow. "With me as bait, I presume."

"You presume correctly."

"Wonderful," I whined. "Grillo comes here, shoots me, and you get to arrest him?"

"Something like that," Riff said. "Except for the part where he shoots you."

I sipped at my coffee while she laid out her thoughts.

"Anthony Grillo's on very shaky ground with the legal system. One more bust and he goes directly to jail."

"Yeah, but for how long?"

"Life without parole if we can tag him for Candy Sprinkles's murder."

"And if you can't?"

Riff's expression told me she understood my concern. "Even if we only bust him for breaking into your house, he's going away for a long time as a habitual."

I picked up my cup, set it back on the table and traced the rim with a forefinger. "You know I want to get rid of this guy, Riff. But isn't entrapping him kind of dangerous for your career? I mean, how would you explain your involvement?"

"I've racked up some vacation time," she said. "If I spend it at a friend's lake house and Grillo happens to break in, it would be my duty to arrest him. Like I said before, it beats using my time off to attend your funeral."

I scowled at her playfully. "Think I don't have what it takes to handle this bozo on my own?"

"That's exactly what I think."

"Me too," I admitted. "What's your plan?"

"First tell me about dinner with Salvatore Grillo."

I ran down my trip to Chicago to meet the senior Grillos and ended with the story of Sophia holding a gun on Anthony.

"So his parents really do think he's lost it?"

"That's the impression I got. Why?"

"Because we want to end this thing here, not set you up for more retaliation."

I understood exactly where she was coming from. Salvatore Grillo had already lost one son during his dealings with me. Losing a second might make him rethink my innocence. "And how are we going to make that happen?"

"First, you call the old man and tell him about Anthony's threat."

Calling the Mafia boss wasn't high up on my list of happy things but I could see why Riff thought it important. After phoning the salon for Grillo's number, I placed the call.

Sophia Grillo answered and recognized my voice immediately. "Hello, Max. How is your mother holding up?"

"She's got her good and bad days, Sophia. How about you?"

"Eh," she said. "Life goes on. Is there something we can do for you?"

"I was hoping to talk to Salvatore if he's available."

"He's out in the yard trimming vines. Hold on."

In two minutes the booming voice sounded on the line.

"Max, my friend. How are you today?"

"Not so good, Salvatore. I need your help with a problem." I told him about finding Candy dead in my pool and Anthony's threatening phone call.

"*Un figlio di puttana*," Grillo muttered when I finished.

"I'm sorry to bother you with this, sir. But I'm sure Anthony intends to try and make good on his threat."

Papa Grillo swore in Italian again before switching back to English. "Anthony is a troubled man. And although my son, I have never had much control over him."

"Kids can be like that," I said in empathy. "I'm sure if you asked Marie, she'd say the same about me."

"I doubt that," Grillo said. "When your mama talks about you, her eyes are alive with love."

"Well, maybe not always, but thank you."

We were both silent for a beat.

"Now," Grillo said, "about Anthony…"

"I need you to talk to him, I guess. Try and get him to understand that I had nothing to do with Olympio's death."

There was a long pause and I pictured Grillo rolling the suggestion over in his mind.

"Why do you think Anthony killed Candy?" The question was quiet but direct.

"Because she couldn't tell him that I played a role in Olympio's death is my guess," I said…at that point, deciding to mix a little fact with my fiction. "And because I gave Candy money to relocate out of town."

"Why would you do that?"

"I'm going to be honest with you, Salvatore. I paid Candy to convince whoever needed to be convinced that Olympio had decided to drop me as a business partner. It was true, he had, but since he was no longer around to tell anyone, I wasn't sure I would be believed."

"You are quite correct in your assumption. But Candy was a good friend to Olympio and to my family for many years. I believe her."

"Thank you, sir. I appreciate that."

During the next hour Riff and I discussed ways of entrapping Anthony. In the end we decided that if I stayed put in the house, he'd be forced to come there.

"I'll position myself in that storage shed out back," Riff said, nodding at the little pagoda-style outbuilding that could be seen through the kitchen window. The shed sat thirty yards from the house and was used to store extra garden equipment. "It offers a decent view of at least two sides of the house, so if he approaches from either direction, there's a good chance I'll see him."

"What about the other two sides?"

"That'll be your job, Shamus. You can keep watch through the upstairs windows, but don't let him see you."

After lunch, we cleaned the shed and outfitted it with Riff's essentials; a stool tall enough for her sit on and still see out the tiny window in the door, an infrared night-scope I had purchased during Andra's murder investigation, and a small electric heater so she wouldn't freeze her butt off.

At 5:16 Riff rechecked the load in her gun for the third time. She slipped on a lightweight parka that I used for cross-country skiing, and barked out some last minute instructions.

"Never be anywhere without your gun, mister. And don't fall asleep. If you spot him, call me on my cell phone."

Without another word she slipped through the back door. I ran up the stairs to patrol the front of the house. A minute later the phone in my pocket rang.

"This is new territory for me," Riff said, in way of apology for her strict manner. "I want to make sure everything goes down the way we want it to."

"No problem, Lieutenant," I said, smiling into the phone. "Your badass cop routine never fails to turn me on."

Riff snorted. "Everything turns you on."

"Yeah. So? You got a problem with that?"

"Not even," she said. "It's one of your more endearing personality traits. Keeps me coming back for more."

"If I had you here with me right now," I said in a low voice, "that's exactly what I'd do."

"What? Keep me coming?"

"Mmm Hmm."

She laughed and the sound was comforting.

"Is this an obscene phone call?"

"We could make it one," I growled. "Can't think of anything better to do while we're waiting."

"You're supposed to be watching for Grillo."

"So I watch one-handed. Go ahead, say something dirty."

"Sorry," she said. "You're on your own. I'll check back in ten to see how it went."

We disconnected and I was looking down on the patio when my phone beeped again. I flipped it open to find Riff back on the line.

"Okay," she said. "You talked me into the phone sex thing. But you start, I'm too embarrassed."

Suddenly I felt lightheaded as blood abandoned brain for crotch. "Let's see," I said, visualizing Riff's tight, muscular body. "You know that star shaped birth mark on the underside of your left breast?"

"Yes."

"And that tiny mole on your right inner thigh…the one just below your…"

"I think I got the picture."

"Well how about I take us on an imaginary connect-the-dots tour?"

After our appetizing experience, I suddenly felt famished and headed to the kitchen to prepare dinner. I buzzed Riff when I was almost finished. She answered on the first ring. "How's it going out there?"

"Not bad. The electric heater keeps this place nice and toasty. What are you doing?"

"Making us some dinner."

"What's on the menu?"

"A stir-fry with chunks of pork tenderloin, yard long beans, shallots, garlic, hot red peppers, and a little *miso* for health and good luck."

"Oohh, I do love a man who can cook."

"And you do a hell of a good job of it too," I said. "Would you like wine with your dinner?"

"Wine would be nice, but I suggest you brew us each a double espresso."

"We can't stay awake forever, you know."

"True. But if Anthony doesn't show tonight, we'll take turns sleeping during daylight hours."

"Can we take a turn sleeping together? That sounds like more fun."

"You just keep thinking about what happens when a .22 caliber slug enters a human skull, lover boy. That should chill out those hot little hormones of yours."

I gulped as the brain-eating Pac-Man image returned. "You really know how to squash a guy's enthusiasm."

"Only when I have to. Now, how are you planning to get that food out here?"

"Well, it's been dark for over an hour now. I'll put it in a bag and walk it out like it was trash."

"Signal me and I'll cover you."

I delivered Riff's food without incident. A half-hour later I called to get her opinion. There was no answer, so I disconnected and dialed again. When there was still no response, I trotted into my spare room and peered out at the shed. The sky was cloud covered, and in the hazy darkness, I saw a figure moving from the shed toward the house.

My first thought was that Riff must be having phone problems. But when the motion detector lights blinked on, they illuminated a different scene. Anthony Grillo stood on the drive directly below me, one hand shading his eyes against the glare, the other pointing a gun in my direction. Suddenly the window in front of me exploded…as did any hope for an easy capture…Glass flew in all directions while the cell phone slipped from my hand. I scrambled into the room's walk-in closet. Seconds later I heard the back door crash open, but there was no resounding security siren. Riff and I had shut it down so Grillo wouldn't be scared away.

"Smart," said my ever ready to complain little voice. "The one piece of your scheme that actually worked is the one that won't do shit to help you."

"Go to hell," I hissed, unholstering the gun on my hip. "I need your harassment now like hole in the head."

"And you're libel to get one too if you don't stop hiding like a rat," the voice taunted. "Get to your phone and call 911."

With no time to consider the wisdom of the advice, I sprinted across the room, plucked up my phone from among the shards of glass, flipped it open and swore when the LED screen remained dark. I tried the triple digits anyway getting only static for my effort. When I lifted the phone beside the bed, dead silence filled my ear.

My mind flew to Riff but I snatched it back, knowing I had to stay focused to stay alive. But when a gunshot cracked dully on the main floor and I heard Blue wail in pain, I raced down the stairs with my gun leading the way. On the main floor, I spotted the cat lying on his side near the entrance to the sunroom; eyes closed, blood oozing from a wound on his right leg. I ran to him, placed a hand on the bloody spot and jerked it back when he yelped in protest.

"What a chump," said Grillo as he emerged from inside the sunroom, gun in hand. "I knew if I whacked your cat, you'd come running. Now drop the gun."

I did, and he kicked it away.

"At least your friend outside put up a fight before I took her out."

"You fucking shit," I shouted, standing to face him, but when his gun pushed hard into my gut, I backed off.

"Don't grieve too much, Max. You'll be joining her soon. If you believe in an afterlife, that is."

A wave of guilt for involving Riff washed over me, and with it went any will to fight. When Grillo prodded me toward the kitchen and told me to sit in a chair tableside, I complied without complaint. A roll of duct tape appeared from his coat pocket. In short order my wrists and ankles were secured to the chair.

Grinning manically, he produced a jeweler's propane torch and a mini tape recorder from a second pocket. "Now," he said, setting them on the table in front of me, "let's talk about Olympio."

Pulling a cigarette from a pack inside his coat, he lit up, exhaling slowly. The blue smoke curling around his face made him look like the devil incarnate; a sight that would have sent me into panic mode ten minutes ago. But the thought of Riff lying dead outside, and Blue, losing his life's blood just a few feet away, downplayed the effect. Grillo shocked me out of my anguished thoughts by pressing the lit end of his cigarette into the soft flesh of my forearm. My breath was cut short by the searing pain. As I tried to push away, the chair went over backwards and my head struck the granite floor with a dull thud. Tiny white lights exploded inside my head like out-of-control pyrotechnics. The next thing I knew, Grillo was standing my chair upright.

"That was only a preview," he said, lifting the jeweler's torch and cranking a knob to start the gas flowing. Holding his cigarette near the tip, the gas ignited with a pop. He adjusted the hissing flame to a fiery, blue point as I pulled in vain against my bonds. "Refuse to cooperate," he said, smiling like he hoped I would, "and it will get worse."

"Cooperate with what?" I heard myself ask. "What do you want?"

"A confession—what did you think?" he said, nodding at the tape recorder. "My old man is going to hear the truth from your own lips."

I shook my head defiantly. "You're not interested in truth, Anthony. So you can go screw yourself."

He smiled and touched the torch flame to the center of his cigarette. The white paper blackened instantly and burst into flame. "That's right, Max," he said bringing the torch point so close to my forearm that the flesh browned like chicken skin, "fight me. I'd be disappointed if you made it too easy."

Jerking back, I struggled to loosen the tape and screamed when he briefly touched the flame to the exact spot where the cigarette had just done its damage.

Chuckling, Anthony walked to the refrigerator and pressed the handle of the automatic icemaker. Scooping up a handful of cubes, he returned to my side and pressed them against the ugly burn. "Better?"

I closed my eyes, savoring the blissful relief.

"You see," he said. "I'm not such a bad guy. All I want is a little cooperation."

"That's all your brother wanted too," I said. "Look what he got for his trouble."

Anthony sneered. "Olympio was an asshole. Not even good enough to break a wimp like you."

"If you hated him so much, why do you care that he's dead?"

"I'm glad the fuck is dead," Grillo spat. "This is about blood."

"Olympio was your father's first born son. I don't see him here torturing me."

"My old man's gone soft. Used to blow people away without blinking an eye."

"Maybe he just got smart."

Grillo barked out a laugh and torqued-up the flame several inches higher. "Enough of this bullshit. You either say what I tell you into the tape recorder, or I start on your face."

I felt my jaw tighten in anticipation while attempting to rally whatever courage I had left. "I am not going to help prove your lies, Anthony."

Grillo's lips stretched tight in a nasty grin. "If you don't, I swear, I'll toast your fucking heart like a marshmallow."

"And if I spew your lies, your daddy will kill me. Not a lot of motivation there."

"*This* is your motivation," he said, waving the torch flame in front of my face. "Which eye do you want fried first?"

As I pulled my head back, I caught a quick movement in the kitchen window behind Grillo. My hopes rose, thinking Riff had somehow survived, but when a pink cap, followed by a head of bushy curls and a face that could double for Mister Ed popped into view, I wasn't sure if I should shout for joy or groan at life's incredulity. Kenny Dougland stood there, smiling at me like a puppy in a pet shop. Beside him was the diminutive lothario, Josh Jackson.

Hope mixed with pain and the scent of burning flesh as Grillo once again touched the blue-white flame to my forearm. A second later, my would-be rescuers came bursting through the door causing Grillo to jerk the torch away. The dynamic-duo were both dressed in what appeared to be black pajamas. If they were trying to come across as a couple of badass ninjas, their act needed a ton of work. The one advantage they did have was the twelve-gage, double-barreled shotgun Kenny-the-crazy-man leveled in our direction.

"Listen up, mister," Kenny said in a very lame imitation of John Wayne. "Hurt my friend again, and you'll find yourself pushing up daisies. Now raise 'em."

Anthony's amused expression was misplaced if he thought Kenny wouldn't fire with me in the way. My friend is whacky as they come. There was no guarantee he wouldn't take us both out, by mistake.

"Yo, Kenny," I said, scooting my chair several inches to the left. "Shoot this son of a bitch if he moves, but aim a little to his right."

Kenny nodded, peering down the barrel at Grillo.

"Josh, grab a knife and cut this tape off me."

The little man had both wrists and one ankle free when a sudden gust of wind blew the damaged back door open. Kenny turned his head to investigate. As he did, Grillo grabbed Josh, dragged him behind me, pushing a gun into the bottom of his chin.

"Fire that shotgun, Horseface," Anthony said. "And your friend dies. Set it down nice and easy and step away from it."

To my surprise Kenny shook his head.

"Do it!" Grillo demanded, "or I blow Tiny Tim's head off."

Josh screwed up his face at the Tiny Tim crack, and with ferret-like speed, brought his heel up into Grillo's groin. Anthony sucked air, Josh squirmed free, and the next thing I knew, the Mafia man's gun had moved to the back of my head. Before he could even think of getting off a round, I rocked back hard and we both crashed to the floor, with me on top. Grillo swore, jerked his gun from beneath me, and scrambling to his feet, got off a shot that sent Kenny's pink cap flying backwards across the room.

Eyes wide with shock, Kenny looked up to where the hat had been. Before Grillo could get off a second round, Kenny pulled the trigger on the shotgun.

A tremendous blast split the air. Buckshot pinged off the wall to the right, and from my position on the floor, I saw Grillo rip open his jacket. He'd been hit. Tiny spots of blood marked each entry point of the hot lead.

Knowing I'd never get a better opportunity, I wrenched the bound leg free of the tape, and dove to the side of the refrigerator. Anthony caught the movement but as he swung his gun in my direction, the second barrel of Kenny's shotgun exploded. Grillo's body jerked puppet-like as a score of the buckshot found their mark. Despite the damage, the tough-as-nails bastard somehow managed to stay on his feet.

"Fun's over, boys," he said as he leveled his revolver at Kenny. "Now all you motherfuckers are going to die."

Slightly unsteady on his feet, Grillo squeezed off a shot. It missed Kenny but slammed into the refrigerator barely two inches from my face.

"Kenny!" I screamed, backing out of range, "Drop, man! Drop to the ground." But Kenny ignored me. He had a determined expression on his face, and before I could yell the order again, he brandished the shotgun like a baseball bat and charged Grillo.

The wounded man leveled the gun dead center at Kenny's chest. The hammer struck home, and as if zapped by a paralyzing space ray, Kenny's body froze mid-stride and dropped to the floor. The scene around me morphed into classic Twilight Zone, all slow-mo and grainy, but my senses back-flipped to normal when I realized Grillo's weapon had misfired.

Screaming out in anguish for his friend, Josh charged Grillo from behind, jammed his head up between the surprised man's legs and to my amazement lifted Grillo right off his feet. Anthony howled in protest and fired downward. The slug punched out a chunk of granite at Josh's feet and, with his rider still in place, the little guy took off, loping in an erratic circle around the wide kitchen area. I grabbed Josh's legs as he galloped by, the two men crashed to the floor, sending Grillo's gun skittering across the room. Chasing after the weapon never entered my mind. I just popped open the refrigerator, snagged a full magnum of Champagne off the bottom shelf, and brought the heavy bottle down hard on the back of Grillo's head.

Epilogue

▼

"I'm fine, Doc," Riff said, as the young female resident on duty at St. Jude's finished her examination of my protesting friend. Grillo had stunned her repeatedly with a 650,000-volt Tazer, bound her mouth, hands, and feet with duct tape and hung her facedown from a hook on the wall.

"Well I can see it was a waste of time going to med school all those years," the doctor said, while noting something on Riff's chart. "I should have just become a cop."

When the doctor left the room, Riff adjusted the hospital bed to a sitting position. "So," she said, raking me with her pale blue eyes, "you really pulled it off, huh?"

"Sure did," I said, breathing on the fingernails of one hand and polishing them on the front of my shirt. "You expected something less from an experienced P.I.?"

"As a matter of fact, yes" she said. "Just before Grillo hit me with that Tazer, I thought for sure if I ever woke up again, the forensic team would find what was left of you in the garbage disposal."

"Grillo ain't so tough," I said, trying to keep my smile from growing. "At least nothing me and the other two stooges couldn't handle."

Riff plucked a plastic water glass off the bedside stand and lobbed it at me. I caught it midair and placed it on my head like a hat.

"How are Larry and Curly anyway?" she asked.

"On their way to stardom, or so they hope," I said. *"Channel 7's Action News* team wants to interview them about what happened at the house."

"How the hell did they know to show up?"

I raised my eyebrows. "Kenny, the psychic-wonder, strikes again."

Riff shook her head. "That is too weird."

I agreed, sitting on the side of the bed. "Thought I'd lost you there, lady," I said, hugging her to me. "Sure you're all right?"

Riff nodded into my shoulder before leaning back against the pillows. "What about Blue?"

"He'll be fine. The bullet only grazed his hip. They're keeping him at the vet for the day to watch for infection."

"And you?" she asked. "Are you doing okay?"

I shrugged and looked down at my bandaged arms. "Yeah. But my kitchen is pretty shot up."

"Where's Grillo now?" Riff asked.

"The doctors are digging lead out of him down in Emergency."

"Does his old man know what happened?"

"Yup," I said, mugging a smile. "Called him myself before I came in here."

Riff shot me a look of surprise. "Damn, Snowman. You are definitely smarter than I give you credit for."

I bowed my head in acknowledgment of the compliment. "So what do you think? Is Grillo going to get life without parole?"

"If we can tag him with Candy Sprinkles's murder, he will. Could you tell what kind of gun he had last night?"

I gave her a "we got that son-of-a-bitch" grin. "A .22 caliber revolver. Probably the same one he offed Candy with."

Riff returned my smile. "Score one for stupidity," she said. "But even his attempt to murder you is probably enough to put him away for a long long time. Plus," she cleared her throat, "he assaulted a police officer."

I glanced at the closed door, then back at Riff. "Anybody ask why you were hiding in the tool shed?"

"Hiding? Who was hiding? I was out there looking for a garden rake when Grillo attacked me."

"Oh yeah," I said. "I almost forgot."

A friendly sheriff's deputy drove Riff and me to my house. We walked in the back door to find Marie standing there, hands on hips, surveying the damaged kitchen.

"Thought I told you to stay out of trouble, baby boy," she said.

"Thought I told you to stay up north."

Marie dismissed the rebuke with a wave of her hand. "A son doesn't tell a mother what to do," she said. "Now what the hell went on here?"

After coffee and explanations, Marie stood, saying she was taking off. She hugged me, and after whispering a rare "I love you, son", picked up her bag and left. Riff filled our cups, then sat across from me at the kitchen table.

"So," she said. "Do you really think the whole Mafia thing is over?"

"According to Salvatore Grillo it is. He apologized for Anthony, and assured me no one in his organization would bother me again."

"You," Riff said, shaking her head, "are the luckiest bastard I've ever met. You know that?"

I sighed melodramatically. "In everything but true love."

Riff rose from her chair, dragged it over to the damaged back door and propped the top beneath the handle. When it was secured to her satisfaction, she turned to face me, brows lowered, blue eyes dark with desire. "I might not be able to give you true love," she said, slowly opening the row of buttons down the front of her shirt. "But we can sure shoot for a reasonable facsimile."

"You're welcome to try, Lieutenant," I said, slipping my arms around her bare waist. "Hope you don't mind if it takes a while for me to notice the difference."

Almost immediately after doing the nasty, Riff and I crashed. It had been a busy, stressful couple of days and we both needed to catch up on our sleep. We awoke just after five the same evening. I nuked some frozen chicken soup for our dinner. Afterward we settled down with coffee in the sunroom.

"That was amazing," Riff said. She looked bright-eyed and content.

"What was? The sex, the sleep or the soup?"

Riff kissed the air in my direction. "Making it with you is always a pleasure, Snowman, but the sleep and homemade soup were close seconds. I could easily make a steady diet of that trio."

"Is that a proposal, Lieutenant?"

"Sorry, but marriage to you isn't in my life plan."

"I'm not surprised," I said. "It doesn't seem to be in anybody's."

Riff's expression turned serious. "You still haven't heard from Zed?"

I shrugged, shaking my head.

"Why don't you go down to Belize?"

"Believe me, I've considered it, but it might be awkward."

"How so?"

"Olympio told me she hooked up with an old lover."

"Yeah?" Riff said, eyebrows rising to meet her sleep tousled bangs. "Well so did you."

I drained my cup and placed it gently on the table between us.

"Face it, Maxie. You're not the monogamous type either. I know you want to be—at least you think you do. But you're a whore."

"A whore?" I said, trying unsuccessfully to repress my smile.

"If the condom fits, friend."

I was about to comment when the phone inside her Coach tote bag announced a call.

Sighing loudly, Riff plucked it out and put it to her ear. "Linda Riff." She listened for several seconds, her eyes widening at one point and catching mine. "What time? Okay. Sign me up."

"Sign you up for what?" I asked, after she had returned the phone to her bag.

"A special agent from Homeland Security wants to meet with me at my office tomorrow."

"*The* Homeland Security?"

She nodded.

"And you're going?"

"Uh, yeah. Is there a problem?"

"No," I said. "I just thought, since you took the time off anyway, we could spend a couple of days together."

Riff smirked. "Doing what?"

"Sailing."

"And having sex?" she asked, folding her arms across her chest and tipping back in the chair.

"Long walks on the beach."

"And sex?"

"Breakfast in bed."

"And sex?"

I narrowed my eyes playfully. "Plenty of sex, Lieutenant. That is, if you can keep up with me."

"If I can't," she said, rocking forward, "I'll just arrest your ass for speeding."

"You mean like, you might cuff me? And rough me up? And throw me into the slammer?"

"Sounds like a plan," she said, fishing in her bag and pulling out a pair of shiny new handcuffs. "Now, get those hands behind your back and spread em', mister."

0-595-32997-7

Printed in the United States
22529LVS00003B/187